Snap

John Burns

Snap

MACMILLAN

First published 1998 by Macmillan

an imprint of Macmillan Publishers Ltd
25 Eccleston Place, London SW1W 9NF
and Basingstoke

Associated companies throughout the world

ISBN 0 333 72131 4

1 3 5 7 9 8 6 4 2

A CIP catalogue record for this book is available from
the British Library.

Typeset by Intype London Ltd
Printed and bound in Great Britain by
Mackays of Chatham plc, Kent

To Rita

Chapter One

It snowed in the night and the place where they found her body was now all white and winter wonderlandish. You could have stuck the scene on a Christmas card. It would have looked even better if Plod hadn't plonked a great yellow tent over her mortal remains. Also, there were dirty-grey patches of slush where the uniforms had parked their hooves.

So far we knew nearly nothing. They'd roped off the area and were keeping us at bay until they got a press officer out of bed to say no comment.

But the betting was that under the big top lay the corpse of one Joni Poelma, last seen, as they say, leaving a disco in Dulwich. Until then none of us knew that Dulwich had a disco. That was a week ago. Since then there had been the usual hullabaloo – TV appeals, posters, back checks on miles of video tape, the full bit. But Joni Poelma had stubbornly refused to reappear.

In the meantime nobody else was reported missing in Dulwich, therefore our lightning brains deduced that Joni had finally turned up.

It is not my usual practice to hang around in the snow waiting for the Old Bill to identify a missing Dutch au pair. But February had been a thinnish month for

news, and we'd run two splashes and three page leads
on the story so far. Plus, in a surfeit of red biddy, our
deranged Editor had stuck up a five-grand reward for
information leading to Joni's whereabouts. He'd
forgotten the proviso that we wanted her alive.

Unless he managed to worm his way out of that,
my bet was the loot would go to the geezer with the
frostbitten poodle nattering away to the Law on their
side of the cordon tapes. We were perched on what in
sunnier seasons you would call a grassy knoll so we had
a ringside seat to all the action, not that there was any
action to write home about. Below us the park fell away
sharply before rolling into a little dip and finally
running out of steam against a row of Victorian railings.
The ironwork had a fine tracery of snow. Very chichi. It
looked like it belonged in Dulwich.

Centre stage in all of this was the big yellow tent. We
had nothing else to look at so we watched it. Every now
and then the walls rippled as some Herbert inside biffed
his head against them. They were either looking for
clues or playing Twister.

The air was brittle and you could hear the forensic
boys panting away in there. Nobody was saying anything. Outside the tent was the lumpish shape of Chief
Inspector Tom Skelly in a red and white ski jacket. He
and the tent clashed. He was standing by the bloke with
the dog but they weren't talking. The dog was playing
dumb too. Skelly had got all he wanted from the body-
finder and pooch. He was just making sure we got
nowhere near the man. Every now and then Skelly
pitched us a baleful look.

I suppose if I was him I would have felt likewise. If

we hadn't all made such a fuss about the vanishing Joni Poelma, a mere Det. Inspector would be chilling his toes out there in the park while Skelly sat in the station canteen, scoffing bacon sarnies and having the Mirror cartoons explained to him.

We weren't feeling too happy either. Everybody was out of fags so we just puffed out white plumes of air and pretended we were smoking. It was still too early for the pubs. Anyway, we had to hang around in the outlandish hope that Skelly or the press liaison officer might say something interesting. We shuffled our feet and looked bored. It wasn't hard.

Down below, a new character trekked into shot. A low moan of dismay escaped us. 'Oddjob!'

He heard it but he acted as if he didn't. Bob Jobley is a Scotland Yard press liaison officer. He is not a copper. Liaison officers know nothing, except what few crumbs the detective in charge bothers to tell them. Oddjob always knows less than nothing, hence our dismay.

Skelly somehow restrained himself from clasping Oddjob to his bosom and telling him all. They had maybe twenty seconds of chit-chat, then the liaison officer turned to face us. This was our signal to slalom downhill and pick his brains.

'Morning, Oddjob,' I greeted him.

He has no pride. 'Morning, Max.'

An agency hack fired the first question: 'Is it Joni Poelma?'

Oddjob simultaneously shrugged, strangled a yawn, squeezed up his eyes and shook his head. The man's a polymath.

'It's not Joni?'

3

We got a repeat performance.

I said, 'Is that on the record?'

Over his shoulder I could see the great pink ham of Skelly's face. He was grinning. The only time Plods like him smirk at us like that is when they have something to smirk about, such as finally tripping over Joni Poelma's body. Or having somebody else doing the tripping over bit for them.

You could see that Skelly had no intention of telling us anything. That's why he was happy. You could also see that they'd found Joni. If it was some other stiff he'd be back down the nick scratching his chilblains by now.

Oddjob said, 'It is a body.' Thereby dispelling any suspicions that the tent might be harbouring Scotland Yard's camping club.

'Male or female?' This from someone behind me.

'It's too early to say,' lied Oddjob.

We ignored that. 'How was she murdered?'

Oddjob waved his mittens about. That meant our guess was as good as his. Better.

'Has she been here long?'

Oddjob said, 'That has yet to be established.'

After that there was a snowball fight of questions. I refrained from taking part and let the kids enjoy themselves. Anyway, I'm a minimalist. I find the less you know about a story the easier it is to write. For starters, you don't find awkward facts getting in the way. Nor do you get useless chunks of information cluttering up the narrative. I mean, right now a local radio hackette was asking Oddjob the name of the dog of the geezer who'd found Joni Poelma. Do the Great British Public really want to know what the dog was called? Indeed not. But just for the record, its name was Jack.

The alleged press briefing wound down to the point where even the bloke from the local weekly had run out of questions. Oddjob promised to meet us all at Dulwich nick around oneish when he should have yet more red-hot news for us. We grunted and shambled off for the pubs had opened. I looked back over my shoulder. Oddjob was standing at the cordon with his mitts sticking out, a forlorn figure that nobody wanted to talk to.

In the nearest bar I was on my second Gordons and halfway through a slanderous story about my News Editor when my bleeper went off. It told me that the very same News Editor wanted me to ring her URGENTLY. I finished the story, listened to someone else's lies, ordered in a new round, and gave her a bell.

'Lo, Angie,' I said. 'You're missing me?'

She wasn't in the mood for banter. 'Yes, I bloody well am. I'm just about to go into conference and I need a schedule line on Joni Poelma. Is it her?'

'Yup.'

She said, 'Scotland Yard have confirmed it?'

'Nope.'

'But you're sure it's her?'

'Yup.'

She said, 'So what's the schedule line?'

I said, '*Gazette* Reader Finds Murdered Joni.'

Angela's a stickler for facts. 'Does he read our paper?'

I said, 'Probably not, but by the time I get to him, even his dog will be a lifelong reader.'

She said, 'OK, that'll do for conference. But before you slope off to the bar, I've got a job for you.'

I didn't like the sound of that. I said warily, 'Oh?'

Angie went all breezy which meant it was a crummy job. She said, 'I want you to go and see the Cardigans and set up an exclusive interview for features.'

'Who's doing the interview?'

She said, 'Beverley Nephews. She'll be down—'

Beverley Nephews! Otherwise known in the trade as Beverley Hills, for two very good reasons. I hauled my mind back to what Angie was saying. ' . . . so we need you to stick your foot in the door and keep every-body else away from the Cardigans until Beverley gets there. OK?'

The Cardigans were the couple who until last week employed Joni to ride shotgun on their children. I remembered that he was big in chemicals and they played happy families in something marginally smaller than Buck House.

Angela said, 'They might need some convincing so we'll go for a buy up.'

And what nutter thought that one up? I just said, 'How much?'

'You can go up to a thousand.'

I said, 'Angie, the Cardigans spend that on dental floss. They probably help the Sultan of Brunei when he's a bit strapped for readies.'

She sighed. 'All right, go to two thou, but no more.'

I holstered my mobile and returned to the bar. There are times when this game is just too silly for its own good.

Meriel, a hackette from the *Mail* was thinking along

the same lines. She said, 'You'll never guess what News Desk have asked me to do.'

I had a very good idea of precisely what but I listened politely.

She said, 'They've asked me to try and buy up the Cardigans.'

I chortled merrily. I said, 'Don't they read the papers? Wedge Cardigan uses fivers for wallpaper. How much are you offering them?'

Meriel stuck her nose in a glass of house white and said, 'Twenty.'

'Twenty thousand?'

She nodded. Now this was serious. The Cardigans might just bite on that. I put on my gravest face. I said, 'I don't think that's a very wise idea.' There was a strange undercurrent in my voice.

She darted me a curious look from under her Shetland pony fringe. 'What do you mean?'

I took a mouthful of gin and lit a Bensons before I bothered to answer. I simply repeated, 'It's not a wise idea.' This time my tones were so laden with sinister nuances that I sounded as if I was talking in slo-mo.

Meriel's fringe eyed me intently. 'Why?'

I took another swig and had a shufti around to make sure no one was eavesdropping. I said, 'Because the police are going to lift Wedge Cardigan.'

The fringe swished hither and thither. 'What!'

I said, 'Keep your voice down. I've just had a tip from a detective mate. Don't tell anyone else.'

Meriel squeaked, 'They think he did it?'

'Sssh. Yes, he's in the frame, so you'd better forget trying to buy him up. Wait for the one o'clock briefing.

They'll probably announce it then. But don't do anything in the meantime.'

The fringe trembled with a pitiful gratitude. She said, 'Thanks, Max. I owe you one.'

Those of you of a more squeamish disposition, that is to say who are not reporters, might regard this as a scumbag trick on my part. But look at it my way: the *Mail* has great buckets of cash to sling at any passing story. We don't. Yet my News Desk requires, no, *demands*, that I deliver the story, regardless of the *Mail*'s megabucks. If I fail, then I am seen to be a lesser hack than Meriel Fringe-face, and that would never do. Therefore I had to use an evil ruse. Besides, it's more fun playing dirty.

I licked my glass clean and said I had to hotfoot it back to the office. Meriel squeezed my arm and gave me a conspiratorial goodbye wink. I winked right back.

Chapter Two

Dulwich is too far from the real world to have itinerant bands of black-cab drivers roaming the streets so I was forced to point my feet in the direction of Wilberforce Crescent and leg it. As I walked, I hauled out the photocopied newspaper cuts on Joni Poelma and read them. I also smoked a cigarette and did some thinking. Oddjob isn't the only polymath around here.

The cuts told me that Joni was twenty-three, a native of Genk, somewhere in the bowels of Holland. Dad was a civil servant of sorts, mum was something else. There were two snaps of Joni. One showed her blonde and chubby. In the other she was blonde and skinny. In both she was reasonably attractive, just a fraction short of tasty. She'd been in England about eight months, loved pop, was always smiling and didn't have a boyfriend. That's all there was on Joni.

There was rather more meat on the Cardigans, or on him at least. His first name was Wedge, but don't ask me why. He was fifty-two, had a three-year-old son, Oliver, and a baby called Ceri. That was a girl, I think. There was also mention of a twenty-year-old son, which didn't make a lot of sense. Mrs C was known to her hubby as Enid. The cuts didn't have her age. Wedge Cardigan, as stated, was the main man at Intraphilyn. Its chief business seemed to be inventing cures for this and that and by all accounts it was pretty good at it too. This explained why Wedge Cardigan had an acre and a half of prime Dulwich real estate, plus a swimming pool, plus a Porsche Boxter, plus a villa in Tuscany, plus a Dutch au pair. Or he used to have one of those anyway. It didn't explain why Wedge Cardigan still looked like E.T. on stilts.

I wheeled up before the Cardigans' gaff. It was called The White House, probably because it was white and it was a house. I pushed open a lofty gate and ambled up a driveway you could land a jumbo on. It curved up to a flight of steps with Greek urn-type things stationed left and right. The house stretched away for a mile or so on either side of the front door. There was no sign of a Porsche Boxter in the driveway, but a cherry-bright Alfa Romeo Spyder was out there with its snout buried in the laurels. I reasoned that Enid Cardigan must be at home, seeing as how she was presently minus one au pair. I bonged on the bell and waited for Enid.

Now I want you to close your eyes and picture an Enid. She's wearing a 1984 Laura Ashley toe-touching frock with cutesy little flowers all over the place. She's got a long nose poking out of brownish hair which needs a good polish. She has eyes that are dulled by something other than a woman's woes. They are set in a pale oval high-cheekboned face that has been too long out of the sun. Her lips are thin and dry and have never bloomed into passion. She looks as if she lives on lentils and brown rice. She is maybe forty-eight or sixty-three. It's hard to tell. That is an Enid. Right?

Wrong. But we were right about the high cheek-bones. The Enid who opened the door to me was the sort of cracker you don't find growing on Christmas trees. If *Country Life* had a Page Three stunna she'd have been it. She was a whisker or so off thirty. She had blonde hair which curled up under her ears and tickled her chin. She was bouncy in all the best places. She had eyes that went halfway round her head. They were green. They knew how to smile.

'Yes?' said her mouth and her eyes, both at the same time.

I pushed my fantasy on to the back burner. I said, 'Mrs Cardigan?'

'Yes. Can I help you?'

I was standing two steps south of her. I took a squint at the house, the cherry Alfa, the wide open spaces of her front lawn, the laurels carefully nibbled by a house-trained army of whatever carefully nibbles laurels. Then I looked at her. She was the sort of shape they build a mega-million-dollar Hollywood movie around. I thought of our stupid offer to buy her exclusive story for two grand. It was just too silly. I looked her dead in her iced green eyes.

I said, 'Mrs Cardigan, my name is Max Chard. My newspaper has authorized me to pay you five pounds for your exclusive story.'

She had the good sense to laugh out loud.

I said sternly, 'Or if you want to haggle about it, I am prepared to go as high as ten pounds. But that is my limit.'

She said, 'You're not serious?'

I said, 'I have never been more serious since the last time I was this serious.'

She figured that one out. She had her hand on the door knob. She swung the door to and fro while she thought. After a pause she said, 'Why should I talk to you?'

'Because I listen.'

She was still smiling. She said, 'I thought reporters asked questions.'

'So far you're the only one asking questions.'

Enid bobbed her head at that. I suppose that meant touché. I could see she was deliberating whether or not to tell me to sling my hook. The smile was fading.

I said, 'Anyways, I'm not the interviewer. That pleasant duty goes to one of our feature writers called Beverley Nephews.' I added as an afterthought, 'Bev gets all the best jobs.'

That sold it. She said, 'I'll give you five minutes.'

She swung her rump for me to follow and I was up those steps like a spring lamb. Her jeans dearly loved her. If she'd had a postage stamp in her hip pocket I could have told you whether it was first or second class. Her bobbly pink sweater wasn't quite so intimate. It just sort of flumped out over the waist of her denims. She led the way through a big airy hall, across a prairie of corn-coloured carpet and into the kitchen. I would like to describe the decor en route but my attention was otherwise engaged. Enid curved round the promontory of a breakfast bar and pointed at a stool on the other side for me to park myself on.

She said, 'Coffee?'

'Please.'

I took in the kitchen. It was big and mostly white and the bits that were not white were chrome. A shade clinical perhaps. Maybe hubby brewed up his top selling potions in there. Out the picture window I could see a child's tree house, the size of a council flat, lodged halfway up a tree.

Enid had her back to me. She asked, 'Are all journalists as pushy as you?'

I said, 'I don't know about journalists. I'm a reporter.'

'Instant coffee OK?'

I said I never drank anything else. She bashed around with cups and saucers. Her bottom wiggled as she worked. She asked, 'How do you like it – black?'

Steady on, Enid, I've only had a couple of gins. She made free with the milk and pushed a sugar bowl at me. She was sitting opposite. She hoisted a chintzy little cup to her lips and said, 'You know they've found Joni's body?'

I nodded yes. We both tucked our smiles away for the present. Enid sighed and shook her hair. 'She really was a lovely girl. I know people always say nice things when somebody's died, but she was honestly really sweet.'

I said, 'What have the police told you?'

She shrugged. 'Only that they've found Joni's body in the park, that they don't yet know how she died, but they're treating it as suspicious.'

I said, 'Did they say if she'd been robbed? Was she still in the same clothes?'

Enid said, 'They also told me not to talk to the Press.' There was a shadow of a smile back in her voice.

'Not even for a fiver?'

'A tenner.'

I said, 'The actual offer is two thousand.'

That didn't make her go all trembly at the knees either. She just whuffed on her coffee and looked at me in a certain speculative way. It was quite cool and appraising. If I had any decency I might have blushed.

Enid asked, 'And what do I have to do to earn my two thousand?'

I thought of several things but I said, 'Beverley asks the big money questions. I've just got one.'

Her eyes opened wide in mock astonishment the way contestants in TV quiz shows look when they learn they've just won a weekend for two in Runcorn.

'Just *one* question?'

I said, 'Why is your husband called Wedge?'

Enid must have thought that was a funny question for she tossed her head back and laughed. It was nice to see her fillings were up to scratch.

She said, 'That's easy. His first name is William – which he's always hated. His initials are W.E.G – William Eskill Gilbert. At boarding school he got dubbed Weegee. It sort of got trimmed down to Wedge. That's it.'

She laughed again. I didn't. Somehow I always miss the point of middle-class humour. Enid dipped a fingertip in her coffee and licked it, which I didn't think was a very middle-class thing to do. She canted an eyebrow at me. She was back in her cool appraising mode.

She said, 'And I have just one little question for you: why do you think you're here?'

I could have answered this several ways, but I had

the feeling they were all wrong so I stayed schtum. Her eyes were shot through with mischief.

She let me stew for a moment, then she said, 'Jason. That's why you're here.'

I don't know any Jasons apart from a geek on our Picture Desk. Somehow I felt he was not the Jason under discussion.

I pulled out my Bensons because that was better than just sitting there looking stupid. She slid me a little porcelain ashtray. It might have been my imagination but I think her fingers touched mine.

Enid said, 'Jason is my stepson.'

She must have put water or something in the coffee for I wasn't following this.

She said, 'Did you really think I invited you in because you offered me ten pounds?'

'Two thousand.'

'That came later. Anyway, the money's got nothing to do with it.'

I said, 'It must have been my magnetic personality then.'

On the pretty side of the breakfast bar Enid examined this as if it were a serious statement. She said, 'Let's say it was more your chat-up line.'

There was no answer to that so I just listened for the rest.

She said, 'I thought it was very clever. You almost had me won over.'

'What's this got to do with Jason?'

She gave me the full blast of her green eyes. 'Jason is twenty, and he's doing media studies at university.'

I said that must be nice for him.

She kept talking as if I hadn't spoken. 'He wants to be a reporter, a newspaper reporter. Just like you.'

I had the bad manners to smile. Enid didn't like that. She scrunched up her nose and gave me a sternish look.

'What I'm saying, Mister Max Chard, is he could learn a lot from someone like you, probably a lot more than he's learning on his course.'

I said, 'I am many things, Missus Enid Cardigan: I am *not* a Joni Poelma, playing nanny to would-be hacks.'

She nearly poured coffee down her sweater. 'What did you just call me?'

I said it again. Missus Enid Cardigan.

This time she totally cracked up. I'd no idea what the joke was. I sat there and smoked and waited for her to fill me in.

It took a while for the last ripples of merriment to subside. Even then she had a mirthful tear or two snagged in her lashes.

She said, 'Do I look like an Enid?'

We've already been through that. No.

More little riffs of laughter. Somewhere in the middle of them she said, 'I'm Gabriella.'

'So who's Enid?'

I had to hang about while she plucked a tissue out of the ether and blew her snoot. She said, 'I'm afraid your newspaper's morgue is rather behind the times: Enid was the name of Wedge's first wife.'

I twigged what had happened. Whoever wrote the first story on Joni had got the Enid tag from some old cutting. Every other paper had just copied it. I felt happier knowing she wasn't an Enid.

Gabriella hauled the conversation back to where we

were. 'But we weren't talking about me. We were talking about you giving Jason some guidance.'

I said, 'Sorry. I don't do that sort of thing.'

She sat up and flicked her bob with both hands. 'In which case, you can forget about an interview . . . but . . .'

'But?'

'But if you simply agree to have Jason under your wing for let's say two weeks, then your paper gets the interview. And it won't cost a penny. And there is a great deal I could tell you about Joni.'

'A great deal?'

'You wouldn't believe it.'

I sat back and chewed the filter. This took some thinking about. First of all, the idea of having a snot-nosed kid hanging on my shoulder for a fortnight was deeply distressing. The upside was that this way we'd have a foot in the Cardigan camp, therefore we'd stuff the opposition. Therefore our crazed Editor would smile fondly on me and maybe forget that barney over my Glasgow expenses. But most important of all, I'd learn what Gabriella knew about Joni.

We hacks are supposed to be cynical, hard-boiled and all that. The reverse is true. We are the most gullible people in the whole universe. So when Gabriella hinted at some deep, dark secret in Joni's background, she had me hooked.

I said, 'So what can you tell me?'

Gabriella waved that away. 'Later. It depends on whether you agree to help Jason. You'll find him a terrific kid. He's a keen learner and he'll not get in your way.'

I snapped a sardonic look at her. She didn't see it. She had another pull on her coffee and said, 'At any rate, that's my offer. But I'm sure if you won't do it, some other newspaper would.'

She was bang on about that but I still wasn't in love with the idea. I put on my seraphically honest face and said, 'OK, our paper will take him, but I wouldn't be the best mentor for Jason. He'd enjoy himself more – and learn more – if he was with one of our features people. Beverley, for instance.'

Gabriella fluted a soprano laugh. 'Nice try, Max. But you're the one. Now, do we have a deal?'

Women are far more devious than civilized folk. I kicked myself, muttered foul curses under my breath, but I nodded yes.

She said, 'Good. Jason's down from university at present so I'll get him to call you tonight.'

I said, 'Now, let's hear it about Joni.'

'Let's see how you and Jason get on first.'

That was a dirty trick. She relented. 'All right. She took drugs.'

'What drugs?'

'I think she tried Ecstasy and one or two other things.'

I narrowed my eyes at her. 'You think?'

'OK. I know. She told me.'

Sure. That's the very first thing a prospective nanny would say. 'Hi. I do drugs. Now can I look after your kids?'

Gabriella picked up on my disbelief. 'You see, Joni used to work for me in another capacity. When I took her on as a nanny I specified she stopped taking drugs.'

'And did she?'

'I'm not sure. I thought she'd stopped but recently . . .'

'Recently what?'

Gabriella waggled her pink bobbly shoulders. 'Just a feeling.'

No it wasn't. I said, 'You found stuff.'

She ducked her head into her cup. 'I'm afraid I looked.'

'What? In her bag? In her room?'

A nod.

I said, 'And what did you find?'

The big eyes were on me again. 'Pills.'

Pills. I've got a pile of pills in my bathroom cabinet. It doesn't mean I do Ecstasy. I said, 'Just pills.'

She wrinkled her forehead and squeezed out a couple of little worry lines to bracket the bridge of her nose. They signified she was being ever so serious.

'I don't want any of this in the newspaper, right?'

Any of what? I agreed anyway.

Gabriella said, 'There was a design on the pills, like a four-leaf clover. I described them to Jason and he said he'd been offered Ecstasy which looked like that.'

'Where?'

She didn't understand.

'Where was Jason offered the pills?'

'Oh, I see. At college. At Sussex University.'

And that's just about all Gabriella had. It wasn't much of an exchange.

She knew it too. She said, 'I'm sure I'll hear things from the police which I can pass on to you.'

Yes. I suppose she could. The deal still stood.

I was in the process of giving her my various telephone numbers when there came the sound of a distant chime.

'That,' I said, 'must be Beverley.'

And so it was. Gabriella Cardigan let me out and Bev in.

Gabriella watched me gird myself up for the slog through the snow.

'You don't have a car?'

I shook my head. 'I drink instead.'

She said, 'Well then, Jason will be able to drive you around – he doesn't drink.'

The boy has much to learn.

I wandered off, my brain firing twenty questions a second. By the time I hit the end of the Cardigans' drive I had them all sorted. All but the big one: was there a link between Joni's death and drugs?

Then a second question bubbled to the surface: how come Gabriella was so singularly unmoved by the murder of her au pair? No tears, no crumpled Kleenex, no tragic stares into the middle distance. Downright callous, I call it.

Maybe she used to be a hack.

Chapter Three

I found myself a bar where no one else was likely to find me and gave News Desk a shout. Angela Whipple whooped with joy and praised me for my cunning in recruiting Jason to our ranks. That's how I played it. In the bar mirror I caught sight of my face. It had a sickly grin plastered all over it.

The next move was to call Mac. Mac is an inspector in the Met. He is unique among his breed because he tells us reporters what the Old Bill are up to. In our gratitude we shower him with stacks of readies. He in turn buys us untold quantities of drink. There is something symbiotic about our relationship.

Mac guessed right away what I wanted – the name of the geezer with the poodle called Jack. For a mere three hundred quid I not only got his name, but his age, his former occupation and his address too. Felix Pegg was sixty-four and used to earn his daily crust as a literary agent. It takes all sorts I suppose. Mac didn't have his phone number which meant I had to swallow my drink and go in search of No. 127 Sackville Road. This time I hooked a minicab.

Sackville Road was a backwater of skinny terrace houses in a street lined with bony trees. No. 127 looked just the same as all the others except it had more snow stacked on the roof. Either Felix Pegg had ace insulation or the heating wasn't on.

Jack the poodle began kicking up hell before I even banged the knocker. I heard a growling and whuffling, followed some seconds later by a rustling and clumping. The latter I took to be F. Pegg. The door swung open and there stood Jack and the bloke from the park. He recognized me too for he started shutting the door on my face. Somehow my foot got in the way.

I said briskly, 'My paper has asked me to verify that you have won our £5,000 reward.'

Felix Pegg had a bristly little moustache which performed handstands when he spoke. 'Reward? What reward?'

That meant he didn't read our mighty organ. I stuck my foot in half a centimetre more.

I went through the whole sorry rigmarole of how the Editor was forking out five grand to whoever found Joni. I ended with, 'And the police told me it was you, so you are entitled to the reward.'

Felix Pegg said, 'Come in.'

I stepped carefully over Jack and followed Pegg down a narrow hallway which featured mugshots of old fogeys with beards and old dears without them but who might have looked better with them. We branched left into a lounge and I peered around. It was one of those manilla coloured jobs but you couldn't see much of it on account of the high rise bookcases. Pegg must have had a sideline in swiping library books. The mystery of the snowy roof was solved – it was stone cold in there.

Now that I was in, he didn't know what to do with

me. He said the first thing that came into his head. 'A cup of tea?'

I'd already had my caffeine quota for the day but I said yes because people don't chuck you out when you've got your pinkie curled around their best china.

He melted away. Jack stayed, just in case I half-inched any of the books. Pegg returned bearing brown beakers with Mississippi swamp water sloshing about in them. I sipped it like it was a single malt.

I said, 'I shan't keep you long. I just have to establish that you found the body.'

Pegg had bleached-out blue eyes that shied away from you. His teeth were too regular. I'll bet they sat on his bedside table grinning at him all the livelong night. He was about five nine and a couple of stone below his fighting weight. He could also have done with a decent tailor. I guessed there was no Mrs Pegg in his life.

He said, 'Chief Inspector Skelly told me I mustn't talk to the Press.'

I said, 'Of course not. Tom Skelly is absolutely right. You know how reporters get in the way.'

'You know Mister Skelly?'

I gave the impression that Peabrain Skelly and I were as close as two men can be without getting indecent.

This puzzled him. 'But *you're* a reporter?'

A light laugh from me. I said, 'In this instance I am here purely to find out if you qualify for the reward. I don't want to know anything about the murder.'

He was still puzzled but the prospect of an easy five grand saw him through it. He told me to sit myself down which I did. He sat opposite on a matching overstuffed chair. His hands hung down over his knees. No sign of a wedding ring. His nails were bitten right back.

Pegg asked, 'What do you need to know?'

I said, 'Were you the first on the scene this morning?'

He thought back. For God's sake it wasn't that long ago. I straightened my creases and waited. After a while he said, 'Well, it was Jack really who found her.'

Terrific. We'll give the poodle the five grand then.

He rambled on. 'I took him out for a walk just before seven. I listened to the headlines on *Today* first. He likes an early run in the park.'

I managed to hold my excitement in check. Pegg was not the most interesting man in this God's world. I bet he could remember where he was when Robert Kennedy was shot.

Pegg was saying, 'I always take him through the side gate for it's always left open. There was no one else around and Jack had run on ahead of me. I could hear him barking so I went to see what was up. That's when I saw it. It was just off the path.'

It, I gathered, was Joni Poelma.

I said, 'I suppose it was the blood that attracted Jack.'

'Blood? No, there wasn't any blood. But I'm not supposed to talk about what happened.'

I purred, 'No, I don't want to know anyway. I just wonder if there were any footprints around the body.'

He flashed me a suspicious look.

I said, 'All I'm trying to establish is whether you were first on the scene. You see, someone might have found the body before you and gone off to phone the police.'

A distant light shone in his eyes. 'Ah, I understand.

No, there were no footprints. None at all. I'm certain of that.'

I said, 'It must have been a shock for you.'

He whiffled through his moustache. 'Yes, it was rather. I had to come home and pour myself a glass of Madeira.'

He must have swigged the whole bottle for he certainly wasn't offering any around.

I was speaking almost to myself. 'She was such a pretty girl too.'

He turned his head away. Whatever he'd seen, it wasn't pretty. I let him think about it for maybe thirty seconds. I said, 'These are violent days.'

Felix Pegg nodded his bonce in vehement agreement but he still wasn't saying anything. I weighed in with, 'The sex killings are the worst.'

He had his head down and I could hardly hear him. He said, 'At least she was spared that I think.'

I laced my voice with 80 proof sympathy and asked, 'Did the police give you a bad time of it?'

'Not really. They wanted to know what time I'd left the house, and where I lived. Just routine, really.'

I said, 'That's good. Sometimes the police – I don't mean Tom Skelly – but the young officers can be very insensitive. They make witnesses feel like suspects, asking them silly questions, like, "Did you see a handbag?"'

The thin edge of a smile rippled Felix Pegg's moustache. 'Funnily enough, they did ask me that. But I didn't mind. Then they asked me why I wasn't wearing a scarf.'

I said, 'Ah, the red scarf.'

He gave me a sharp glance. 'It was green.'

I goggled. 'I'm sure Tom told me it was red.'

'No, he must have meant the coat. The scarf was patterned, but it was definitely green. Paisley patterned.'

And that, basically, was all Pegg had to say for himself. I promised him we'd have the cheque posted post-haste. On the way out I lingered in the hall before the whiskered snaps just so that I could steal a glance at the phone and memorize the number.

Behind me Pegg was saying something, speaking so softly I could hardly hear him. He said, 'She was smiling.'

He was not being chatty. He was just reliving the scene out loud.

I said, 'Smiling?'

'Well, I suppose it couldn't have been a smile. More a sort of death rictus.'

Rictus is a word that our readers don't have hanging about their houses.

I said, 'Like a grimace?'

He preferred rictus. I looked closely at him but his eyes were far away. He said, 'Her face, her cheek was in the snow. She was just lying there, smiling.'

I didn't say a word. Pegg was still back there in the park. 'She was on her side, facing the path. I could see her eyes. She was a dreadful colour. You knew right away there was something wrong. But she was smiling.'

He left it like that for a moment and then he got himself together.

'Sorry,' he said.

He pulled the front door open for me. We didn't

shake hands but Jack wagged his tail. I turned as I hit the street and said, 'Don't forget what Tom Skelly told you.'

'What?'

'You mustn't talk to reporters.'

'Oh, I wouldn't open the door to them,' Pegg promised.

Now that I'd got the day's funny business out of the way, it was time to write the story. This needed a stiffish Gordons or two to coax the brain out of hiding. I grazed through the cuts until I had all the relevant facts, ages and so on. I fetched out the mobile and phoned Mission Control. They patched me through to copy and Dorian, whose real name is Ernie, but we needn't go into that right now.

I told him to call the story 'Joni'.

Dorian said, 'Is this for News, Max?'

No, you fool, it's for Sport. I started dictating:

MISSING disco girl Joni Poelma was found strangled yesterday in a kiddies' playpark.

I'd got as far as 'Poelma' before Dorian chipped in, 'Spell that.'

I said, 'P as in ptarmigan, O as in Oedipus, L as in Llandudno, M as in mnemonic, A as in aisle.'

Dorian said, 'Stop mucking about, Max.'

I spelt it properly and got on with the story:

And last night police were quizzing pushers after it emerged she was hooked on rave drugs.

The nationwide hunt for the stunning blonde was called off when a *Gazette* reader stumbled across her body.

Joni – au pair to multimillionaire scientist Wedge Cardigan – was half-buried in snow.

A shocked Felix Pegg who found her said, 'At first it looked like she was smiling.

'But the smile was only her death grimace. It was chilling.'

Forensic experts are now probing a silk paisley-patterned scarf found knotted tightly around Joni's throat.

The vivacious 23-year-old Dutch girl was murdered less than a mile from the smart-set disco where she was last seen.

But detectives are baffled over where Joni was in the seven days since she vanished in the upmarket London suburb of Dulwich .

Gazette reader Mr Pegg made the grim discovery while taking his poodle Jack for an early morning walk in Victoria Park.

He said, 'We follow the same path every day and if Joni had been there before, we would have found her. She was lying just beside the path, her cheek in the snow.

'Her eyes were open but she was a dreadful colour and I knew right away there was something wrong.

'Her death smile will haunt me forever.'

A senior officer said, 'She was not the victim of a sex attack.

'Her handbag was stolen but we have also ruled out robbery as a motive.'

Police suspect that Joni – a known Ecstasy user – was killed after a drugs deal went sour.

They are quizzing clubgoers and . . .

And about another 300 words, among which were snappy quotes like '*She was a pretty girl but it was an ugly crime*' (Pegg), '*The children keep asking me where Joni is*' (Gabriella Cardigan), and '*She may have double-crossed a drug pusher*' (our old friend, the senior police officer).

After I'd filed it all, I did a routine check with Press Bureau. The story was already all over page one of the *Standard* so they were forced into confirming that it was indeed Joni. But as to the cause of death, they were heroically unhelpful.

I said, 'I have it on good authority she was mauled to death by a polar bear.'

They told me to go away. People sometimes think I am hypercritical of Scotland Yard's press officers. But I ask you, who else in the world believes that alsatians have fingers? I know for a fact that Press Bureau does, because one night back in the eighties, an emergency plumber called Mike was tackling a blocked drain in Muswell Hill when he found human fingers poking out of it. He called in the Old Bill and somebody tipped us off. I gave Press Bureau a bell.

'It's only an alsatian,' they said.

It was nothing of the kind. The fingers were the first

human remains of serial killer Denis Nilsen's many, many victims.

Some hours later I was sitting in Hampton's, drinking something which pretended to be champagne, when my mobile gave voice. At first I pretended not to notice in the fond hope it would give up. It just kept on keening. I clicked on.

'Hello,' said a voice.

I'd never heard this voice before but I groaned anyway. It was a middle-class voice and it sounded too young to be awake at this time of night.

I said, 'Hello, Jason.'

'How did you know it was me?'

'It's a gift I have.'

He wanted to know where I was so I told him. I even gave him directions on how to get there.

He said, 'How will I recognize you?'

'Don't worry, I'll recognize you.'

This wouldn't be difficult. Hampton's, as usual, was knee deep in Fleet Street's less discriminating drunks, their numbers swollen by a jellied mob of blokes who put on black frocks during the day and act like lawyers. The appearance in this charnel house of a fresh-faced teetotal youth would be as unusual as finding intelligent life on News Desk.

I forgot about Jason because I was seriously involved in trading blank meal receipts with a circle of hacks. This was very important as I'd just blown a thousand quid more than I owned on clothes and I needed to rack up a few weeks' expenses. The time passed merrily. Suddenly I looked up and there was Jason, standing just inside the door with his eyes bright and his mouth agape.

This much I'd expected. What I didn't expect was the earring and the pigtail. For more than a moment I was tempted to knock the whole thing on the head. But curiosity got the better of me. I slid from the bosom of my cronies and made myself known.

Up close Jason was as previously described. I've left out the facts that he was tall and made up entirely of bones. His chin was speckled with week-old stubble. The overall effect was enough to frighten the horses. Jason split his mouth in an amiable beam. 'Hello, Mister Chard,' he said.

Behind me I could hear Hampton's roar diminish to a startled hush.

I said briskly, 'Follow me', and marched to the tacked-on restaurant at the tail end of the bar where illicit lovers mauled each other between mouthfuls of E-Coli. I knew Jason was following me from the way the lovers looked up in morbid curiosity.

I sat him down in the dimmest most distant corner of the dive. He said, 'I've got the car outside now.'

I said, 'Good. They don't like you parking inside.'

Jason was oblivious to the stir he'd caused. He rubbernecked around the bar. 'Is this your local, Mister Chard?'

'Call me Max.'

'All right.'

I said, 'Your name is Ben.'

He looked as if he was going to dispute that.

I said, 'Your name is Ben and you're my nephew. I don't want anybody here knowing who you really are.'

He said, 'Why?'

This was going to be harder than I feared.

Chapter Four

My glass was empty. I waved in the direction of Babs the marauding waitress who promptly came over and sat on my lap; she's friendly like that. She ruffled my hair and fiddled with my tie, but a man has priorities. Besides, Babs is heavier than she thinks. I dislodged her gently and told her to unbung a bottle of house champagne for me. She tilted her head interrogatively at Jason.

He said, 'Just a coke, please.'

I said, 'In a clean glass.'

Jason and I were silent for a moment while we watched Babs weave and wend through the tables. She was worth watching.

He said, 'What did you write about Joni?'

He had brown eyes, as soft as a little floppy bunny's. In another age he might have been a poet. Maybe he still was.

I just shrugged. 'The usual. Plus a bit your mum told me about the drugs link.'

'Ah,' he said.

Not 'What!', not 'Drugs!', not anything. So the boy Jason knew what connected Joni with drugs.

I said, 'What was she on?'

He opened his mouth to say something but Babs breezed up clinking glass. She made a production out of serving us, leaning right over the table as she poured. One of these days she really ought to get herself a bigger blouse. Either that or industrial strength buttons.

We watched her go again.

I said, 'You were saying?'

He said, 'Wow! She's up for it.'

Babs has that effect on first time viewers. I rolled bubbles around my mouth and waited for his brain to find its way home. After a while he remembered me.

Jason said, 'Sorry.' When he grinned he showed you his teeth. They were probably still milk teeth.

I said, 'We were talking about Joni and drugs.'

'Ah, yes.'

I wasn't sure whether he didn't want to tell me or he was just plain woolly-headed. I changed direction.

'Tell me about your media course.'

That gave him a push start. He said, 'I was wondering if you could help me – I've got a thesis to do by Easter.'

'What about?'

'Chequebook journalism.'

I flashed him a look but he wasn't taking the mick. I said, 'How much have you got to write?'

'About five thousand words.'

Five thousand! How in the name of heaven do you train someone to be a reporter by getting them to write more than anybody can read? The very essence of our job is getting it fast, getting it short, getting it clear. Getting it right is a bonus.

I marvelled at the stupidity of media studies courses.

Their whole point seems to be to teach waffle and padding and flimflam. All the things the subs chuck out.

But as I mused thus, a little diamond-studded idea stuck its head up and said, 'Why don't you get Jason to *write* what he knows?'

I ran with it. I said, 'The first thing we've got to do is have a look at your style. Then we'll tighten it up.'

Jason said, 'You want me to show you what I've written on the thesis so far?'

'No. I want to give you an exercise. You know, I give you the facts of a story and you write it up as if you were a tabloid reporter.'

He liked the sound of that. 'What's the story?'

I went all vague, as if I was casting round for an idea. Then I sat up with a big bright smile. 'I know. Write the story of Joni's murder. You already have the background.'

Jason wavered. 'I don't know . . .'

I steamrollered right over him. 'It's bang on. And if you're unsure about any of the details, just make them up. Pretend you're a real reporter.'

He still wasn't red hot for it but he was getting there. He said, 'OK, I'll be able to have it done by tomorrow night.'

Sometimes you just despair.

I said, 'No. It's like I said: pretend you're a real reporter. Write it now.'

'Here?'

'All the best stories are written in bars, though usually better bars than this.'

I dug out a notebook and ripped off half a dozen sheets. I said, 'Please use both sides of the paper.'

I had to give him a pen too. I stood up and looked at my watch. I said, 'I'll give you half an hour.'

Jason nodded dumbly and took the top off the Bic. At least it was a start.

I collared my bottle and returned to join the resident bar props. I gave him all of forty minutes. When I got back to the table he had three sheets of paper covered in arty looking writing. He was still scribbling.

I said, 'Let's see what you've got.'

It kicked off like this:

A 23-year-old Dutch visitor was discovered brutally murdered by police in Dulwich, south-east London yesterday morning after being missing for some days.

I sighed and lit a cigarette. This was going to be a three-Bensons problem.

I said, 'The word "A" in an intro is a dead word, and "23-year-old" is three dead words. You need to open with a word that jumps up and bites you, like "Sexy", or "Gunmen" or "Evil". That way you've grabbed them from the start.'

He looked hurt. I didn't care. Stories are important to me, more important than tender sensibilities. And the deal with his stepmum was for me to tutor Jason.

I breezed on. 'You've called Joni a Dutch visitor. That doesn't even tell you her sex. What was her job?'

Jason mumbled, 'She was a nanny.'

'No she wasn't: she was an au pair.'

He dug his heels in on that one. 'She was a nanny.'

I said, 'Which sounds sexier – nanny or au pair?'

He didn't have to think long. 'Au pair.'

'Right. So Joni was an au pair. Now she was not "discovered", she was "found".'

'Because "found" is a smaller word?'

'You got it. OK. What's next? She was *brutally* murdered? Now if she was *tenderly* murdered, that's a story. Otherwise—'

'—It's tautology,' said Jason.

'Yes, one of those things. Plus she was *not* murdered by the police. Even they have got more sense.'

He gave a crooked smile. I took some more fizz on board and cracked on. 'Dulwich you don't need. Our readers in Hartlepool and Kirkcudright think Dulwich is a town in Bosnia.'

Jason said, 'But I've said it's in London.'

I rolled my eyes. 'When a reader in Hartlepool sees that a story is in London he couldn't give a toss. He wouldn't care if every man, woman and child in London was topped. I know. I've been in Hartlepool. You stick London way down the story.'

He tried out the crooked smile again. 'Otherwise it's all right?'

I can be a right sod at times. 'No. You said she was found yesterday morning. You've just made the story twenty-four hours old. All right, so we know it's that old but you've got to *bury* that, make it sound as fresh as their morning pinta. And then you've said she was missing for "some" days.'

'Well, she was.'

I said, 'No she wasn't. She was missing for *seven* days. Or, if you're not sure, stick in five, eight, ten days whatever. They won't even notice if you've got it wrong.

37

But if you write "some" days, that means you don't know. Whereupon your reader will not trust another word you write. "Some" is not a word.'

Jason said in a small voice: 'They don't teach you it like this in media studies.'

'That's because they're teachers, not hacks. If you think I'm being too tough on you it's because you've got to get the intro right. After that it writes itself.'

'And what do you think of the rest of it?'

I went through it quickly. There were lots of words that nobody ever says, like 'however' and 'declined' and 'despite', but I let them pass. I didn't want Jason to burst into tears. This is what he had written.

The young woman victim, whom the police have identified as Miss Joni Poelma, a native of Genk in the Netherlands, was stated to be a friendly girl with no enemies.

She went missing after visiting the Silver Lino club in Dulwich where she was described by clubgoers as a 'raver' who loved British Indie bands like the Doncha and Tuf Luvvin'.

One clubgoer who declined to be named said that Joni frequently 'partied till dawn' in the well-known club where she had made many friends despite only recently coming to London.

A police spokesman said that so far there had been little progress in the search for her killer. However he was hopeful that her little green address book might provide them with clues. It includes the names of some friends she had met on the club scene.

Joni was a nanny to the family of leading indus-
trialist Mr William –

Jason had crossed that out and made it

Wedge Cardigan whose home lies almost a mile from
where she was last seen alive.
Her employer's wife, Mrs Gabriella Cardigan,
said, 'We all miss Joni very much and send our
deepest sympathy to her parents . . .'

It ran on for another page and a half without going
anywhere in particular. But I already had plenty to think
about. I tapped the first sheet and asked, 'What's this
crack about her little green book?'

He grinned all over his face. 'I made it up. Just like
a reporter. Anyway, every girl's got a little address book,
so it's probably true.'

It wasn't bad. I said, 'And the raver girl line; did you
make that up too?'

Jason said, 'No. Joni was really into clubbing. She
was there every weekend.'

'At the disco?'

'At the club. They're not called discos anymore.'

I frowned at him. 'Listen, our readers think a club is
what you hit somebody over the head with. It's a disco.'

'OK. Call it a disco, then. But it's still a club. I thought
we might go there tonight.'

We? Some bubbles, make it twenty-five bubbles,
went up my nose.

Jason said, 'Yes. The Silver Lino. That's the last place

Joni went. Maybe her mates know something they haven't told the police.'

I said, 'I have a better idea. You be my leg man – my researcher. You go and see what you can find out and I'll meet you here same time tomorrow. OK?'

He fell for it. 'All right. What are you going to do?'

I told him some fanciful yarn about me having to shoot off to see a contact on the Fraud Squad. He swallowed that too. I signalled to Babs who trotted up with the bill. Thirty-eight quid for two bottles of blanc de blanc, shot through with soda water, plus a coke.

Jason said, 'Oops. I almost forgot.' His hand shot into his jacket pocket and came out waving a creamy envelope. On the front of it somebody had written in black ink with an italic nib, 'Max Chard.'

He handed it over. I hoisted an eyebrow.

Jason explained, 'Mum said to give this to you – to cover your expenses.'

I slid a thumbnail along the flap. Inside there wasn't a letter or a thank you card or anything personal like that. There was just a thick wad of orange fifty-quid notes. I counted, even though I already knew how many there were. There were forty of them. That came to bang on two grand. Precisely what I'd offered Gabriella for her story.

And they talk about chequebook journalism.

Chapter Five

The taxi driver agreed to transport me down to Battersea only on the clear understanding that I didn't smoke. Next thing he wanted to yak all the way there. I threatened, 'You talk, I smoke.'

That shut him up. We journeyed on in mutual frustration. But at least I'd plenty to think about. Item One was the vellum envelope stuffed with cash which was presently ruining the cut of my Daks. Of course I couldn't take Gabriella Cardigan's lolly. But then again, why not?

I pushed that one aside and took a look at Item Two: what Jason had told me about Joni and drugs, or rather, what he had signally failed to tell me. Why so coy? I stuck it in the pending file and moved on to the next: Joni's little green book. Every girl's got one, Jason had said. No they don't. Some girls have a little black book, or a little yellow book, or even one in heliotrope. But Joni had a little green book. Jason didn't make that bit up. That meant he'd seen the thing.

And that took me on to the next question: where had he seen it? Where does a girl keep her book of red-hot names – in the top drawer under her Janet Reger flimsies? In the glovebox of her GTi? In the freezer? I thought about Rosie, the woman whom I know more than slightly. She's got an address book the size of the electoral roll and she parks it in her handbag. That sounds about the right place for it.

Then I thought about Jason. Barring the pigtail, the earring and the stubble, he seemed reasonably all right for a teenager. Maybe a bit young for his age. And maybe that was why he didn't seem at all bothered about Joni's killing. I gave up.

Anyway, Battersea had popped up on the starboard bow, there was a light in her window, and I had far better things to think about.

Rosie is not an easy girl to describe because every time you describe her, she goes and changes the way she looks, the way she dresses, the way she acts. On this particular night she was acting uppity on account of me rolling up on the wrong side of midnight. There was a hint of flame in the smoky blue eyes.

Sometimes it's better to come clean and admit, 'Sorry I'm late – I've been on the toot.' Other times it's better to spin out a long convoluted excuse and hope that it does the biz. The trouble is, with Rosie anyway, you never know which time is which.

Therefore I compromised by telling her the saga of Jason, tossing in a line about meeting some old drinking mates from the Law. I didn't tell her about the knock-you-down-dead looks of Jason's stepmum, for there are some things it is safer to keep from Rosie. She heard me through in silence. I prefer it when she yells and shouts and chucks things at me. Though not the ice bucket. When I was done she said, 'You sleep on the sofa.'

A bit harsh, I thought. But I just nodded glumly,

hoping she might take pity on me. Rosie was fresh out of pity but she had a whole heap of grievance in stock. She unloaded it in a way calculated to make a man feel sadder than is good for him. First off she padded away to the bedroom. I poured myself a Gordons and listened. There followed the rustly sounds of a woman undressing herself. My imagination popped up with a gleam in its eye. 'Hey!' it shouted. I stood on its head.

Rosie reappeared, clad only in an ivory kimono thing, which, if she had stood still long enough, would have told you what my imagination was kicking up such a fuss about. She skipped lightly through the lounge, her black curls bobbing in synch with everything else. Then she was gone.

Next came the splatter of her nuclear-powered shower, and above that, a clear soprano singing something by Annie Lennox. She sounded deliriously happy. I sighed. This gin was missing the spot.

I hung around smoking and drinking for close on twenty minutes. The shower shut up. She went on singing. Another ten minutes ambled past on the legs of a three-toed sloth. She reappeared. There was a saffron towel wrapped round her head and it kept all but the wildest curls in check. The towel's big brother was draped over just about every inch of the rest of her. But my imagination told me that underneath it she was pink, and fresh and naked. If we were married I could have got a divorce on the grounds of mental cruelty.

She plonked herself down on the sofa, three inches or less from my left knee. She said without inflection, 'I've got to be up early, but I'll try not to disturb you.'

Now, wasn't that decent of her? I didn't think so either. I said, 'What's on tomorrow?'

I said it to the back of her head for she had produced a make-up bag from somewhere and was busy doing something to her nails.

'Just some designs.'

Rosie, I'd better explain, is arty. She draws lizards and frogs and terrapins and things like that which gambol playfully across curtains and wallpapers. She also knocks up the occasional tie for me, which is more than any of my other girlfriends ever did.

I said, 'An early start then. I'll rustle up my own breakfast.'

'Yes, you will.'

It was getting chillier by the minute in there. I suppose I could have flung a careless arm around her and said 'Sorry', but she wouldn't have believed me anyway. She finished what she was doing to her cuticles and toddled off bedwards.

I called out over my shoulder, 'What – no night-night kiss?'

She didn't answer for a good twenty seconds. When she did, her voice was back to its usual smoky purr. 'It's your turn to kiss me.'

I was in the bedroom before my imagination even twigged.

Rosie woke me in the morning with a cup of something that tasted like it had been brewed by the Druids. I'd forgotten she'd switched to herbal tea. I swigged back a mouthful anyway, for I am a considerate soul. Then she planted a kiss on my forehead, shrieked 'Byeee!' and she was gone. That left me alone, but for Blue, her rancid old cat. 'Morning, Goebbels,' I said, giving him/it his/its proper anatomical name. He stuck his tail up in the air and minced off in offended dignity.

I popped down to the corner newsagent's to get my daily fix of newsprint. Joni's murder got a decent show all over, though nobody else had the stuff I had. My chum Ali in the *Mirror* had a good line about the DISCO DEMON – linking Joni's killing with that of Sandra Wade who vanished fourteen months back on her way home from a girls' night out. Nice line, shame about the facts. Sandra was killed the night she went AWOL. Joni was not. Sandra was bludgeoned and knifed to death, Joni was strangled. Sandra, a granny, had been at an old-tyme dancing thrash, and, whatever the Silver Lino was, it was not the place to go if you fancied a quick waltz. Apart from these minor details, Ali's story made perfect sense.

Skelly had opened up to the *Mail*, to the effect that Joni's murder was a vicious and senseless crime. He added that somebody out there, a wife, perhaps a mother, might be shielding the monster, and if they would be so kind, would they come forward and grass on him. He was already hitting the desperation button.

I took my time about getting to the office because there was nothing on the morning news to make my heart go pitty-pat. And, if the day behaved itself, I reckoned there was a more than reasonable chance I could slope off for a long lunch with sundry dissolutes. Which just shows what a bum fortune teller I'd be.

My desk is tucked away in the extreme right-hand

corner of the newsroom. The nearest window offers a prospect of Southwark across the Thames, but I didn't choose the spot for its view. What makes my little corner so appealing is that it is the furthest point from News Desk, therefore I am least likely to be saddled with tomfool stories. Also, it is the closest point to the back stairs, meaning I can slip out for a swift one without them noticing.

Today the assorted News Desk inadequates didn't even glower in my direction. They just sat around staring at the incoming stories on their screens. You could tell they weren't reading them because their lips weren't moving. I spent the morning phoning mates in other sleeping newsrooms. I was scheduled for a follow up on the Joni story but so far nothing had changed. If I'd been feeling more energetic I might have given Gabriella Cardigan a buzz and asked her to tell me what she'd got from the Law. Instead I just filled in the time helping a couple of monkeys fiddle their expenses. Monkeys, in case you're wondering, is our euphemism for photographers.

I also grabbed a copy of our great newspaper and flipped over to Beverley Nephews' features page thing on Gabriella Cardigan. It got off to a slowish start.

THEIRS is a house built for laughter and gracious living.

But yesterday there was only heartache in a home touched by tragedy.

Behind drawn blinds Gabriella Cardigan was never far from tears as she talked about Joni Poelma, the nanny who lived and laughed with her family.

There were about another nine hundred words in like vein. Buried away in the slush were a couple of things I didn't know. Like I didn't know Gabriella Cardigan was wearing Ellesse trainers. Nor was I aware that she was a qualified biochemist. Even more astonishing was the news she had a heated swimming pool, a forty-foot dining room and a painting by somebody called Palmer. It just goes to show how informative our features pages are. I must read them more often.

I was interrupted by the sudden arrival of Angela Whipple off my right elbow. Angie is our News Editor, and, as the species go, is less awful than most. She's also a reasonable piece of totty. Take an inch off her nose and a stone off her weight and she'd be a very reasonable piece indeed. Angie used to be a hack of sorts herself, though her speciality was the netherworld of showbiz where you just make it up as you go along.

She perched herself on the corner of my desk and flashed a leg or two. 'OK, Max. What's the Joni Poelma line today?'

That's another thing about News Editors. They think we're clairvoyant.

I told her the police were rifling through Joni's little green book and she nodded sagely, as if she knew what I was talking about.

I looked closely at Angie and guessed she was not her usual romping, stomping self. It couldn't be a hangover because these News Desk people have forgotten how to enjoy themselves. I put her gloom down to one of those hideous internal political intrigues that are God's punishment on newspaper execs.

Still, I felt sorry for Angie, for she gives me a longish

leash. I tried to coax her into telling me what was bothering her, but she was in no comment mode. She drifted off with her head down.

I was sufficiently moved to do some work. I had a vague idea I might get something more on Joni from Holland so I phoned Karl, our stringer in the Hague. We usually bother him only about twice a year, when we feel the need to run another two-page exposé on drugs, sex and squalor in the back canals of Amsterdam. He always writes the same guff but nobody's noticed it yet.

'Joni who?' he asked, demonstrating once again that his news instinct is remarkably undimmed by a lifetime passion for genever gin.

I took him patiently through the story and somewhere along the way he remembered something or other but he couldn't remember what. But he'd let me know when he did.

So much for Karl. I was pondering whether it was time for an early livener when in the distance I spied the wobbling bulk of Belker, our despised executive editor. His Easter Island gaze was battened on me.

Automatically I picked up the phone and tried to look busy. It didn't work. Out of the corner of my eye I saw him advancing with all the innate grace of a slag heap until he was there bang in front of me, blotting out the rest of the Newsroom.

I glanced up casually and to my horror he was smiling. Tony Belker *never* smiles at me. He never even talks to me. Our usual conversational exchanges start with him bellowing and stamping a cloven hoof. After that things go downhill.

I put down the phone with great care and gave him

my full attention. He was still smiling. I'm pretty sure I wasn't.

'I liked your Joni Poelma story today, Max.'

I waited for the sting. It didn't come.

Belker said, 'I suppose you've got a good follow up.'

This was said without menace, without sarcasm. It didn't make me feel any happier. I eyed him warily. He was outwardly the same pasty-faced, two-ton heap of sweating blubber and malice that I'd met on Day One at the *Gazette*. My impression then had been, 'Quick, grab a shovel: there's still somebody buried in there.'

I just nodded and said, 'It's coming along.'

Belker nodded back. 'Good, good. I thought we might have a word.'

A couple of words sprung instantly to mind. I thought it safer not to say them.

He was getting matier by the minute. He shifted his bulk and for one terrible moment I thought he was about to plop his backside on the corner of the desk, thereby catapulting me, my computer screen and plastic cup of plastic tea into the middle of next week. He thought better of it. I eased a fraction.

Belker said, 'What have you got planned for lunch?'

This meant that he had something planned for my lunch.

I said, 'I'm on a diet.'

Irony is not his strong point.

He said, 'You can break it. I thought we could go to Joe Allen's and have a chat.'

Frankly I'd rather have lunch with Lucrezia Borgia, Hannibal Lecter and the entire Arsenal first team squad, but there are some things you don't say.

Belker shifted from one haunch to the other and flapped his trousers. 'Good man. Let's say half-past one.'

He trundled off, leaving me to smoke several cigarettes and try to figure out what the hell was going on. I didn't get anywhere.

Belker turned up five minutes later than threatened which just meant I had five more minutes of fruitless puzzling.

I let him pay for the cab, and I let him lead the way down the stairs into Joe Allen's. He gollomphed down them like a rhino to the waterhole. The place was as usual packed with Fleet Street mini-execs. Several raised a cheery face to greet me, then, when they saw who I was with, rapidly turned away again. I would have done the same.

Belker had booked a table for two. It was tucked away round the back, and for this I was grateful. He was in no hurry to get to the point, and so while we waited for the Chablis (his) and gin (mine) to arrive, he ran through a string of daft questions – was I married yet, had I my holidays planned, had I seen the new *Prime Suspect* movie. This was his idea of friendly conversation. I answered no in three different ways.

The drinks arrived but he just kept waffling on. I realized he was waiting for his nosh. Mine was the chicken estragon. He went for the Lincolnshire sausage. God help us, he had chips with it.

There now followed a period of silence on my part and a noisy performance from the human fork-lift truck as he got stuck in. No one had ever told him to shut his mouth while he ate. I averted my eyes.

He was halfway through the pile when he came up for air.

'We had a think-tank last week.'

I sipped delicately, dabbed my lips and said, 'Oh?'

Every couple of months the paper's A List of halfwits lock themselves away for a weekend in some snooty hotel and drink the joint dry. They call these beanos think-tanks. The general idea is that, safely cocooned from the hurly-burly of the office, the assembled wastrels will come up with some grand plan to halt the paper's plummeting circulation and to make life more hellish for the rest of us. Though not necessarily in that order.

What usually happens is they come away so addled with drink that they've forgotten everything they planned.

Belker slid his little flat eyes this way and that. He said, 'Max, this is just between the two of us.'

With his bulk we looked more like three. He was staring straight at me. I had my eyes fixed firmly on my plate.

He said, 'Some questions were raised about the News Desk operation.'

Good. That meant it had nothing to do with me.

Jabba the Hutt opposite got busy with his gnashers again. I think he was expecting me to say something.

I said, 'Nice hotel?'

'Great,' he said, flashing me a sausage and chip smile.

There was something worrying me. It took me a sip or two to work out what: if News Desk were this week's whipping boys, why was he telling me?

Belker resurfaced. 'The feeling is the wheels have come off News Desk. It's lost its cutting edge.'

He waved a fork around, 'It needs more ideas. It needs to interface with reporters better.'

'You mean, talk to us.'

'Exactly,' said Belker who had just realized what interface means.

It is never a smart move for a hack to badmouth News Desk to an alleged superior. I said, 'It's been a quiet month.'

'Doesn't matter. The lifeblood of a newspaper is its ideas men. Take you.'

'Me?' There was something seriously wrong going on here.

Belker said, 'That was a terrific idea getting that kid Julian so we've got a beat on the Joni Poelma yarn.'

'Jason.'

'That shows thinking.'

It also shows how a pretty woman can con me into anything.

I said, 'Angie was all for it.'

This was intended to give Angie a generous plug. I was beginning to understand the reason for her morning gloom. They'd been having a pop at her.

Belker said, 'She's a good admin exec but we need a more hands-on approach.'

In short, Angela Whipple is a crummy News Editor. I raised a pained eyebrow to signify I disagreed.

He sucked his teeth. He said, 'In this game you've got to run with the ball, Max. I can tell you, though you mustn't onpass it, News Desk is scheduled for down-sizing.'

Normally this is the sort of news which brightens a hack's day, but not when it comes from Belker. Anyway, it still had sod all to do with me. My glass was empty. He didn't notice.

He said, 'The game plan is to streamline the operation, possibly giving Angela an exec news editor role . . .'

That meant pushing her out on a limb. The next step is you saw off the branch.

' . . . which means we need a good proactive man in her slot.'

That's when it hit me. He wanted *me* to go on News Desk.

Maybe it was the way my face went white, maybe it was because I dropped my fork. At any rate he knew I'd caught on.

'What about it, Max?'

What about it? This was the worst idea since Pot Noodles. There is something the outside world doesn't know about reporting. It is the very best job in the entire universe and the bit beyond. Give me the choice of romping nude with Michelle Pfeiffer in a jacuzzi or covering a fish 'n' chippy murder down Catford, and Catford wins every time. No regrets.

Any proper hack feels the same. But here's the odd thing: into our enchanted world there come strange people who somehow fail to appreciate the wonder of it all. They spend their sad lives chained to desks in the pursuit of executive status. Poor deluded fools, they eventually get to thinking they are superior to us hacks. Really.

'Well?' Belker prompted.

The honest response was to tell him to get his head examined. But honesty and newspapers are mutually incompatible.

I rooted around for the nearest cliché. 'It's a bit sudden, Tony. I'd have to think about it. What exactly is the job?'

His eyes popped. 'Job? I've just told you. Number One on Desk.'

I popped my eyes back at him. 'News Editor? You want *me* to be the News Editor?'

'What do you think I've been talking about?'

Hell's teeth. The prospect was just too awful.

I heard my voice coming from a long way away. It was saying, 'But Tony, I don't have any Desk experience. I've—'

He gave me his village-idiot grin. 'That's precisely why you're the ideal man for the job. You have an overview of the operation. You can bring a fresh eye to bear. So, what do you say?'

I said several things to myself but for his benefit I contributed, 'It's something I've never considered. I'd have to think about it.'

'Excellent. You do that, Max. There'll be a *very* attractive pay rise in it, plus there's a chance I can put you on the share-option scheme.'

He wittered on about the delights in store – no more night work, an office jam jar, my own parking space and so forth. I wasn't listening. I was trying on the title of News Editor for size. It didn't fit.

I was also thinking about the Chard Theory of Fleet Street Executivedom: those whom the Gods destroy, they first give a title.

Chapter Six

We got back to the office with Belker still acting like we were blood brothers. I marched straight over to my desk, taking care not to glance in Angie's direction. But I felt the combined gaze of News Desk firing darts into my back. Even they had to suss something must be up if Belker was talking to me.

I pushed the whole shambles out of my head and read through my on-screen messages. Jason had phoned. Twice. Also, Karl in the Hague wanted words. I got to him before the genever rendered him incomprehensible.

He was sounding sparky which meant he had something. He took his time getting round to it. First off, he read out a string of plain boring quotes from the Dutch papers. I got to hear what everybody from Joni's mum to her ex-headmistress had to say. I could have made up better stuff myself. I probably would.

Karl took a deep breath. 'And then there's her sister.'

Sister? I didn't even know she had one of those.

'Yeh, Astrid. She's in Lille right now.'

I said that must be nice for her. Karl said it wasn't. And why not?

'Because the French police have lifted her.'

She and four others were in a VW Combi the gendarmes pulled in on the E3. Just for the hell of it, the cops stuck a sniffer dog in the minibus. It came out with half a bar of cannabis. Small beer, but they hauled the famous five off to the lock-up and got their blokes with the screwdrivers to take the Combi apart.

That's when they found the 80,000 tabs of acid.

I said, 'Who else has this line?'

Karl said nobody. 'It only happened on Wednesday. I got it by chance from a local paper guy down in Genk. Nobody's running it because drug busts don't mean anything here. It's too ordinary.'

And to prove it, he cited the fact that last year the Lille drugs unit had nicked 109 Dutch day trippers on the E3.

So I had the edge of an angle for today's Joni story. Just as I put the phone down it started ringing again. Jason.

I said, 'Did you know Joni had a sister?'

'Astrid? Yes.'

'Did you know she's been lifted with enough acid to trip out half of Holland?'

People should know better than to whistle into telephones.

Jason said, 'That's a neat angle, isn't it? By the way, I did like you said. I went to the Silver Lino last night.'

I said, 'Is that your whole story?'

'No. I found out something very interesting.'

I shook my head in sorrow. 'Jason. You're meant to be a reporter.'

'So?'

'So you don't start a story by saying you've got something interesting to say. You say the interesting thing first and waffle about later.'

'Oh, yes.'

'Well?'

'Well, there's a guy there dealing E. You know, Ecstasy and cannabis and stuff.'

I said, 'What's the connection?'

'With Joni?'

'No. With the Queen Mum.'

'I'm not sure. He hangs around with a bunch of guys and I think I've seen Joni with one of them.'

I said, 'So you go to the disco too.'

He hesitated. 'Yeh. A couple of times just.'

I said, 'What's the dealer called?'

'Fez, but that's not his real name.'

Well ain't that a surprise.

I said, 'What's he charging for Ecstasy?'

Jason edged and hedged for a moment. Then he said, 'I heard it's twenty.'

'Twenty quid a tab? That sounds steep.'

'Yeh, but this is Dulwich.' You could hear he was smiling.

I said, 'Anything else?'

'Not really. There were a couple of cops in, asking people about Joni again. They saw me.'

'And what did you say?'

'I told them I was working with you.'

And Gabriella Cardigan had told me her Jason was bright.

I said, 'That was so stupid it deserves a mention in the Guinness Book of Records.'

He was so dumb I had to explain why. 'Because if
the Old Bill think you talk to me, they'll tell you nothing.'
'Oh.' He went away bruised and tearful.
And serve him bloody right too.

I made my round of check calls, got nothing new there,
and hammered out five hundred words of follow up on
the lines of:

> ARMED drug busters are holding the sister of mur-
> dered au pair Joni Poelma.
>
> They are linking her to a crime syndicate plot-
> ting to flood teen clubs with designer drugs.
>
> Astrid Poelma, 24, was seized when police
> swooped on a minibus carrying LSD with a street
> value of £1.5 million.
>
> Last night undercover drug officers joined
> murder squad detectives hunting the killer of her
> 23-year-old sister, Joni.
>
> One officer said: 'Joni might have been mixed
> up with violent drug dealers.
>
> 'We have no other motive for her murder.'

I tossed into the mix a couple of quotes about Joni
hanging out at raves where merchants of death flogged
Ecstasy at £20 a throw. I took good care to bury the fact
that Astrid was in chokey in Lille way down the story. I
didn't want to faze our readers in Hartlepool.

By now it was fourish and time for a quick sharp-
ener. After all, I'd had only two gins at lunchtime. I
nicked down the back stairs and into the dive bar of the

Stone. There was a couple of clusters of news subs in for
a bracer before they started their night shifts. Subs are
the bottom feeders of our business so I pretended not to
know them. The only other drinker in sight was Frankie
Frost and the temptation to ignore him was nigh on
irresistible. But that would have left me with only Deke
the barman for conversation and Deke is not the
brightest of God's children. So I said hello to Frankie.

Frankie is a monkey, a snapper, a smudger; or, as he
prefers to style himself, a photographer. Lest anyone
mistake him for a brain surgeon, Frankie, like all the
other monkeys ever born, wanders the streets of this
city with a battered Nikkon wrapped round his neck.
That one's just for show. The real tool of his trade is a
Canon Sureshot in his pocket. What makes it so special
is that, unlike Frankie, it can actually take a snap in
focus.

Frankie was lingering over a half pint of McEwans,
because that's the cheapest lager the Stone sells and it
was a half pint because they don't sell it in quarter
pints. Monkeys are prodigious drinkers but only when
somebody else is getting them in.

He kindly let me buy him a pint of Fosters. I asked
him what he was up to and he said nothing worth talking
about. He talked about it anyway.

Subbing it down, what it came to was Frankie was
bored, hadn't had a decent show in the paper since
Christmas, hadn't had a foreign since the Spanish train
crash in November. Foreign trips mean a lot to monkeys,
their chief attraction being you can fiddle big exes. Plus
monkeys are the only people I know who find places
like Heathrow, JFK and West Midlands Airport

romantic. I expect it's just the prospect of duty-free drink.

It was Frankie's round. He bought himself another half and made a big production out of getting me a gin. A single. Luckily I'd some tonic left or he might have thrown a fit.

He got round to asking me what I was doing, and, looking back over the winter so far, my track record was every bit as dull as his. Only I wasn't making as much fuss about it.

Frankie said, 'What you and I need, Max, is a decent foreign.'

I nodded soberly. My immediate horizon was none too bright, what with another meet with the boy Jason scheduled for the evening. That's when I started thinking. That's when I remembered my new-found chumminess with Tony Belker, He Who Approves The Foreigns.

I said, 'It doesn't have to be anywhere special.'

'No. Just anywhere away from the office.'

'Yes, maybe even Holland.'

'Holland?'

I said, 'It's next door to Belgium.'

Frankie pretended he already knew where it was.

I put my glass down. 'I'll bet you twenty quid I can set us up with a foreign tonight.'

'Bollocks.'

'Bet me.'

In the end the last of the big-time gamblers bet me a quid. I left him to his half and fairly scampered back upstairs. Evening conference was only three minutes away. I just had time for a quick audience with Belker.

I gave his door a hearty blam and he snarled a 'Come in'.

As soon as he saw it was me, his great pumpkin face went all squishy and smiley. But I kept my nerve.

I said, 'Tony, this Joni Poelma story, I've just had a tip from an Interpol guy in Holland and he reckons we could get a good line there.'

Normally I have to wrestle Belker to the floor to get him to authorize a foreign. This time he didn't even ask me what the line was.

'When do you want to go?'

'Now. Tonight. I'll need a monkey too.'

The smile thinned a shade. 'What for?'

This was a toughie. There are three unanswerable questions in the world: Why are we here? Where do women come from? And why do you need a monkey?

I bluffed it out, saying I thought there was a stack of naughty pix of Joni, which, if we got our mitts on them, we could syndicate to like-minded muck-raking tabloids around the globe, thereby making a vast profit for ourselves.

The smile fattened out again. 'Good thinking, Max. Like I said, we need an ideas man like you. Thought any more about the offer?'

An apologetic grimace from my corner.

'Never mind. We'll sort it out when you come back.'

I think I thanked him but things got fuzzy after that. Two minutes later I was briefing the Foreign Desk clerk to set up flights, hotels and so forth. I collected my overnight bag and woke up News Desk to tell them Belker had the bright idea of sending me to Holland. Angie gave me a look which might have meant anything. And three minutes after that I was prising Frankie loose from a freshly bought half.

We hopped a taxi and were tooling up at the Docklands airport even before Frankie had stopped griping. They were expecting us. A honey blonde in blue pushed a couple of tickets into our sticky little dabs. She proceeded to totter on ahead of us on a matching pair of prize pins which made Frankie forget his duty-frees and which was just as well, seeing as how our pilot was already out there on the runway, tapping an irritable tattoo on the joystick.

I have never had to suffer the company of a hyperactive seven-year-old child on a long car journey. But I imagine it is very much akin to having Frankie Frost as your co-passenger on a plane. The only real difference being that Frankie is about nine foot tall.

'Wot's the airline?' said he.

'VLM.'

'You mean KLM.'

'No. KLM is Dutch. VLM is Belgian.'

'But we're flying to Holland.'

I said, 'Frankie, Aero Mexico fly to Moscow.'

'So?'

I gave up and started reading the in-flight bumf.

Frankie said, 'What is this anyway? It isn't a Boeing.'

'No, it's a Fokker.'

That gave Frankie the chance to demonstrate what a subtle punster he is.

I passed him the duty-free tariff to shut him up while I studied the map.

'Bugger,' I said.

'What is it now?'

62

I said, 'Genk is on the German border.'

'Where's Genk?'

'Genk is where we're going: and it's on the German border.'

'So?'

'They kick us off the plane in Rotterdam. That's the other side of Holland.'

'Don't worry. I'll do the driving.'

Which is precisely why I said bugger in the first place.

The drinks trolley rattled up alongside and a nymph with a seductive smile somehow coaxed us into loading up with miniatures.

The Fokker swung out over the estuary, canted a wing and the lights of Essex vanished beneath a torn blanket of cloud. A heartwarming spirit of gin and freedom descended upon us. If they'd let us smoke, we could have stayed up there forever.

Rotterdam was windswept and rainy and pitch black. Though if you've ever flown into Rotterdam in daylight, you'll agree darkness is preferable.

We had only overnight bags so we didn't have to eff about waiting for our luggage to be shunted up. The flat hat in Customs gave Frankie an alarmed look, then he slanted a sniffy glance at me. He didn't say anything. But I knew what he was thinking: why haven't you got that thing on a leash?

I phoned our Foreign clerk who reported he'd got us booked into the Golden Tulip hotel in Maastricht. Before I even asked, he said, 'That's just twenty minutes from Genk.'

There was also a car lined up with Hertz but no

dough. I wasn't worried. I still had all of Gabriella Cardigan's two grand in my breast pocket, giving the outward appearance I was halfway through an oestrogen implant.

I'd already talked myself into handing all of it back to her, but right now I needed to borrow some of it. I went off and changed £500 into guilders, leaving Frankie to frighten the Hertz girls.

I caught up with him in the underground car park. He was caressing a cheesy chunk of silver metal.

'What is that, Frankie?'

'A Citroen Xantia.' The light of love was in his eyes, his voice had gone all husky.

I said, 'Do the bloody doors open?'

He glared at me but pressed the gizmo and the locks went plikkkk. We got in and shut the doors. I belted myself in because that's the very first thing you do when you drive with Frankie Frost.

He for his part slid the driver's seat back as far as it would go, adjusted the rake, fiddled with the mirrors and stroked the steering wheel. So there we were, ready for the off, ace lensman Frankie Frost and globetrotting crime hack Max Chard.

That's when Frankie dropped the keys. It was dark in that car park, slightly darker than midnight at the Black Hole of Calcutta during a total eclipse. There followed several minutes during which the only sound to be heard was that of Frankie rutting around in the floor well.

Then I had a brainwave. I opened my door. Click. The courtesy light came on. And there were the keys, nestling between the front seats.

Frankie said, 'Urph.'

I closed my door.

'Open your door again,' he said.

'Why?'

'Because I don't know where the ignition is.'

I rolled my eyes and opened the door.

'Got it,' he said.

I closed the door. He got the engine going at the third try. The next bit was more difficult. He couldn't find the lights. But he found everything else: the windscreen washer, the horn, the rear window demister, the horn, the steering wheel rake, the air conditioning, the horn. We both opened our doors.

I said, 'Maybe it hasn't got lights.'

He took me literally. 'It's got them all right.' And just to prove it, he knocked on the rear fog lamp.

Another five minutes peeled by. I said, 'I'd prefer to get to Maastricht while I'm still a relatively young man.'

I fell into a dreamless reverie from which I was roused by a jubilant cry. I opened my eyes. We had lights. We had action.

I did the navigating bit because monkeys can't be expected to do two things at once. I reckoned we had around 120 miles to do in all and the way Frankie was driving that should take about fifteen minutes top whack. We tacked south on the E10 to Breda, further south to Antwerp and then hung a left on to the E39.

I spent most of the journey peering at the map or diddling around with the radio. I spent an hour or thereabouts listening to last year's Eurovision losers, but at least it kept me from thinking about the carnage unfolding in our wake.

Genk came and went in a blare of horns. Then the Maastricht slip road. And then Maastricht, which, as far as I could judge at 5,000 miles an hour, was a pretty burg with more than its fair share of jaywalking burghers. We skimmed round a corner on one-and-a-half wheels and there before us was the Golden Tulip Derlon hotel.

It was a solid looking party, built in a more gracious age and fronting on to a skinny rectangle with a gang of spindly trees mooching about in the centre. It would look better in the summer. But you could say that for just about anything, barring the Sahara Desert. I checked in, leaving Frankie arguing with the doorman about whether he could park on the cobbles. The receptionist, a slim young thing from somewhere east of Java showed me her teeth and fetched out a key.

I got to the room, flung my bag down and phoned Night Desk. I interrupted Vic in the middle of his nightly prayer for a cure for alopecia and a lottery win.

'Where are you?' Accusingly.

'In Holland. Maastricht, to be exact.'

'What are you doing there?'

'I'm phoning you.'

Wherever we go in the world, even on our hols, it is our bounden duty to let the Desk know our where-abouts. God knows why. They always sound pissed off when we tell them where we are. I expect they think we're enjoying ourselves or something.

I said, 'I'm polishing off a bottle of champagne while having my lithe young limbs massaged by Miss Thailand.'

Vic suspected as much. He told me to get lost. In short there were no messages for me.

I rang off and promptly called Rosie. She sounded if anything even more narked. The rule with loved ones is very different. You must never *ever* let them think you're having a good time. And so I launched into a tirade against Belker, blaming him for sending me to this benighted spot. In the end she was almost feeling sorry for me.

But she's ever vigilant. 'What's the talent like?'

'Great hulking brutes with pigtails and buck teeth.'

'I was talking about the men.'

'So was I.'

After that the conversation got all twee and I don't feel like repeating it. A sudden battering on my door showed that the Hotel Derlon had decided to drop its standards for the night and let Frankie in. End of phone call. But I rang Jason's home number to apologize for standing him up. All I got was an ansaphone. I apologized anyway.

We dined halfway across town in the Wong Dynasty, which came highly recommended by reception. They also highly recommended a string of other nosheries, but it was Frankie's idea to go Chinese. Like most of his brainwaves, it was a bummer. The speciality of the Wong Dynasty was their refusal to dish out blank receipts. Frankie packed away the nasi goreng and remembered something that had been troubling him.

'How come Belker agreed to this?'

'Maybe he likes me.'

Much mirth from the monkey side of the table.

Frankie said, 'How did you sell him the idea?'

I said, 'I've got a confession to make.'

'Confession?' Three-syllable words always have him foxed.

'I told Belker there was a stack of nudie pix of Joni kicking around.'

Frankie said, 'Are there?'

'Probably not.'

There was silence, but for the sound of a monkey gnawing a prawn cracker. He was thinking. He said, 'No problem. We just get some other bird that looks like her to flash her boobs for us.'

He was quite serious.

I said, 'No we don't.'

Frankie looked hurt. 'We don't have to say she's Joni.'

'So who's she supposed to be then?'

He thought some more. 'We could always say she's Joni's mate.'

I said, 'You could. I couldn't.'

He went back to chewing the cud. I had a ringside view of his tonsils chomping away.

After a while he tried again, with a touch of wheedle. 'But just say she *is* Joni's mate?'

'I'm still not playing.'

Frankie got crabby. 'I don't see nothing wrong with it. I mean, if we could find some bird who knows her you might get a story out of it.'

'That bit's OK.'

He said, 'So we do that then, we go looking for her mate?'

'Yep, and anyone else who knows her.'

Frankie didn't give a toss about them. He said, 'OK, but this bird . . .'

'Her alleged friend?'

'Yeh, she might give you some good quotes.'

'And naturally you'd want a snap of her?'

He bobbed his head. 'Sure. Something to go with the story.'

I rested my chopstick and stared him straight in his beady eye. 'So tell me, Frankie: why do you need her to get her kit off?'

He smiled a truly horrible smile, 'Because that way I get a big show in the paper.'

I said, 'And you expect me to write a caption saying this is Joni's bosom pal, and here's her bosom to prove it?'

'That's it. We'll look around for some bird with big knockers. The office will love it.'

He was right about that bit at least. I looked at him pityingly. 'Doesn't it bother you that the story is missing certain points, like facts for starters?'

No, it didn't bother him.

I said, 'I prefer to confine my fiction writing to my exes.'

He wasn't listening. He was thinking out loud. 'Or maybe we could get a *couple* of birds . . .'

There's not much you can do with him really. I've been around snappers for years and years and still their capacity for mischief never fails to appal.

We sauntered back through the cobbles to the Golden Tulip and poured ourselves into the teensy bar where we sampled various bottles of this and that until we found something we could each live with.

Frankie swigged on his Remy Martin and said, 'So the plan is?'

'The plan is first thing we go to Genk, grab a few quotes from Joni's old man, then we find a friendly smudger. It's easy. We'll have it all done and dusted by lunch.'

Which prediction once again shows that this Nostradamus of the Newsroom has his off moments just like the rest of us.

Chapter Seven

The first inkling that anything was wrong came at twenty to three in the morning when the bedside phone went off in my earhole.

'Max. It's Vic.'

He sounded happy which is always a bad sign.

'Sorry to wake you,' he lied, 'but we've got one for you in Dortmund.'

'What? Now?'

'It's only just happened. It's a bomb at an army base. Looks like the IRA.'

I switched on the light and reached for a pen. 'OK, Vic. What have you got?'

He had precisely three lines of a Reuter's snap: *An explosive device has gone off outside a British Army base in Dortmund, Germany. Early reports indicate it has caused damage to installations but there are as yet no reports of injuries.'*

I said, 'Is that it?'

Vic said, 'That's it.'

We didn't wish each other good night. I showered, got dressed and went along to kick Frankie awake. He opened the door wearing nothing but a pair of boxer shorts. They had – and I'm not making this up – a grinning Mr Man motif on the front. Mr Old Slapper Fancier, I think it was. I didn't look too closely.

Frankie grunted and grumbled and staggered off to the bathroom to splash water on his chops. The fool had left his room key on the bedside table so I helped myself to a Gordons from his minibar and got out the map. I reckoned Dortmund was about seventy miles east. We'd be there long before breakfast.

We tootled through the deserted streets of Maastricht with the river Maas keeping us company on our left. For once Frankie was driving like a semi-normal person. This was largely because I told him the Dutch execute drivers with more than a half glass of shandy in their systems. There was a token police and Customs border post but they seemed to have called it a day. We ambled through unchecked.

Out on the Euroroute, Frankie forgot all about the Law and stuck his foot down. I closed my eyes until we squealed into Dortmund. There was no problem finding the army base. It was the size of a small town. We spent fifteen minutes cruising the perimeter until a far off sprinkling of flashing blue and yellow lights told us we'd found the spot.

Like most of these things, when you eventually got there you wondered why you'd bothered. On the far side of the road there was a buff Merc with its nose stove in against a tree. Just about opposite it was a twenty-foot hole in the perimeter fence and beyond that what looked like the mortal remains of a bike shed. There were army cars, civvy cars, police cars, fire engines, ambulances and God knows what else all clustered around the hole.

Frankie strung fifteen cameras around his neck and went off to make a nuisance of himself. I collared a bomb disposal bloke who refused even to disclose his name, rank and serial number. But he did say that a Major Carty was looking after the 'meeja'.

It didn't take long to find him. He was the red-faced geezer with a doughnut of quivering hacks hanging on his every word. He wasn't saying anything so they were just quivering.

I pushed through and introduced myself. I was the only Brit present. Carty blinked. He said, 'You got here fast.'

I said, 'I'm from my paper's rapid deployment unit.'

Military types like it when you speak their language. He nodded and promised to brief me in half an hour. Better still, he arranged the meet in the officers' mess.

I conned him into writing me a pass and he assigned a perfectly square squaddie to escort me thither. En route we talked. The squaddie was from Belfast so I suppose Dortmund must have seemed like Sleepy Hollow to him. At least until something went boom on his doorstep. I bet that made him feel homesick.

I asked him about the bomb. He was a talkative type. It went off at zero two hundred local time. There was no warning. The base was already on alert for attacks, but it had been that way for years.

'Was it in the Merc?' I asked.

He laughed. 'No, that was just some *hausfrau* who was driving past when it went off. The bomb was in a rucksack or something like that.'

'Was she injured?'

No, just very pissed off.

Why did the IRA pick Dortmund? No idea. A thought struck me. 'Have you got 14th Signals Intelligence here?'

Probably. They'd all sorts here.

There are people who still think the SAS are the blokes who do all our shooting for us. That's the way it used to be, before MI5 took over the show. The real bang bang boys now are the 14th Sig. Int. lot. The trouble with them is they don't go writing books about their escapades therefore we don't have much idea of what exactly they get up to. We just know they're the business.

By now the squaddie and I were at the gate and saying good morning to a regiment of sentries. They must have thought I was the master bomber come back to gloat because they frisked me all over in the most intimate way. They got me to demonstrate that my tape-recorder was indeed a tape-recorder and not a cunningly disguised 1,000-pound landmine. After that I was through and in the officers' mess.

Despite the early hour there was a fair turn out of guys in green pullovers knocking back halfs of lager and talking in initials. I got the feeling they didn't trust my Balmain double-breasted because they went quiet and looked at me with their twenty-twenty eyes.

I ordered up a pint of Heineken and mooched around admiring the regimental trophy cabinets. For soldiers, those blokes played an awful lot of golf.

Carty duly arrived with a clipboard under his arm. No, he wouldn't have a pint, just a coffee. We moved downwind of the Royal Corps of Green Pullies.

Carty told me slightly less than the squaddie, though

he had the info that the bomb was a couple of pounds of Semtex. And what about the building it had pulverized? That was just some old storage 'facility', used by the REME. What you and I would call a shed.

And what did it contain?

'Nothing of strategic significance.'

I took this to mean it wasn't holding Britain's nuclear weapon arsenal at the time.

The woman, Carty said, suffered trauma and minor abrasions after she ran her car into the tree. Yes, she was German. No, he didn't have her name. No one else injured. That was about it.

I said, 'We – my photographer and I – have just driven here from Maastricht. We didn't see a single guard at the border.'

Carty's teeth framed a little tight smile. 'You wouldn't.'

'Because of the Euro Community's no frontiers policy?'

That, plus the fact that the Germans didn't give a toss who sneaked across the border. Carty didn't exactly say that, but his shrug did.

I tried him on the 14th Sig. Int. line, but he wasn't giving anything there. So we talked about the price of fish until Frankie loomed up, putting a full stop to any sensible conversation.

I'll say this for the British Army: they look after us hacks. We got breakfast (free), a couple of frames of snooker and severalish pints at prices that made you happy to pay. Try getting service like that at Stoke Newington nick. They even printed out Frankie's negs for him and wired them through to London. I gave Norbert,

our xenophobic Foreign Editor, a wake up call. I had to
tell him where I was because he hadn't bothered to read
the night log.

He said, 'What's the schedule line?'

'Army Bosses On Warpath Over Euro Terror Havens.'

'What does that mean?'

Norbert still lives in the days when ours was a broad-
sheet newspaper. I talked him through it slowly so that
he could go into morning conference and act as if he
knew what was going on.

Then, my glass replenished, I sat down to write the
guff.

ARMY chiefs last night slammed Eurocrats after a
cowardly IRA bomb blitz on a British base.

Top brass savaged the EC's open borders policy
for handing terrorists a passport to murder and maim.

Fury erupted after a night attack on the giant
British camp at Dortmund, Germany.

Terrorists targetted the base because it is the
hush hush HQ of Britain's undercover troops from
the secretive Signals Intelligence corps.

After planting a bomb outside its perimeter
fence, the Provos' active service unit fled back to
their safe haven in Holland.

The border crossing was unmanned.

Last night the three men in the terror cell were
toasting the raid in the seedy clubs of Amsterdam.

And a seething Army officer warned: 'These
bastards can hit and run as often as they like.

'The Dutch give them sanctuary. The Germans
don't even try to keep them out.

'But our boys are in the firing line.'

The bomb – a holdall stuffed with two pounds of Semtex – blasted etc. etc. etc.

OK, maybe it's not the most interesting story you've ever read but it would do all right for a foreign page lead.

I filed it, finished my drink, and said to myself, 'Now, where was I before I was so rudely interrupted?'

What with one thing and another, we didn't get back to Maastricht until early evening, by which time we felt we'd earned a rest, therefore Joni Poelma's family could wait for the morrow. The day had solved one pressing problem. On our way west we'd taken the back roads, stopping every now and then for a glass of something and picking up blank bills at every halt.

We shared them out across the pink linen of Au Premier on the Brusselse Straat. The food was Dutch/French/Belgian/German and the decor was similarly hotchpotched. If you looked at the plain walls, dotted with still lifes, you were in your auntie's best room. Raise your eyes to the ceiling, and you're in some Anglo-Saxon nook, with great chunky beams all across the ceiling. The old Dutch mood of that was somewhat marred by a whacking great chandelier that dangled centre stage. And looking south, you chanced upon a patio window framed with soft looping curtains, giving the impression you were looking into milady's boudoir.

If I sound a mite liverish, it's because the Au Premier didn't stoop to hooky bills.

After it we staggered on to a club, or what Frankie in

his quaint old fashioned way called a disco. The club was downstairs in what looked like a condemned cave. The music was sort of Edith Piaf meets the Sex Pistols in a head-on crash. It was loud. We looked down from the top of the stairs. Between us and the bar there was about a hundred people giving it all they'd got. My eye was drawn naturally to the bar where there was a dark girl sitting alone and looking bored.

I pointed to her and bellowed in Frankie's ear, 'I'm taking her. You get one of your own.'

He nodded and went off to ogle. I threaded through to the bar and mouthed a big hello to little miss lonely-heart. She mouthed something similar. We were off to a promising start.

I know what you're thinking, but you're wrong. My intentions were strictly dishonourable. All I desired was a pretty woman yearning to tell me she was Joni Poelma's dearest chum. The rest I could make up.

The music was fairly non-stop which made chat-up lines redundant. Does nobody write twelve-bar blues anymore? I just gestured towards her glass and smiled. She shrilled something at the barman and he fetched her another glass of green stuff. I screamed 'GIN!' at him. He howled something back. It was probably Dutch for 'WHAAAAT?' I ended up pointing at the bottles and he got the right one at the fourth go.

So now the dusky beauty and I were facing each other and grinning like loons. You would have had to be deaf and dumb to communicate in that place. But we were getting on famously, having a glug apiece, beaming at each other, having another glug, and back to the beams. She was worth it. She was maybe a smidge skinnier than she ought to be and I like them an edge taller, but she had great big black eyes and a mouth ripe with eastern promise. I guessed she was from the Dutch East Indies. She was decked up in a sawn-off halter top and micro mini which seemed to be the standard gear in these parts, for the girls anyway. Both skirt and top were in nuclear-powered lilac. On a white girl they would have looked godawful; on her, they were terrific.

She mouthed something at me but seeing that (a) I can't lip read and (b) I certainly can't lip read in Dutch, it went clean over my head. I had a sudden inspiration. I drew out a notebook, pointed at myself with my left hand and, with my right hand wrote MAX in capital letters.

She took the pen from me and wrote EVA just below it. So now we were introduced. My turn for the pen. I scribbled ENGLISH. Over to Eva. She came back with LONDON? Not so fast, dear, I ask the questions around here. I nodded and spelt out MAASTRICHT? She nodded.

All this talking had made us thirsty. I shrieked at the barman and he did the necessary. I got writing again. DO YOU KNOW GENK? She did. JONI POELMA? That put a thoughtful pucker on her brow. I supplied helpfully: MURDERED IN LONDON. The pucker went away. She'd obviously heard of her, but she wasn't the bosom pal I needed. I was going off Eva pretty rapidly. She was also giving me a funny look. I wrote NEWSPAPER REPORTER and that made her happy again.

She took the pen from me and scrawled WAIT. She slid off into the heaving throng and I lit a Bensons and waited. I was just stubbing it out when there was a tug at my shoulder. There stood Eva along with a couple of blondes, a little geezer, and, inexplicably, Frankie.

She got busy with my notebook again. MARGRIT, she wrote, and pointed to the taller blonde. Margrit said cheese. She had wide open eyes in a pink round face, and shoulders that looked like they did a lot of swimming. But you wouldn't say no.

The little bloke yelled in Eva's ear. Eva bobbed her bean. She turned back to me and mouthed GOODBYE. I watched her shimmy off with the little bloke and my heartstrings went plong.

Margrit, an accomplished mime artist in her spare time, took over. She turned her head, gestured thataways and somehow conveyed that we should follow her. We snaked our way across the floor until we came to a rough sort of archway. Beyond it was a low-ceilinged room about twenty foot square. Along its walls were wooden benches where the ravers of Maastricht were exploring each other's tonsils.

I raised an eyebrow at Frankie. He smirked and licked his lips. Margrit led us to the furthest gloomiest corner. It was a lot quieter in here, just about the level of two pneumatic drills and a concrete mixer. We could hear each other if we shouted.

'You are journalists?' Margrit said.

I said more or less.

'You want to know about Joni?'

I said to the other blonde, 'I'm Max. Who're you?'

Frankie smirked. 'I don't know her name. I sort of picked her up.'

She just giggled. I forgot about her and turned back to Margrit.

'How do you know Joni?'

Margrit had a cool, grave gaze which made you feel she knew what you were thinking. I sincerely hoped she didn't because right then Frankie was thinking of how he could con her into popping a couple of those buttons on her top and posing for a snap.

He started on the foreplay, banging off a couple of head shots. He switched cameras and moved in for the close ups. Margrit promptly forgot what she was supposed to be thinking about and started acting all Pamela Andersonish.

I let them get on with it. As long as Frankie grabbed the pix I could always cobble together a quote or two. My glass was empty. I got them all to tell me what they wanted to swill and I headed back to the bar with the giggle girl in tow. She either fancied me or she was dying for a drink.

It took us all of fifteen minutes to get them in. We returned to the square room just in time to see Margrit buttoning up her top. I glanced at Frankie. He was openly salivating. So we'd got the smudges. My turn now.

'Tell me about Joni.'

'She was in school with my sister. They are friends.'

Close enough. 'Did she come here?'

'My sister?'

No, Joni, you cretin.

Apparently Joni had been here a couple of times. Boyfriend? No one special, but there was one in London. I blinked and said, 'What?'

Margrit said, 'She told Hanneke – Hanneke's my

sister – she had an English boyfriend. But there was some sort of problem.'

I said, 'What problem?'

'Maybe I'm not sure. I think there is a problem because Joni is not rich.'

'And her boyfriend is?'

Margrit said that was about the size of it.

I said, 'So what was the problem?'

She said, 'It is your English class thing. I don't think his mother liked him being with Joni.'

'Do you know this boy's name.'

'Maybe it begins with M. I go and ask Hanneke.'

She pitched off into the outer darkness. Frankie and I sat in the corner drinking our drinks and thinking what clever little clogs we were. The other blonde had already wandered away.

Margrit returned with big sister Hanneke, who had if anything an even skimpier top. The difference was there was nothing to brag about under it. It didn't matter. At least Frankie had got the right sister for the snaps. All I had to do was get Hanneke's quotes and stick them in Margrit's mouth.

She was a slow talker and an even slower thinker. But after I plied her with a stonking huge margarita she got motoring. Joni, she said, had a boyfriend called George. So much for something beginning with M. No, Hanneke didn't know his surname, how they met or anything useful like that. But she did know his family were rolling in it, that Joni was loopy about him. She'd said as much when she came home at Christmas. But then he'd given Joni the bum's rush because his parents said so. Yes, Joni was a bit brassed off about it.

The lout who was operating the sound system suddenly turned it down by three thousand degrees. We could actually talk without screaming.

Hanneke frowned. Screams she could live with.

I asked, 'Anybody after George?'

She had to think about that one. Then she said, 'Perhaps someone called Villi or Billy.'

'Billy?'

Hanneke said, 'Joni said she was having much fun with Billy and when she comes back she'll bring Billy and we will have a good time together.'

Billy sounded an accommodating type. I yelled: 'Billy is her boyfriend?'

'Perhaps he is a friend only. Perhaps Joni was making a joke.'

'What's the joke?'

Hanneke tossed her chest about. I think that meant pass.

The rest of the stuff was mainly background colour, how Joni's old man was some sort of paper pusher for the council and her mother did something at an old folks home.

And what about Joni's sister, Astrid the acid queen? Hanneke rolled her eyes and said, 'She is in big trouble.'

'Drugs?'

Yep. Drugs.

'Was Joni into drugs?'

A laugh which you could take anyway you wanted. Then, after a moment. 'Maybe a little. Everybody in Holland takes drugs.'

So the next time you see the Dutch Euro commissioner bleating on about mad cow disease, just bear in mind that he's probably out of his socks on something or other.

I took Hanneke's phone number in case I remembered anything else worth asking her and after that I'd run out of things to say. She and Margrit were equally bored with me. But not with Frankie. It's amazing what a camera round the neck does to enhance a man's sexual allure. I loaned him a pile of guilders and left him to play. I returned to the Golden Tulip in search of a decent Gordons and a quiet life. Rosie has spies everywhere.

Chapter Eight

Great fat blots of rain splatted against the windscreen as we rolled Genk-wards the following morning. I was a shade subdued as it was still short of eight-fifteen local time which is only seven-fifteen in Battersea. Frankie, alas, was filled with all the vim of his sub-species. He was still rabbitting on about his exploits of the previous eve.

Stripping away the exaggeration, it appeared that he had fallen into the company of three nymphomaniacs, each clamouring for his body. There was a blonde, a redhead and a brunette. The redhead, I gather, was the most demanding. The toothsome trio were built on the lines of the Three Graces, though with fewer clothes. And just by the way, each had a zillion guilders to her name. I expect they all owned Ferrari Testarossas, but he just forgot to mention that.

I allowed Frankie his little fantasy, reckoning that the closest he got to the above scenario was watching the late night Red Hot Dutch movie in his hotel room.

We trundled into Genk and mowed down a passing cyclist to ask the way. He was strangely disinclined to help us. Fortunately a rain-lashed local steamed up and told us to go left at the roundabout, right at the furniture shop, right again at the crossroads, over the railway line, left at the junction, upside down at the lights, and . . .

I gave up and left it to Frankie. We'd just got to the bit where the redhead was showing him her butterfly tattoo when Frankie interrupted himself to announce, 'This is it.'

I sat up and paid attention. We were in the middle of a small estate of square-built white houses, each with a bright-red roof that somehow made you think of apples. The place looked like Legoland off season.

Frankie hoicked a thumb over his shoulder at the nearest box. 'That's the one.'

There then followed ten minutes of fussing and fumbling on his part as he decorated himself with ropes of cameras. I merely patted the pocket of my Aquascutum to check I had a notebook on board.

The Poelma house, like its neighbours, was fronted with a plain rectangle of grass. Hexagonal paving stones, laid flush with the lawn, staggered up to a front door. It was green.

I hit the doorbell and took in the scene. The windows all featured venetian blinds which were slanted so that the inmates could see out but you couldn't see in. There was nothing in the way of outside embellishments. There wasn't even a car parked out front. I began to get anxious. I pushed the bell again.

Frankie was already into the spirit of things, zinging off snaps of the frontage. The green door opened. A Twelfth-century Viking glared out at me and growled, 'Ja?'

I said, 'We're English – English Press.'

'Ja?' he said again.

'I'm a photographer,' Frankie contributed, just in case the bloke was blind.

The Viking was somewhere in his mid-twenties. He sported a long straggly blond beard and matching hair. He had weird blue eyes that made you think he was staring right through you at something twenty-five miles away.

I said, 'I want to talk to you about Joni.'

'So?'

At least it sounded English. I pushed on. 'My name is Max Chard. I'm the crime reporter for the *Gazette* in London. This is my photographer, Frank Frost.'

The Viking looked through Frankie and didn't like what he saw.

'What do you want?'

I'd already told him that, but I told him again. This time it got home. 'You want to talk to me about Joni?'

'You're her brother?'

He gave a half nod. 'My parents are not here today. They have gone to London.'

Frankie raised his camera to squeeze off a mugshot and then thought better of it.

I said, 'Perhaps we might come in.'

'Why?'

Because this rain is pissing me off and a cup of coffee would make my morning. I said, 'So that I can write an accurate story.'

The faraway blue eyes zeroed in on me. 'Maybe it was you who write about Joni having business with drugs?'

Frankie said, 'No, that was some prat in the Currant Bun.'

I translated, 'The *Sun*. They always get it wrong. Nobody believes Joni was doing stuff.'

'Stuff?'

'Drugs.'

'No. No drugs.'

So far all I'd got was a denial, and a denial is not a story. I said, 'The police tell me they don't believe she was on drugs.'

He said that was good. This wasn't going anywhere. I said, 'We've got two pictures of Joni, but we don't know which is the more recent.'

'You have them here?'

No, they were back in our office, but perhaps he had a recent shot?

'Vait.'

He vanished stage left and ve vaited. I gave the door a gentle prod with my toe and it swung lazily back to reveal a prospect of blue-carpeted stairs. Frankie banged off a few snaps just for the fun of it.

The Viking reappeared holding an eight-by-ten framed pic. 'This is Joni,' he announced.

It was just a head and shoulders job and as far as you could tell, she had all her clothes on. She was wearing a stripey little knitted cap pulled down to her ears with wisps of blonde hair sticking out either side. Her face was thinner than in either of the pix we'd been using, but she was looking fairly tickled with herself.

I said, 'May I?' And before he realized it, I was holding the photograph. I turned it towards Frankie who took half a dozen pops at it. Then, ever so accidentally, I angled the photograph so that the face of the glass got splattered with rain drops.

'Ooops,' I said. 'It's all wet. Maybe we could take the pix inside.'

He wasn't keen on the idea but he let us in. As soon as we were through the door, Frankie pushed it shut behind us. That meant there were three of us clogging up the hall. I sort of naturally drifted into the living room, my eyes still intent on the snap of Joni. Her brother was forced to tag along.

I said, 'When was this taken?'

'There was a birthday for my father last month. Joni was home for that.'

'She was a pretty girl.'

He said he thought so too. Frankie took the pic from me, laid it on a table by the window and got clicking again. I pulled out my Bensons and offered them to Erik the Viking. He hesitated and then helped himself to one. He lit it with his own Zippo.

I said, 'I met Joni's friend, Hanneke, last night and she mentioned you. Erik, isn't it?'

'Rudy.'

'Rudy. Yes, of course. Hanneke said that Joni had an English boyfriend, George.'

The faraway gaze took on an arctic blue. 'So?'

I said old George must be pretty broken-hearted what with losing his girlfriend. Rudy made it clear he didn't give a toss for how George was taking it.

'It is very sad for all of us.'

Frankie chipped in, 'Mind if I open the blinds? There's not enough light here.'

There was lashings of light over the table but I knew what he was really up to. Along the far wall – where it was a touch gloomy – there was a wood-framed fireplace affair. And on top of that there was a whole stack of family snaps. As long as I kept Rudy otherwise distracted, Frankie could bag them as well.

So we got him to open the blinds and I launched into a blitz of useless questions. Which school had Joni attended? Did she like England? Was she fond of children? I had taken out my notebook so that Rudy could watch me write all this tosh down. In the background Frankie went clickety-click unnoticed.

After a while he said, 'That's it.'

Now it was my turn to get the captions. I glanced idly along the row of pictures. In the middle there was a big one featuring a couple with matching grizzled hairdos.

'Your parents?'

'My mother and father.'

To its immediate left was a shot of a barrage balloon in a frock with a football for a face and a thatch of blonde curls atop.

Rudy saw me staring at it. 'Joni,' he said.

I stared harder. By God, he was right. It was a human being. It was hard to tell, but I reckoned she was about eighteen when it was taken.

'Joni?'

A nod. 'She used to be, what you say . . .?'

Fat? Obese? Gargantuan? Belker-like?

'Maybe not so thin,' he supplied.

I ranged over the other snaps. There was one of Rudy, dressed as he was today, in blue denim shirt and jeans. He was probably wearing the same Y-fronts. He had a spanner in one beefy mit and half a motorbike in the other. Further west along the shelf there was a normal-sized girl in a red shift dress, posed over the aforesaid motorbike and giving it a lot of leg. She looked a right handful.

'Astrid?' I asked.

'Astrid,' he said. And his lips clamped shut. I gathered that Astrid the drug runner was not up for discussion right now. Or that's what he thought.

I gave him a sidelong glance and reckoned the odds. Our Rudy struck me as being a bloke with a low boiling point. Plus he was chunky in places where I don't like blokes with low boiling points to be chunky. He didn't look fast, but in a space as small as that you don't need to be fast. I began plotting a strategic withdrawal. The question of Astrid could wait until I had a clear getaway.

And so I changed the subject by asking him about his motorbike. But Rudy had used up all his small talk. I cocked an eye at Frankie and he got the message. I ambled out into the hallway, prattling all the while, with Rudy half a step behind me and Frankie snatching a general shot as he backed out.

I opened the front door and stepped out into the rain. Frankie squeezed past him. Rudy was glad to see us go.

I calculated the distances. Yep, it was safe enough here. Especially with Frankie between me and him. I said, 'Thanks for your help, Rudy. Just one final thing . . .'

His brow furrowed and he switched on the laser stare.

I said, 'Astrid's in jail for drug smuggling: was Joni running drugs too?'

That's when he lost it. If I'd been close enough he would have smacked me right in the jaw. I was well out of reach. But big daft Frankie, with a horsey grin all over his face, was still standing there. So Rudy thumped him. He caught him bang in the throat. Frankie's eyes popped. He reeled back, tripped over his own feet and ended up on his backside on the grass. I legged it for the car.

Rudy came after me. At which point Frankie staggered upright, bumped into him and this time they both went down. Frankie's bum renewed its acquaintance with the tufty grass. Rudy landed with a smack on the concrete path. He lay there and said something like 'Argghhh'.

I'd reached the car, but the fool had locked it. 'Run, Frankie!' I yelled. Well, it sounded better than, 'Throw me the keys.'

He got up on his hind legs again and came a-clanking and a-clunking at full throttle. 'You gastard!' he growled through his fractured larynx.

'Just open the door. Quick!'

There was no need to hurry. Rudy was still lying on the path groaning horribly.

We hurried anyway. Frankie was screeching off down that street before I'd even got my door closed.

I said, 'I think you've killed him.'

'I hope so.' Frankie massaged his adam's apple. 'The bugger nearly killed me.'

Then he thought about that and amended it. 'No, *you* bloody well nearly had me killed. What did you want to do that for? That bloody hurt.'

I wasn't all that bothered. It's a well known fact that these monkeys don't feel pain the way we do.

*

Back at the hotel, I rustled up a glass of what called itself white beer but was the same colour as ordinary beer and phoned Norbert on Foreign Desk.

'What's the story, morning glory?' he asked, displaying his finger was right there on the pulse of the pop scene.

Now if you tell Desk you've just done an interview, they'll bitch at you to put it across immediately, or preferably sooner. So what you always do is you say you are *trying* to get an interview. Then, when you come back on and tell them you've got it, they're happy and so are you.

I said, 'Joni Poelma's parents have shuttled off to London but I've an address for her brother and I'm on my way to see him.'

Norbert asked, 'What do you think he's going to say?'

Funny you should ask that, Norbert. I've just been consulting my crystal ball and it says he's going to say bugger all.

I said, 'I won't know until he opens his mouth.'

Norbert said, 'It's not much of a schedule line. Anything else?'

Of course there is. Has Chard ever failed you? Well, apart from that time in Naples.

I said, 'This one's a long shot, so don't push it too hard in conference. I was having a drink with a local Plod last night and he said there was a whisper going round that Joni was running drugs.'

'That sounds better.'

'Plus, I've got a tip off from a Dutch hack that she had an English boyfriend. I'm still trying to stand that one up.'

I left Norbert to piece that all together in one simple
sentence for his schedule line. I summoned up more
drink. Frankie was applying it liberally to his injured
throat. Every now and then he massaged the spot and
gurgled painfully just in case I forgot.

He said, 'What now?'

'Now you sit here and drink until you don't feel any
pain. Me, I'm going shopping.'

'What for?'

On our heedless charges through the streets of Maastricht I'd spotted a string of familiar names. Austin Reed,
Next, Principles, Jaeger, that sort of thing. I wanted a
prezzie for Rosie, and besides, I had fallen out of love
with the shirt I was wearing.

So I left Frankie in the tender loving care of an
unwitting barmaid while I took my wallet off for a
workout.

I returned about a hundred or so pounds lighter
which was better than feared. I'd got Rosie a little
chrome-yellow teapot she could stick her foul herbal tea
in, and various flimsy bits and pieces I looked forward
to seeing her blooming out of. I also came back with the
story sketched out in my mind. A drink, then a call to
Copy.

ONLY days before her murder, Dutch au pair Joni
Poelma was callously jilted by her posh English boyfriend.

He dumped the pretty blonde because his snooty
parents sneered at her humble background.

Last night Joni's best friend said: 'They said she
wasn't good enough for their son.

'It broke her heart for she was crazy about him.'

Now murder squad detectives are anxious to interview the boyfriend.

A senior officer said: 'He might help us fill in the missing seven days between her disappearance and when her body was found.'

And last night in Holland it emerged that 23-year-old Joni flirted dangerously with the drug scene.

Close friend Margrit Lommen said: 'She dabbled in drugs – everybody here does.'

Joni's sister Astrid is in jail in France charged with smuggling £1.5 million in LSD tabs . . .

Add to that Erik the Viking running amok – with a few tasty quotes thrown in – a chunk more from Margrit, an unnamed 'friend' revealing what a little raver Joni was, and there you have it. Stick that under a five-column snap of Margrit with her cleavage grinning out at you, and you just have to read it.

Nitpickers might hum and hah over it, but then nitpickers don't read our paper. Anyway, the Desk loved it and that's all that matters.

'You're coming back now?' Norbert asked.

I was in no particular rush. I still hadn't figured out how I was going to respond to Belker's indecent proposal of a News Desk slot. So I said, 'I thought it might be worthwhile to try to see her sister Astrid. She's in Lille.'

'In France,' said Norbert, who knows these things.

He said it was worth a shot, which it probably wasn't, so I went off to detach Frankie from his beer. He wasn't keen until I pointed out it meant another night away from the funny farm with the prospect of even huger exes. He downed the glass in one.

The rain dogged our tyre tracks all the way west through Holland and Belgium, giving up the chase just as we hit Lille. That was the only bright spot of the afternoon. We fiddled around until we found a block-house masquerading as the town nick where I donned my sweetest smile and asked questions.

I tried them out in English first. No, the language was evidently foreign to their tongue. I then gave them the benefit of my best French. They didn't speak that either. Frankie turfed in a bit of Anglo-Saxon but they just squinted down their snoots at us. We were rescued by a woman civvy who told us to go and see a bloke called Maitre Le Sueur, who, I gathered, was Astrid Poelma's brief. She even got us the address.

So we went knocking. But French briefs lead an even cushier life than those in Britain. They put in half an hour in the morning and then go off to get razzled, at least that's the impression I got.

It was pitch dark outside and the rain had eventually caught up with us. It was time we forgot about the Poelmas and started thinking about ourselves. We found a crusty old back-streets hotel which Frankie hoped might be a brothel. It wasn't. I consoled him with Lowenbrau and phoned base.

Norbert had cleared off, leaving the world and Britain in the incapable hands of Vic on Night Desk. He didn't want to speak to me but he knew someone who did. Angela Whipple.

'Bon soir, ma petite choux,' I greeted.

'Where are you?'

No merry quips, none of her celebrated sauciness.

I said, 'In Lille.'

'Why?'

Frankly this was none of her business. On a Foreign you are the exclusive property of the Foreign Editor. But I told her anyway.

She said, 'You're wasting your time. Come back.'

'Now?'

'No. Next year. Of course now.'

Oooh. Touchy, aren't we?

I said, 'Angie, it's—' I looked at my fake Cartier '—eight-fifteen over here. The trains have stopped, the planes have stopped, and by the time we get to Boulogne, the ferries will be stopped. And I don't think I can swim it. Besides, we've been on the go since six this morning.'

I don't think she cared. She paused. It was a pause with icicles dripping off it. She said, 'Then I want you on the first available ferry or plane tomorrow.'

'What's up, Angie - has somebody scrumped the Commissioner's apples?'

She said, 'They've got someone for Joni Poelma's murder.'

'Who?'

'You know the guy who had the poodle.'

'They've lifted the poodle?'

That didn't raise a smile either.

She simply said, 'So what you're doing there is just a waste of time - and money. Be back tomorrow.'

And down went the phone. I took a pull at the Lowenbrau but I don't think I tasted it. I knew what this big chill was all about and there was sod all I could do about it. Angie thought I was out to stab her in the back and nick her job. Now, if we were working for some sensible organization like the Broadmoor Escape Committee or Barnum's Circus, this could all be sorted in no time. I would simply have to say, 'I don't want your silly old job, Angie. This is that cretin Belker's idea.' But newspaper politics are too murky for simple solutions. If I told Angie, she'd go storming into the Editor, weeping buckets and chucking computers all over him. He, fearless pillar of truth that he is, would deny there was a Stab Angie Campaign in the offing. Whereupon Angie would say, 'Bollocks. Max Chard says Belker's offered him my job.'

'Has he now?' the Editor would say, crunching his knuckles and narrowing his eyes.

And two hours later Belker would be in Joe Allen's with some dipstick reporter offering him *my* job. That's the way it works in newspapers.

Therefore, until I'd worked this thing out, I had to get used to the grim reality that Angie loathed me and Belker loved me. I could understand it all right, but by God, it wasn't natural.

Chapter Nine

Rosie crooned over her chrome-yellow teapot. That was good. She also modelled the various flimsies for me. That was downright wonderful. And she just loved the idea of me as News Editor.

That was horrendously bad.

Bright-eyed and bouncing around the place, she ticked off all the good bits: I wouldn't have to go on Foreigns anymore, there'd be a stack more money in it, I could be home for eight every night, I wouldn't have to spend hours and hours drinking with contacts, there'd be great freebie holidays, and so it went on.

Meanwhile I started drawing up a list of all the bad bits about being News Editor. Mostly they were just about the same as her good bits.

The only thing that appealed to me was when she said, 'Just think, you'd be telling other people what to do instead of being bossed around by those idiots on News Desk.' I briefly entertained the idea of me sitting in the big centre swivel chair and getting Vic out of bed at eight o'clock in the morning to bollock him for missing the *Mirror*'s page-five lead. Now that would be fun.

After a while Rosie wound herself down to a steady

hum of excitement. It was only then she saw I wasn't up there sharing cloud nine with her.

The smoky blue eyes narrowed. 'What's wrong with it?'

A braver or a more stupid man might have told her. I told lies.

I said, 'Angela Whipple is only thirty-two.'

She's thirty-six.

Rosie blinked. 'She's not!'

'She is. She's aged four years since she got the job. And she and her husband split.'

'Yes, because he was having it off with somebody else.'

I shook my head slowly and sadly. 'That's the story Angie puts about. The real reason is they never saw each other, and when they did, she was always under the cosh about busting her News Desk budget or missing big stories. The pressures blew them apart.'

Rosie was looking flinty, getting suspicious. 'But *you're* always under a lot of pressure.'

'The kind I can handle.'

'Yes, that's why you stay out half the night drinking.'

This was heading towards dangerous territory. I needed a smoke screen. I said, 'All right, think of it like this: some big buyer comes to you and says, "We need half a dozen new designs and we need them last week." What do you do?'

Rosie said, 'I tell him to get lost.'

'Yes, but then you go ahead and do them.'

Rosie sniffed but didn't really disagree.

I said, 'But then some company, Liberty's or somebody, says, "Hey, Rosie. We want you to be our chief buyer." '

'Head buyer.'

'All right, head buyer. They say there's a company jam jar, twenty grand a year more, and your very own dyslexic secretary thrown in. What do you say to that?'

This time she knew the answer. 'I'd tell them thanks, but no thanks.'

I waved my arms wide. 'But why should you turn down all these riches and power?'

It was such a daft question she laughed. 'Because I *design* things: I don't buy them.'

I said, 'Ex-*act*-ly.'

'What's that supposed to mean? Ex-*act*-ly?'

'It's exactly the same with me. I *write* things. I don't get somebody else to do the writing for me. It's the same difference.'

There was a flaw but she couldn't find it. She went very quiet and started pulling it this way and that in her head. I poured us both a Gordons and sat back to enjoy it in all its junipery glory.

I realize the above little exchange might not matter a hoot to the world at large. But it mattered to me. It was the only time since records began that I've ever beaten the pants off Rosie in an argument. Be happy for me.

So far the day was not shaping up too badly. Frankie and I had been funnelled out of the Chunnel at Waterloo just gone noon. I called the office and Angie told me to take the rest of the day off. Well, she didn't tell me. She got one of her underlings to break the glad tidings. It was hard work holding back the tears of gratitude.

I lost Frankie and took a cab down to Battersea, arriving just in the nick of time: Rosie was halfway out the door on her way to do the week's shopping at Waitrose. Her idea of what constitutes food is to be found almost exclusively in the fruit and veg section, though she makes occasional forays into the deli for low-fat cheese, goat's milk, yoghurt and olives. Great grub for girls, but it doesn't exactly feed the inner man. I coaxed her into beefing up her shopping list with proper food, like sausages, steak and other essentials. She gave in because she was so happy to have her loving Max home again, and safely out of the clutches of all those lustful harridans who prey on innocent Englishmen abroad.

I was chancing my arm with the shopping list because this is really Rosie's territory, just like her flat. Some nights I'm welcome to hang my hat there. She greets me with hugs, kisses, the full monty. Other nights, she doesn't want me within miles of the place. Sometimes it's a full-time job working out which night is which. But there have been grim occasions where I've reeled into Battersea early, been greeted with all the trimmings and then been subjected to Rosie's idea of dinner. The last such event saw her dishing up *cold* watercress soup, grilled peppers and rubber cheese, and a nectarine for afters. I thought she was taking the mick. No, she explained, this was the sort of nosh you need to keep your body in the pink. Much though I adore and admire Rosie's body, I have no desire to have mine looking like it. Hence my coaxing her into stocking up on a sausage or two.

She relieved me of a chunk of my/Gabriella Cardigan's cash and off she toddled, leaving me to have another gander at the morning papers. Buried way in the back of ours was my Dutch copy. They'd hacked it to shreds and Frankie's boob shot was cropped to a mere double-column affair. I suspected sabotage by Angie. Up front there was a ten-paragraph piece on the lifting of Felix Pegg, with a quote from a copper that the celebrated poodle owner was 'assisting with enquiries'.

This is a useful catch-all term much favoured by Plod. It means that if they've got the wrong man they can always say they never suspected him at all. He was just helping them pinpoint the right man. Or, if by happy chance, he is Mr Right, it looks like they're good at their job. Sometimes if they're getting nowhere with a case they just nick somebody anyway. This means we hacks can no longer write embarrassing stories on the lines of: *Baffled police last night admitted they haven't got the foggiest who topped Joni Poelma.*

So what I needed to know was: is Felix Pegg in the frame for the murder or has he been collared just to take the bad look off things. I gave Mac a call. I caught him refuelling in Hampton's.

'How's about ye?' he asked. Mac is Irish, the Northern variety, so you've got to make allowances for the way he talks.

I said I was all the better for hearing his dulcet tones. Now, what was the inside stuff on Felix Pegg?

'He's got previous,' said Mac.

'What, he's a serial au-pair strangler?'

Nearly. Pegg had a ten-year-old conviction for showing his rude bits to a neighbour.

I said that didn't add up to much.

Mac said he had no idea what size it was. I let him do the laughing. He always enjoys his own jokes better than anyone else.

I said, 'So Pegg's not really up for it?'

'Maybe. Maybe not. Somebody says they saw him in the park an hour or so before the body showed up.'

'Who this somebody? Why he not arrested too?'

Mac said, 'She. And she's beyond suspicion because she's an off-duty WPC.'

'Personally my money's on the Killer Copette. She probably strangled Joni just to keep her hand in.'

'What – you're accusing her of police brutality? I'll have you know that is a foul canard on Her Majesty's upstanding WPCs.'

I asked what else was happening. Mac licked his lips and began describing the new barmaid in Hampton's. You could picture his hands slicing curves in the air as he spoke.

I wasn't interested in his latest target. I said, 'I mean what else is happening with the Poelma murder. Anything from the autopsy?'

Nothing to stir a flicker. Yes, she'd been strangled. No, she hadn't been raped. Maybe she'd been robbed. There was still no sign of the handbag.

Mac was already bored with the topic. He got back to his present specialist subject, the likelihood of his romping with Kirsty, the new barmaid. In many ways Mac reminds me a lot of Frankie. Like my monkey, his conversation is firmly tethered to groin level. Unlike Frankie, Mac talks from experience. I gave Kirsty seven to four against her surviving a Mac attack for more than a week. They trip over each other to get to him. I've seen prim young solicitors' clerks, Teflon-coated hackettes, barmaids with fortified bosoms, the lot, all queuing up to gaze woozily into his foxy eyes. After that, they're lost. Mac confesses there is a downside to his fatal attraction; he doesn't have any fantasy life worth talking about.

I have thought long and hard and I still can't figure out what he's got that the rest of us haven't. Mac is dark and skinny and so is his hair. He's got a thin pale face like an upturned triangle. He has a pair of black eyebrows that are arched in perpetual surprise. Does that sound like a photofit for Mr Love Machine? No. Indeed not. He also dresses in black which does nothing for his pasty face. And yet this man never sleeps alone. Come to that, he doesn't get much sleep at all.

I once asked Rosie what made Mac the killer king. She fluffed about a bit and then she said, 'Maybe it's his eyes.'

I haven't really mentioned them. They're green, or maybe light brown, slanty, and about as romantic as a snake's.

'What about his eyes?'

Rosie said, 'I don't know . . . it's just when he's talking to you, he looks at you as if you're the only person in the room.'

'Don't I do that?'

She squeezed my arm. 'Of course you do.'

So I was none the wiser.

Mac never brags about his conquests. His victims do that for him. But if pressed he will go into the shameless details. The only episode he refuses to talk about is the

one that led to him being kicked out of the Royal Ulster
Constabulary. But we have other sources. The general
theory is that a fast track Det. Insp. in the RUC came
home from a border stakeout several hours before he
ought to. Enough of Mac.

I was debating whether to do my Dutch exes or slope
off to Hampton's when my mobile went.

'Hello. You're back.'

I didn't sound as thrilled as he obviously was. I said,
'Hello, Jason.'

I'm not even sure he heard me. He said, 'I've been
doing a lot of digging and I've come up with some stuff
that might be interesting.'

'Like?'

'Do you remember you were asking about drugs?'

I did.

'And you remember I mentioned a guy called Fez?'

I remembered that too.

'Well, he's definitely dealing. A mate of mine said he
scored a nine-bar off him last summer.'

I wouldn't know a nine-bar if you hit me over the
head with one. I called for a translation.

Jason laughed merrily at my ignorance. 'It's a
regular drug deal. It's a quarter kilo of cannabis resin.'

I said, 'If it's a quarter k, why's it called a nine-bar?'

'Because it weighs nine ounces.'

'Oh.'

You learn something every day.

I said, 'Who's George?'

'George?'

'George. As in Best, as in Bush, as in Boy.'

'Don't know. Why?'

'Because Joni was madly in love with an English kid called George. Know him?'

A chunk of silence from his end. Then: 'Never heard of him.'

'Did you know Joni had a boyfriend?'

He was faster off the mark this time. 'No.'

He wasn't very good at telling lies.

I said, 'What about a Billy? Have you unearthed one of those in your "digging"?'

'Billy who?'

I said, 'If I knew I wouldn't be asking. Doesn't matter anway. What else have you got?'

'I thought we could both go to the Silver Lino tonight. I can get you in all right. Then you could see Fez.'

I remembered the heaving, sweating racket of the club in Maastricht. Not bloody likely.

I said, 'Where do these people – Fez and his mates – go before they go to the club?'

Jason chirruped, 'Mostly they meet up in the pub.'

Now that sounds more like it.

'Which pub?'

A place in Herne Hill called Clutterbucks. Never mind, it was a pub.

Jason wanted to know where he could collect me. And as if by reflex I said Hampton's.

He said, 'I'm looking forward to it.'

I wasn't. I could think of far better things to do on my day off.

*

Rosie returned with the vittels and started right away on knocking up dinner. 'I've got you something nice to eat,' she carolled amid the clanking of pans.

Knowing her idea of nice, that meant that lobster thermidor, Aberdeen Angus and a haunch of venison were definitely not on the night's menu. I let her get on with it while I rang around various cronies to learn what bilge they were inflicting on the newspaper-buying public.

Harry, my mate on the *Star*, had a police gun guard on Pamela Anderson while she went shopping in Harrods. There wasn't a pick of truth in it, but the pix were corkers. The *Express* were teasing out some guff on a shire police force starved of cash by a softy Labour government. The *Mail* had a buy-up on the nurse nicked brewing up beer in a Saudi hospital. I suppressed my yawns.

Rosie traipsed in brandishing a flat pan in which reposed a great chunk of something white. Whatever it was, it wasn't steak.

'Mako shark,' she proudly announced, as if she'd landed the thing herself.

The poor fool was so chuffed with herself I had to act ecstatic.

'You don't eat enough fish,' she said.

I don't eat enough steak either, but I let it pass.

She uncorked a bottle of Vouve de Vernay and we got chomping. Actually the ex-shark was more edible than feared, especially as she'd knocked up a coriander and lime mayonnaise to take the edge off. But there was an awful lot of it.

We were noshing away merrily when she said, 'What shall we do tonight?'

We?

I kept my head down. 'I've got a meet with a contact about this Joni Poelma case.'

She put her glass down very slowly. 'Who?'

'Jason. Jason Cardigan. I told you about him. He's taking me to a pub to point out some drug dealers.'

'A pub. You're off to a pub.'

This wasn't a question. It was an open accusation.

I looked at her with pained eyes. 'Rosie, I'm going to the pub because that's where the dealers are. If they met in the local church, I'd be going to the church.'

'Only if there was communion wine handy.'

'All right. What had you planned?'

She tossed her curls back. 'Oh, nothing much. Maybe have Kieran and Chris round for a drink.'

Kieran and Chris are both in the same lark as Rosie. They are normal human beings which means their conversation is somewhat lacking in reminiscences of drunken debauchery, fist fights, murky deeds and dirty doings. I'm not saying they're boring. They're just, well, normal.

I said, 'Maybe tomorrow night. But I do have to see Jason.'

We tipped back our glasses in silence. Rosie was thinking. There was a sharp little light in her eyes.

She said, 'OK. I'll come with you.'

I argued this way and that but she wasn't having any of it. The upshot was the usual abject surrender on my part. She bubbled off to get herself kitted out for the evening, leaving me to junk a nine-bar of mako shark in the flip-top bin.

She resurfaced in a long jacket the colour of the bloom on a grape with a mushroomy cashmere sweater under. The trousers had also been run up by the same bloke who made the jacket. But it was the sweater that quickened the heart. It sort of billowed and hugged. Cashmere sweaters always get me like that. Maybe I'm just kinky. I began thinking of other ways I would rather spend the night.

'Not now,' said Rosie the mind reader.

I shrugged on a jacket and checked my tape-recorder batteries were still sparking.

'Now, where's this pub?' she asked.

I said, 'We've got to stop by Hampton's first.'

'Ha! I knew it.'

It was National Take No Prisoners Night in Hampton's, but then I suppose it's like that most nights. Mac was crooked over the bar trapping a little blonde rabbity girl in his green headlights. This I guessed was Kirsty. I revised the odds on her survival down to ten to one against.

He caught sight of us in the bar mirror and waved a skeletal hand. Before we could join him, Tommy, my mate on the *Express*, shanghaied us with a story I couldn't repeat without breaking the laws on blasphemy, obscenity and slander and maybe some other laws I don't know about.

He had plenty more where that came from but we'd been there at least three minutes and we still hadn't a drink. I squeezed through a scrum of barristers to the corner where Mac had a couple of glasses waiting. We settled in to enjoy ourselves. We were joined by a clump of hacks from the *Sun*, including Kev who's too nosy to have around you for any length of time.

Out of my left ear I heard Rosie gaily tell him, 'We're off to see Jason Cardigan and a bunch of drug dealers.'

I swivelled right round. 'No we're not. We're off to see my nephew Ben.'

'Who's Ben?' This from Rosie.

I tossed her a frown but it slipped right by her.

'Who's Ben?' she asked again.

Kev had me locked in a sharp stare.

I said, 'Ben is my nephew. He's at hack school and I've promised to help him with his thesis.'

It sounded so stupid that Kev nearly fell for it. But not nearly enough.

He said, 'Who's Jason Cardigan?'

Rosie looked as if she was about to tell him. This time she caught the frown. She dipped her head and busied herself tossing back the Bratislavan Merlot.

I said, 'No idea. What are you up to anyway?'

Apart from being nosy, Kev also does a strong line in cock and bull stories. He cranked himself up and embarked on some tosh about him having lunch with the head of the Anti-Terrorist Plod. He was thus engaged when I saw Jason's ponytail bob over the horizon.

'Ben!' I yelled.

The idiot Jason looked around to see who was called Ben. It took maybe three seconds before it got through to him. He gave a big dopey smile and came threading his way through the ruck. Meanwhile Keyhole Kev had gone schtum and was watching his arrival through slitted eyelids.

I made the introductions. Jason looked as if he fancied a Coke, but I knew that if he stayed there Kev would soon have him telling all.

I said, 'How's the old thesis coming along?' Frankly I didn't give a tinker's, but I needed a line from him to stand up my cover story.

'Not bad. I took a couple of hints from you and I think it's a bit sharper. By the way, mum sends her regards.'

'How is Aunt Anne?'

Rosie came within a whisker of asking who Aunt Anne was. Jason got the idea. 'She's fine. She's off skiing in Aspen at the moment.'

Not bad, Jason. Maybe you will make a hack after all.

Mac asked, 'Have you got a sister?'

I don't think he was joking. But enough small talk. I drained my glass and pushed out a sigh of regret.

'Well, I've got to go and read this thesis while I still can.'

I turned Jason around and started pushing him out the way he had come.

'Night everybody,' I called over my shoulder.

They hurled their usual pleasantries at my back. All except Kev. I could feel his stoatish eyes on me all the way to the door.

Chapter Ten

I'm a connoisseur of pubs. I collect them. Clutterbucks is one I would happily drop from the collection.

Go back a couple of years and this would have been one of those big grotty boozers so beloved by the punters of Streatham. You know the type. It's been painted fifty different colours but it's still nicotine brown. There would have been a length of mahogany bar with a dozen squashed leatherette stools in front of it. Maybe a snug with burgundy flock wallpaper off to the side. An over-grazed snooker table filling the hole in the middle of the bar. A bank of one-armed bandits against the wall. Behind the bar a guv'nor with a busted nose and too much pork. And over everything a melange of odours that made you wish you had a head cold.

That's the way it used to be. That's the way I'd have preferred it.

Now Clutterbucks was panelled in black pretend wood. The lights were about three watts dimmer than the Blackpool Illuminations. You couldn't drink at the bar. You couldn't smoke at the bar. Instead there was a thicket of pillars, around each of which was a perilously narrow ledge. This much I could live with. I could even swallow the prices. And I suppose I could just about get used to being bumped against every five seconds. What made Clutterbucks more than a man could bear was the alleged music. It came at you from everywhere at about 15,000 decibels a second.

Jason seemed to like it though. He bobbed his head to the beat, which made shouting in his ear somewhat difficult. Whenever it came within range I yelled into it. I wanted to know what this Fez bloke looked like.

He told me. Fez was either a skink's thigh with a pig's mishmash or a skinny guy with a big moustache. I plumped for the latter. I looked around. There were easily half a dozen such characters in the offing. They all wore floppy lumberjack shirts over vests.

'Anything else?' I mouthed.

'No thanks.'

For a moment I toyed with the idea of doing the same trick I'd done in Maastricht and writing questions in my notebook. But Clutterbucks wasn't the sort of bar where they look kindly on intellectuals. I gave up.

I was on my second warm gin when Jason jogged my arm thereby nearly shattering my incisors. I followed the nod of his head. Over against the bar was a new skinny guy with a big moustache. He also had a lurid tattoo on his arm. Jason hadn't mentioned the tattoo.

Fez was swigging Sol from the bottle. There was a hunk of lemon stuck in the neck just to show what a sophisticate he was. Fez was in breezy conversation with an undernourished looking skinhead. They were laughing a lot. So now I'd seen Fez. Somehow I didn't feel as if new vistas had suddenly opened before me.

And what did I do next? Ask him if he had any E's for sale? The idea didn't appeal.

At that moment the music stopped. That was the first time I realized that everybody in the place was screaming at the tops of their voices. I'd seen and heard more than enough. Besides, I'd already copped too many suspicious looks from punters who had never seen a bloke in a suit before, except in court. I said, no I didn't, I *howled*, 'Let's get out of here.'

I led the way, deliberately plotting a course that took us alongside Fez and the skinhead. Rosie was stepping on my heels and Jason was the tail gunner. I drew abeam of Fez and that's when he did something strange. He stopped talking and gave me his undivided attention. There was a touch of streetwise arrogance in his look. He soaked up every detail of my appearance, right down to the claret-hued lizards frisking on my tie. He would remember me all right.

Naturally, I've been stared at by blokes before. But not when I'm with Rosie, particularly not when Rosie's wrapped up in a cashmere sweater. That was the strange bit. I stared back at Fez. He was about five ten or eleven with a hooky nose hanging over the moustache. His hair was darkish and so were his eyes. He had the sort of swagger you usually get in a roadie for a heavy metal band. Or a street corner pusher.

I stared back just as coolly and mooched on. I got about a yard past him when by some quaint quirk of the accoustics I heard him say, 'Hi, Jason. How's it going, man?'

I didn't hear the answer. I ploughed on through the lumberjack shirt forest until we made the street. Then I looked back at Jason. He squeezed off a half-embarrassed smile. 'Fez recognized me.'

He didn't just recognize you: he knew your name too. I tucked that away somewhere to look at later.

Rosie said, 'Jason, that place is godawful. Where do you drink normally?'

But Jason doesn't drink normally: he drinks Coca Cola.

We got back into his motor and made him drive us some place where we could actually talk and drink at more or less the same time. We ended up in a dinky Dulwich bar with mock-Tudor beams and tapestry-covered chairs. Still, it was a legit bar.

I lodged Rosie and Jason in a corner lit by fake candles and went to whistle up some drink. The guv'nor, who was not Speedy Gonzales, eventually twigged that I was gasping for liquor and was on his way to do the necessary when from over my shoulder somebody bawled, 'Two more large scotch and a pint of best, Hector.'

Hector forgot about me. I swung around to vent contempt and bile on the queue-jumper and, blow me down, I knew that face. The last time I'd seen it, it was glaring at me from behind the police cordon in Dulwich park.

"Ello, 'ello, 'ello. It's Chief Inspector Skelly,' I said sweetly.

He was chewing the end off a panatella and trying to stuff his shirt into his waistband. He paused and squeezed up his eyes at me.

'I know you.'

This shows how you get to be a Chiefie in the Met.

I said, 'That's good.'

You could hear his brain trying to figure out who I was. A brief? No, too respectable for that. Another Plod? Ditto. He gave in.

I said, 'Max Chard.'

'Ah.' It was an 'Ah' that could have meant several things, none of them pleasant.

Hector popped up with the drinks and Skelly took his time about paying. You could see there was something he wanted to say to me but he couldn't remember what.

I ordered in a brace of gins and a Coke while he tried to work it out. He eventually ran it to ground in some dusty pigeonhole of his brain. 'Drugs! What's all this crap you've been writing about drugs?'

I said, 'Let me get these drinks in and I'll tell you all about it.'

I left my own glass on the bar and cruised across to Rosie and Jason. He was looking at her with his cuddly toy eyes and she was doing all the talking. I told them to look after each other because I was otherwise engaged at the bar. Jason didn't seem to mind anyway.

And so back to Skelly of the Yard. He was in the company of a couple of other representatives of the Thick Blue Line. They'd evidently been briefed that I was a scumbag hack because they squared their shoulders and stuck their noses in the air. Skelly accused, 'You just made up that drugs thing for a bit of sensation.'

I smiled. 'You're right. I also totally fabricated the line that Joni Poelma's sister is banged up in France for drug running. And I verballed her best friend to say Joni was into drugs. And if I told you there was a geezer flogging, E, acid, blow, Charlie, the whole bit at the Silver Lino, I'd be making that up too.'

Skelly has marbles where other people have eyes. He said, 'What's his name?'

'Don't know.'

'Huh.'

I said, 'That makes two of us who don't know. But he exists. And have you found George yet? Or Billy?'

I had to explain that George was the ex-boyfriend of the ex-Joni and that Billy was probably his successor. Skelly pretended he wasn't interested but he poured too much water into his scotch. He unfurled another panatella and whoofed smoke in my face.

He said, 'George. Billy. Some drug pusher. All this other business. They don't mean a toss. What you're looking at is a straightforward murder.'

I lifted an eyebrow. 'And you think it was Felix Pegg what done it?'

Skelly bristled. 'No. He was just helping with enquiries.'

So Pegg was loose again.

I said, 'Well, what have you got on it?'

A blustery laugh from my least favourite CI. He had nothing.

He said, 'I'll tell you one thing – now this is off the record.'

I nodded assent and clicked on my tape-recorder.

Skelly said, 'It wasn't drugs. There was nothing on her, nothing in her handbag, nothing in her room.'

Handbag. He'd said handbag. Now where had that been hiding itself?

I said idly, 'I suppose you've been turning over her friends, all the names in her little green book.'

'What little green book?'

I sighed. If the Law only bothered to read the papers they might catch a murderer now and again. I explained it to him. He wasn't interested in that either. Besides, he'd just run out of scotch and he was looking at me thirstily. Somehow I didn't feel like topping him up. I made my excuses and left.

A couple of hours later Rosie and I were back in Battersea warming ourselves around a glass or two. I was silent, largely because I was glooming over my plans for the morrow. In a moment of insanity I had kindly offered to show Jason what we ripsnorting hacks get up to at the Old Bailey. He'd jumped at it.

Rosie was a touch preoccupied too. She twirled an artistic curl round an artistic finger and mused aloud, 'They sound an odd bunch, the Cardigans.'

She's an expert on strange people. She's one of them herself.

Rosie said, 'I mean, there's his dad who spends his life inventing miracle cures, yet he won't even take an Aspirin if he's got a headache.'

'How incredibly odd.'

She wasn't listening. She said, 'And they've got absolutely heaps and heaps of money, but guess where they went for their last holidays?'

I guessed Scunthorpe.

'Nearly. They went fell walking in Cumbria, you

119

know, where it rains all the time. And the holiday before that they were off riding bikes in the Pyrenees.'

I said, 'I'll bet that was Gabriella's idea. She strikes you as one of these body beautiful types.'

Rosie shot me a look but kept going. 'Yes, she's even got her own fitness studio. I don't mean her own private one. She actually *runs* a sort of health place for all her rich friends. You know, aerobics and all that.'

I pictured Gabriella Cardigan bopping about in a leotard. It was a pretty picture.

I said, 'I suppose the idle rich need something to while away the hours.'

Rosie said, 'You make it sound like a hobby. But Jason says the fitness centre is her pet lamb. And it's really raking it in.'

'Maybe Wedge Cardigan isn't as loaded as he's cracked up to be.'

'Uh-huh. It's got nothing to do with him. It's Gabriella's baby. She spends half the week there. You know she's a dietician *and* a biochemist?'

'And a multi-millionairess.'

Rosie said, 'Yes, but I think that's the whole point of the fitness place. It's her sort of independence. OK, it makes a lot of money but I think the independence thing is really what it's all about.'

Frankly I was bored with the oddities of the Cardigans. She wasn't. She said, 'And our Jason, he doesn't quite add up either.'

'How so?'

'Well . . .' she began, ' . . . it's hard to pin down. He doesn't seem all that upset about Joni's murder, yet he knows her better than he lets on.'

I said, 'He also knows the mysterious George, but he says he doesn't. And he has an inside track on the drug thing but he's holding back on that too.'

'So what does all that mean?' asked Rosie.

'I don't know. Maybe he used to buy stuff for Joni, or he may even have helped her sell it.'

'Maybe,' said Rosie, the great romantic, 'it's got nothing to do with drugs. Maybe they were lovers and they were having naughties.'

The woman has a one-track mind.

I said, 'Maybe it's time we went to bed.'

The Old Bailey is a good old place. It may not churn out much in the way of Justice but five days a week it fills half the pages of every daily in the land. You just wander around the place picking the stories like so many plums.

You don't even have to go into any of its courts. Way down in the bowels of the Bailey is a clutch of press agencies which let us use their phones, files and notes when we're too hungover to decipher our own scribbles. You can sit there and file half a dozen stories on the trot, thereby giving News Desk the impression you've spent the entire day chasing like a mad thing from one court to another. And Desk can't even pester you because your bleep and your mobile are both switched off, lest they disrupt the majesty of the court.

I turned up half an hour before the kick-off to find Jason kicking about on the steps. 'What's the story today?' he asked.

First up, in Court 18, was a tasty one: a big noise in the anti-abortion lobby was accused of killing an unborn child. Well, that wasn't exactly the charge but that's the story anyway. We bowled along to Court 18 and I smuggled Jason into the Press benches.

Our killer was not the usual type you find glowering over the Old Bailey dock. He had tiny eyes that skipped nervously all over the place, not much in the way of hair and a suit two sizes too big. If you were to guess his occupation you'd have said he was a chartered accountant who'd failed the charisma test. His name was Endel Loy. We sat back to relish the ritual blood-letting.

A woman brief who looked like a raven got up and started pitching into him. Endel Loy, she told us, was an outspoken crusader against abortion. That bit we already knew so we dozed off until she got somewhere interesting.

We come now to the morning of September 25, when E. Loy set out to stage a 'wanton and reckless' protest at an abortion clinic in Feltham. The protest involved him driving his seven-year-old Nissan through the front doors of the clinic. It probably seemed a good idea at the time.

All went more or less as planned, except for one petty detail. A Miss Avis Falklender chose that very self-same morning to visit the clinic. She was due to have an op there the following morning when, quoth the Raven, 'her pregnancy would be terminated'.

But, and that is a heavily ironic 'But', Avis had under-gone one of those sudden changes of mind, so common to her species. She had decided to have the baby after all. She went to the clinic that morning to tell them to call the whole thing off. They said OK, have a nice baby and see you around sometime.

Avis strolled out. At which precise point Endel Loy and his seven-year-old Nissan rolled in. Oooops. When the dust cleared they found Avis urgently in need of prolonged intensive care. She was now no longer hospitalized but still not sparking on all four cylinders. Our eyes swung round to Avis, a dark waif of a girl with half a zimmer frame tucked under her arm. She'd make some good snaps later.

The Raven was still in full flight. Miss Falklender, she said, was so grievously injured she tragically lost her unborn child. The tragedy was wholly due to Loy's wanton disregard for the lives and safety of others.

In the dock, Endel Loy sort of shrunk.

The case clicked on at a breezy pace. Avis hobbled to the stand and said about the same as the Raven only she wasn't so addicted to adverbs. She also chipped in with some good lines about how her life had been ruined and she had lost the baby she so wanted. (It would have been a boy.)

Next a vulture flapped his wings and got stuck into telling us what a fine, upstanding, deeply religious, even more deeply contrite man Endel Loy was. You could see the jury having a good laugh at that one. Up on his high chair Mr Justice Kamblin rolled his eyes and looked at the clock.

After a while everybody had had their say, including Loy. ('Every night I pray for forgiveness. Nothing I can do or say will bring her baby back.') You can say that again. The judge told the jury to go away and think about it. We gathered up our notebooks and went off to Harry's bar to think of something altogether more pleasant.

The timing was ace. The case had run out of steam just after twelve-thirty, and Mr Justice Kamblin is a man who likes his tucker. Therefore he instructed the jury to come back at two if they'd made their minds up. That gave us time for a healing glass or four.

The other hacks looked sideways at Jason until I explained that he was my idiot nephew Ben whose heart was set on being a big bold reporter just like them. Grim smiles all round. We got started on the latest scuttlebuck from the Street of Shame. Somebody said that a *Star* sports guy had got the heave-ho for fiddling his expenses. A shiver ran through the company. There but for the grace of God . . .

It dawned on me presently that I was being less than considerate to Jason, so I grabbed him by the elbow and steered him further along the bar.

'Well,' I asked, 'what do you think of the show so far?'

He thought it was 'safe'. Safe? That meant it was 'pukka'. Pukka? That meant great. These kids don't even speak English anymore.

He insisted on buying me a drink and I didn't put up too much of a fight. He said, 'So have you got the whole story now?'

I gave him an odd look. 'Not quite. We need to know that the bugger's guilty before we go around saying he killed an unborn baby.'

'But the jury's bound to convict him.'

People, I mean ordinary people, have such a touching faith in Old Bailey juries. I've seen multiple murderers, serial rapists, Arsenal fans, the works, walk free from the Bailey because jurors deemed them of incapable of doing what they did. Most jurors still believe in the tooth fairy.

But this lot got it right. They paddled back into Court 18 and said, yep, Endel Loy was a bad lot. Mr Justice Kamblin gawped and praised them for their rare percipience. Then he turned on the wizened Loy and gave him a right old bollocking. Five years for grievous bodily plus a couple of concurrent jobs for this, that and the other. Loy wept buckets.

'That's it then,' Jason announced brightly.

Oh no it wasn't. The next bit was us getting hold of Avis Falklender and making her say something snappy. She knew what we wanted.

'He's a murderer!' she screeched. 'He killed my baby.'

She warmed to the theme, so much so that you came away with the impression that Loy was Feltham's answer to King Herod, only nasty with it. There was also a lot of stuff from Avis on namby-pamby judges and wishy-washy sentences.

By now we were outside in the wishy-washy sunshine and the monkeys joined in the circus. Avis obliged with a flood of tears. So that was it all done and dusted. All we had to do now was write the thing.

We went back inside and borrowed a desk in a news agency. I had my Toshiba laptop with me and got tapping on the story while Jason fetched coffee.

He returned and started reading it aloud over my shoulder.

'CRAZED anti-abortionist Endel Loy killed an unborn child in a bizarre publicity stunt, the Old Bailey heard yesterday.

Jason clicked his tongue. I snapped my head round at him. 'Yes?'

He said, 'If you dropped "Crazed" from the intro, would that not make it tighter?'

Oh dear. It was tutorial time again. I explained it patiently. 'You don't intro a story with a hyphenated word. It looks stupid. The first half is in big type, the second bit in lower case. Anyway, "Crazed" has a bite to it.'

I turned back to my laptop but he was still hovering. 'Anything else?' A more worldly man might have noticed the sardonic emphasis on 'else'.

Jason said, 'Well, you told me that if you stuck in things like Dulwich and London high up the story, it put off readers in Hartlepool. But you've got "Old Bailey" in the intro.'

I sighed. 'The Old Bailey isn't a geographical place: it's a thing. It means something. It tells the reader this is a big, big story.'

He still wasn't convinced.

I said, 'Look, the Bailey is where Crippen was sentenced to be hanged from the neck until dead. It was where George Blake copped forty-two years for having forty-two British spies killed. It was where Ruth Ellis was weighed off. That's how important it is.'

I don't think he knew who any of them were, but he caught the drift. He shut up and let me get on with knocking Avis Falklender's quotes into shape. It took the best part of twenty minutes. I pressed ENTER and squirted five hundred blistering words down the line. Time for a livener.

I looked around for Jason but he'd gone off to snoop over other people's shoulders. I dragged him away before they beat him to a pulp and we nipped back to the bar.

He tucked into a Coke as if he liked the stuff and said, 'I was reading the other's intros.'

'And?'

'One of them started: "*A mother wept last night as she told how a religious fanatic killed her unborn child.*" '

'That,' I said, 'would have been Ian, the bloke from the *Mirror.*'

'How do you know?'

'Because Ian claims to have copyright on the intro "*A mother wept . . .*" If any of us use it, we've got to buy him a bottle of champagne.'

Jason said, 'You're kidding.'

'I'm not. Furthermore, Liz from the *Standard* holds the rights to "*Police faced a wall of silence last night . . .*" '

'So you have to buy her champagne too?'

'That's the deal. And Alvin from PA gets miffed if anybody else uses "*A deadly cocktail of drink and drugs . . .*" '

'Wow!' said Jason. He glugged meditatively on his Coke.

I said, 'And you still want to be a hack?'

'Absolutely.'

We put in another appearance at the Bailey and I tricked out a couple of up-and-downer murders. There wasn't much chance of them making the paper but at least they told News Desk I wasn't spending all my time in the pub.

After which I thought I'd better give Jason a guided tour of the nuthouse that passes for our Newsroom. As soon as we got out of the lift I knew something funny was going on. People were actually smiling. Even the News Desk riff-raff were looking reasonably happy in their work. Angela Whipple glanced up as we came eddying by.

'Hello, Max,' she said. 'You've got a Page Three top on the abortion killer. Nice job.'

Something was definitely going on.

She flicked a coquettish eye at Jason.

'And you must be Julian,' she said.

'Jason,' said he.

News Desk people are used to making mistakes. She gushed on. 'Nice to have you with us. If you'd like to sit in on News Desk anytime, just let me know.'

Jason said he would like that very much. Any more of this and they'd start kissing each other.

Angie said, 'And how's Max looking after you? He's not leading you into too many pubs, I hope?'

A light laugh from the youth. 'Just a dozen or so.'

Thank you, Jason.

I said, 'Has everyone been on the sauce or something? There's a certain mood of merriment in the air.'

Angie said, 'GAGA.'

Suddenly all was explained. GAGA is our shorthand for the *Gazette* Actors' Galaxy Award, an expensive and futile publicity stunt. Every year we get our gormless readers to vote for their favourite luvvies. Then we hire

128

the banquetting hall at the Grosvenor and invite the nominees to a beanfeast. The whole show gets televized, giving the Editor the excuse to say *Gazette* every third word.

We hacks of course are not welcome, but the pathetic rabble which masquerades as our showbiz department get the chance to put on monkey suits and sequins and drink the house red.

I said before that GAGA is a futile exercise. This is not strictly true. It serves one very useful purpose: it gets the Editor and Belker out of our hair. For the best part of a week they whoop it up in the Ivy and the Groucho Club with various lowlife thesps.

As the full meaning hit me, a slow seraphic smile lit my rugged jaw. This meant that Belker would not be around until Friday at least. It probably meant his liver would need a few days off to recuperate. And that all meant I didn't have to give him my answer on the News Editor's job until next week.

Angie eyed my wall-to-wall grin and fired a mischievous dart. 'I thought you'd be going to GAGA with Belker.'

I said, 'He invited me. But when I heard that guests were rationed to four bottles apiece, I wasn't interested.'

'That I could believe.'

I was heading off to show Jason the hacks' ghetto when Angie called me back.

'Max. I've got you down for one tomorrow.'

'Anything interesting?'

She ruffled through her news diary. 'Should be. It's Joni Poelma's inquest. Dulwich coroner's, ten o'clock.'

I glanced at my watch. Bugger. It was gone four-thirty, so I couldn't ring the coroner's clerk to see whether the inquest had anything promising on the menu. If it was nothing more than the formal opening, I'd be wasting my time going to it.

Angie saw what was running through my head. She said, 'Joni's parents might be there. I should have let you know earlier so you could check. Look, we don't need you for anything more right now, so if you want, just knock it on the head for today. Take Jason for a drink.'

She was smiling at me and it was a proper smile. I let her have one of my toothiest ones back. We were mates again.

As I wandered away I mused on how the absence of Belker always has such a heartwarming effect on people.

Chapter Eleven

Next morning I wasn't feeling quite so tender-hearted towards Angela Whipple. I'd phoned some dork at the nick in Dulwich who told me the inquest was in Croydon. Time was getting tight so I shuttled off there in a minicab.

A kingsize cop at the door happily informed me I was in the wrong place. The inquest was in Southwark. He seemed to find that funny. I growled and hunted another taxi to take me back to London proper.

And when I got there, the whole bloody thing was over anyway. Not that I'd missed much. It was only the formal opening. So I'd blown twenty-five quid on cabs and thrown away a precious hour of my life chasing nothing. I was in a rare old mood.

I collared the coroner's officer, a rustic-looking Plod with straw hair. I've never quite figured out why, but apart from the uniform, these blokes are a breed apart from the usual Met minions. For a start, they are only too keen to help us hacks.

I asked him the score and he told me it was all very routine. Joni's dad had given the formal identification, the clerk had read out a line or two from the pathologist's report, to the effect that Joni's death was caused by asphyxiation due to suffocation, due to strangulation, which sounded thorough enough. Tom Skelly put in a guest appearance as the investigating officer. Skelly fibbed and said detectives were following several avenues of investigation.

The only lively spot in the whole proceedings came when Mum and Pop Poelma said they wanted their daughter's body back. The coroner said tough titty, we're hanging onto it for a fortnight anyway. Maybe longer. Mrs P was taken over all tearful and the coroner, deeming that everyone had had enough fun for one day, adjourned the inquest for a month. That was it.

I thanked the coroner's officer anyway and was turning for the door when he said, 'There's Doctor Grasmith now.'

I blinked. Dr Paul Grasmith is the Home Office pathologist. You don't normally find heavyweight bods like him wasting their time at inquest openings.

I said, 'What's he doing here?'

The coroner's tame Plod knew that too. The pathologist was showing a new assistant around.

I thought about it. Maybe Grasmith might throw me a crumb or two. It is not in the nature of pathologists to grab passing hacks and whisper hot news in their ears. There's probably something against it in the Official Secrets Act. But Grasmith and I are blood brothers. He is forever in my debt.

This all goes back to an inquest a year or so ago when he was the star turn at Westminster Coroner's Court. He'd given yards of evidence and then been cross examined for more than an hour, after which he'd reeled out into the corridor in dire need of a soothing smoke.

I was already out there and a quarter of a way down a Bensons. He flashed me a tight, conspiratorial smile. The smile of one nicotine addict to another. Then he whipped a lighter out of one pocket and patted the other for his fags. Suddenly his face fell and he took over all twitchy. I knew the symptoms: he'd left his cigarettes back at the morgue.

Without saying anything I proffered my pack. In broken words and with fumbling fingers he snatched a Bensons. I even lit it for him because his hands didn't seem up to the job. A couple of puffs later and he was his normal self again. I gave him the rest of the pack because I was going to the pub anyway, and, while there might not exactly have been tears of gratitude coursing down his cheeks, you could tell he was deeply touched.

So Dr Paul Grasmith owed me.

I wandered over to the corner where he and a fetching Asian girl were talking. At least he was doing the talking. She was just nodding her head and looking reverential.

He broke off when he saw me. 'Ah, the Good Samaritan,' he said.

So he remembered me. I went straight for it. 'I got here too late for the inquest. Did I miss anything?'

No. Not a thing. Straightforward strangulation. You got the impression he would have preferred the odd bullet hole, machete slash and minute traces of a rare poison to make it interesting.

His assistant had sort of made herself invisible against the wall. I said, 'I'm a shade surprised it was so ordinary.'

Grasmith had deep-set eyes under heavy lids. But

there was nothing sleepy about them. He asked, 'Really? What did you expect?'

'Drugs.'

From the way he went quiet I knew I'd hit on something. Grasmith's voice was quite precise. 'And what made you think drugs might be involved?'

I cobbled together some stuff about talking to Joni's friends and how they'd said she was into illegal substances.

Grasmith tapped a long bony finger on his jaw. His eyes never left mine. He was making his mind up about something. After a while he said, 'I suppose you think you know how a coroner's court works.'

Think? I've been to so many of them I could write the verdicts before they've reached them. But there was something about the way he'd said it that gave me pause.

He continued evenly, 'A pathologist submits a report. That is correct?'

Yep, that's the way you do it.

Grasmith smiled at my ignorance. 'No. What a pathologist does is submit a *partial* report. The coroner does not see his full findings. What he reads is only that area of the report which deals exclusively with the cause of death.'

I didn't see where this was going. So?

'Therefore any other condition the deceased might have is not deemed relevant. It is not reported.'

Ah. I was beginning to see.

Grasmith asked casually, 'What sort of drugs was she supposed to be on?'

'Ecstasy.'

'Our old friend methylenedioxymethamphetamine. Yes, that sounds logical.'

It didn't to me. I said, 'So Joni Poelma would have failed a drugs test.'

Grasmith went coy. 'Did I say that?'

'No, I did.'

'You *guessed* it,' he corrected.

I said, 'All right. I guessed that she was out of her tree on Ecstasy. That's what I'm writing anyway.'

He shook his head in sorrow. 'And you'd be quite wrong.'

'Wrong?'

He said, 'Let's see what else you can guess. Do you know what repeated abuse of MDMA can tend to cause?'

I guessed for a start that MDMA was Ecstasy. After that I was stuck.

He enlightened me, 'It leads to renal and hepatitic damage, even renal failure.'

I looked suitably agog.

'That means your kidneys pack in,' he added helpfully.

I said, 'I'm guessing that Joni's kidneys packed in.'

'Not quite. But imagine that someone has a congenital renal impairment and that person proceeds to abuse regularly MDMA or any other of the amphetamine family.'

I imagined. 'That person would have pretty ropey kidneys.'

'Indeed, yes.'

I strung it all together. 'So Joni Poelma was in fairly bad nick even before somebody topped her.'

He didn't disagree.

'Would she have known?'

He hesitated over that one. 'It is possible. She would have been in considerable pain. She did not have a GP in England and I have not been able to obtain her medical record from Holland.'

I pushed it. 'And what caused the pain was she was popping Ecstasy all the time.'

Grasmith frowned. 'Now you're guessing again. But there are amphetamine indicators present.'

I was already starting to shape it into a story. Grasmith guessed as much. He said smoothly, 'Naturally one would hope you do not attribute any of this to the pathologist.'

'Naturally. But just one other thing. You said this won't even come out at Joni's inquest?'

'That's right. It might be very interesting, but it has certainly nothing to do with the cause of death.'

And so saying he handed me a cigarette. We were evens now.

I sniffed out a bar and emptied a glass or two to get into writing mode. I was feeling fairly tickled with myself. I suppose there was a certain malicious pleasure in it. I was imagining what the cretinous Chief Inspector Skelly would say when he read the story.

Here was proof positive that Joni was awash with drugs. All right, they didn't kill her, but Skelly had been so pigheadedly cocksure that drugs didn't enter the picture anywhere.

I got on the mobile and rang it through, putting as much top spin on the story as I could. There was a bevy of muscular quotes from senior officers, and, just for badness, a line saying, 'On the record, police have repeatedly denied a drugs link.'

The only inference to be drawn from this was that *off* the record, they were confirming it. That would make Skelly blow a head gasket.

I trickled back to the office, timing it so that I got there just as everyone was about to stagger off for lunch. Angie was happy to see me. After all, she'd sent me out on a no-hoper and I'd come back with a tasty little story, all wrapped up and tied with a bow. She said, 'It's been a while since we've had a drink together. How's about if I buy you lunch?'

I put on a plastic smile and said nothing could make me happier. I knew what this was about.

She grabbed her coat and hauled me off to a wine bar which had too many woman execs all shrilling at each other over their Chardonnay. I stuck with gin.

Angie came at me from an oblique angle. 'You know, Max, I'd hate to lose you.'

Eh?

She said, 'Have you heard about the changes at the *Daily Mail*?'

I'd heard but I let her tell me. The headline item was their crime bloke was leaving, or at least he was taking a year's sabbatical to sail a boat around the world or some other place.

I said that must be nice for him.

Angie fiddled with her glass. These News Desk people are so long off the road they've forgotten how to be devious. She said, 'I hear the *Mail*'s looking for somebody to replace him. They're offering top dollar.'

I didn't say anything.

She flashed me a look from under her lashes. 'They haven't approached you?'

Oh, Angie. Whatever happened to subtlety? What she was really saying was why didn't I approach them. And the subtext to that was if I joined the *Mail* I couldn't pinch her job.

I shook my head. 'I like the *Gazette*. And the *Mail* News Desk is bloody awful.'

She sifted through this for a hidden meaning. There wasn't one.

She said, 'I'm glad you're staying. You're the best crime man in the street.'

That was newspaperspeak for 'You'd be rubbish on the Desk.'

It's not right, it's not kind, but hacks can't resist winding up News Desk execs.

I said, 'There's only one problem with my job. I don't earn enough.'

Angie widened her eyes. She could dig only one message out of this: I wanted to stay at the *Gazette* and earn more money, therefore that meant her job.

She asked: 'How much are you on now?'

'Fifty.'

'That's a lot of money.'

I said, 'I earn it.'

She went quiet and I didn't want to interrupt her. She gave it another try. 'The *Mail* would pay more than fifty-grand. Maybe fifty-five.'

'But who wants to work for the *Mail*?'

Another two-minute silence rolled by, enlivened only by the waitress weighing in with more drink. I lit a cigarette and began eyeing up the local totty. There was a lot on show. One in particular . . .

Angie broke in on my reverie. 'You know that I'm already running 12 per cent over my news budget?'

That was her problem.

'But . . .' she said, dragging her heels over it, 'I just might be able to squeeze you some sort of discretionary pay rise.'

'What sort of rise are we talking about?'

'Maybe fifteen hundred, maybe two grand.'

Two grand. Forty quid a week. Take away 40 per cent tax, the added pension rake off, and that left me with what? Just about enough to pay for another bottle of Hampton's Croatian champagne. I did not burst into song.

'It's the best I can do,' Angie said in a little voice.

I smiled to let her know I appreciated it anyway. But I was careful not to say that two grand would do nicely. For I knew precisely what she was up to: she was trying to buy my loyalty for a crummy £40 a week.

After that the conversation moved on to general office slandering. Angie contributed a lulu about the Editor getting a feature writer to research his idiot daughter's local government thesis for her.

We strolled back to the office still matey but hardly talking. She was busy plotting other pretty ploys to stop me moving into her chair. If only she knew.

I for my part was thinking of coincidence. This was the second time in less than a fortnight that for no good reason a woman had offered me two grand.

*

I hadn't lied to Angie about needing more money. My overdraft was getting close to Third World Debt status and I'd stopped reading my mail. I'd also somehow frittered away half of Gabriella Cardigan's bounty and I had to pay her back. On the plus side, the office owed me two months' expenses, enough to shut the bank manager up for a while and sort Gabriella. But the snag was I had to write the damn things first and my imagination wasn't up to it today.

So I phoned the bank manager. He refused to speak to me and I was shunted through to a woman who talked through her nose. She liked saying no a lot. I embroidered the facts a little, hinting that a vast wodge of exes was winging my way. She'd heard it all before. It was still no.

That left me with just one alternative, putting the squeeze on Rosie. The drawback there was I'd have to put up with a smarty-pants lecture on my spending habits. But in the end she'd cough up. The woman's a fool with her money.

It was a quietish afternoon. I zinged up a couple of agency court stories and phoned a mate here and there but nobody could come out to play. I began seriously abusing the office tea and thinking over what Dr Grasmith had told me. There was a loose strand in there that I wanted to have a tug at. It was the bit where he said he hadn't been able to get hold of Joni's medical records.

I turned up my notebook from the Maastricht trip and dug out the number for Hanneke Lommen, Joni's erstwhile chum. I let the phone ring for nearly a minute and was on the brink of giving up when a breathless woman barked into it.

I said, 'Good afternoon. May I speak to Hanneke please.'

I said this in my best English and she promptly came back with a helping of double Dutch. I tried again. This time I think she got the idea. She didn't say anything to me, but I could hear her hollering '*Hanneke!*' at top treble.

I lit a cigarette and waited. After a while on came another voice, every bit as breathless. What on earth were they getting up to out there?

'Hanneke. This is Max Chard. We met last week in the club in Maastricht. Remember?'

She remembered all right. She also remembered she'd landed herself in a hell of a row for speaking to me.

'Why?' I asked with pained innocence.

There followed a rant about my story on Joni doing drugs. I cocked an eyebrow. I didn't know they read our newspaper down Maastricht way.

They didn't. But Joni's dad did in London. He'd griped about it to his son, Erik the Viking, who had gone pounding on her door, threatening rape, pillage and God knows what else. So she didn't want to say anything to me. Ever.

I said I wasn't surprised. I was every bit as angry.

She said something like huh?

'Yes, some idiot in our London office messed up the story. I've made a formal complaint about it.'

She didn't believe me and who could blame her.

I dived in before she could hang up. 'Anyway, I didn't ring you to ask you anything. I thought you might like to know how the inquest went today.'

Hanneke said nothing. I explained to her what an inquest was. She still said nothing but at least she was listening.

I gave her the sketchiest outline, placing all the emphasis on Joni's mum breaking down when the coroner refused to release the body.

'That is terrible,' said Hanneke.

Isn't it just. I said, 'Part of the problem is the British authorities haven't been able to get Joni's medical records from Holland. If they had them, her parents could take her body home.'

'Oh.'

I pushed on. 'But the authorities don't even know who her doctor was. Do you?'

She didn't.

I said they'd found that Joni was suffering from a strange illness, that she must have been in a lot of pain.

Hanneke forgot her vow of silence. 'Joni said there was something wrong. I don't know the English word.'

'Kidneys?'

'I don't know.'

'But she went to see a doctor?'

Hanneke thought so.

I said, 'There's one other thing that's stopping her mother getting Joni's body. The authorities haven't found George yet.'

Hanneke wanted to know why they needed him. I went all silky. 'It's just a formality. They want to interview anybody who knew Joni well in London. And he was her boyfriend.'

'But that was finished.'

I sighed sorrowfully. 'I know. But that's the way

they operate here. I suppose they think he gave Joni something which made her ill.'

Over in Maastricht a two-megaton thermonuclear device went off. 'I know what you're doing. You're trying to get me to say George gave her drugs, just because he . . .'

'Just because he what?'

The phone went down with a bang that hurt my ears.

Now, where had all that got me? Not much further, except for that one unfinished sentence. Just because he what? Just because he was up to some mischief or other. And the betting from my end was it involved drugs. Enough useless pondering. Time for a quickie.

I was down in the Stone with a glass to my lips when my mobile chimed in. I took a swig before answering it. Jason. They'd just let him out of hack school so he was full of pent-up vim. It made you tired to listen to him.

He wanted to know what I was doing tonight. I was on the point of inventing an Important Contact whom I had to see when I changed my mind.

'Nothing,' I said.

That was super, because he'd spent the day being taught interviewing techniques and he wanted to know what I thought of them.

'Hampton's?' he suggested.

No. I needed to get him somewhere without distraction, for I suddenly felt the need to practise my interviewing techniques on him. I didn't tell him that bit.

'What about a decent pub down your place? But not

143

the one we were in the other night. I don't want to meet Skelly right now.'

He said he'd think of something and he'd pick me up around eight.

I returned to my Gordons and forgot all about Jason. It wasn't hard.

The place he chose was not the liveliest spot I've ever been in, but it was bang on for the purpose. There was a large semi circular bar holding up a couple of estate agents or sales reps. Beyond them was a low, wide lounge, dotted with high-backed seats. They formed horseshoes where the punters could spill out their hearts without the world at large lending an earhole. In the centre of each was a round table with a green-shaded lamp perched in the middle. All very Dulwichy.

The overall mood was about as upbeat as the inside of Dracula's coffin, largely thanks to a crimson carpet, crimson curtains and crimson cushions. If you ordered red wine in there you'd never find it.

Three of the horseshoes were already occupied. I shuffled Jason off to one out on its own and I rattled my change to let the barman know I wasn't there just to drink in the atmosphere.

While he got popping among the optics I listened to the muzak. It was that godawful bland cocktail jazz you always associate with an empty hotel lounge about three in the afternoon. It's nearly enough to put you off drink. Maybe after a while I wouldn't notice it.

I returned with the goods. Jason helped himself to a gulp and said, 'They were teaching us today about how to use silence as an interviewing technique.'

I was silent.

He said, 'What do you think of it – I mean, to get information from somebody who doesn't want to tell you anything?'

'It works OK for television. People get self-conscious when there's a camera stuck in their face. They have to say something. But it's not so useful in newspaper interviews.'

Jason absorbed this and nodded wisely. He said, 'How do *you* do it then?'

That's a daft one. It's different every time.

I said, 'All right, let's try an interview. You pretend you're the interviewee and I've got to coax something out of you.'

He liked this game.

I lit a cigarette. I looked away at an angle and said, 'They had the inquest on Joni today.'

'I thought you were going to interview me.'

'This *is* an interview.'

'Oh.'

I faced him again. 'I went to the inquest.'

He wanted to ask questions but he remembered I was supposed to be doing the asking.

I said, 'It was only a formal opening. Nothing much. Except for one little thing.'

He practically had to sit on his hands.

I said, 'They wondered who was feeding Ecstasy to Joni.'

This time he was stone silent.

I took a pull on my cigarette. 'I reckon it was George.'

Jason's mouth was a straight line. Lips tight together.

I said, 'Your friend George.'

145

He couldn't help himself. 'I don't have a friend called George.'

I said, 'I didn't ask you that. I *know* you have a friend called George. Shall I tell you how I know?'

I told him. 'When I came back from Holland I had the names of two blokes involved with Joni. One was George, the other was Billy. I asked you if you knew George. You said, "George?" And then you said you'd never heard of him. Next I asked you about Billy. You said, "Billy who?" Note the subtle difference.'

Just in case he'd missed it I explained it. 'You did not ask "George who?" Now I'll offer you five to one that you know at least one George. London's full of the buggers. All I have to do to prove it is to phone your mum right now and ask her the surname of your good friend George.'

All of a sudden Jason had gone right off me. It didn't matter.

I said, 'And after we get that sorted, we move on to why Joni was topped, because I'm betting it's all about drugs.'

He got up abruptly and said, 'I need to take a leak.'

I watched him putter off towards the bogs. His step lacked its usual bounce. If it hadn't been a story I might have felt sorry for him. But it was, so I didn't.

I got myself another gin and smoked another cigarette. He was taking his time. I looked at the locals. That was when I saw the bloke. He was sitting on a stool at the bend in the bar, off at an angle to me. He was younger than the other drinkers. I'd say around twenty-five. He was also not the snappiest dresser in the place. Dark chino trousers, reddish or brownish sweater. That wasn't what made him interesting. What intrigued me was that as my gaze fell on him he swung quickly round to face the bar.

OK, people are often embarrassed when you catch them staring at you. But it was the way he was now sitting with his shoulders hunched up round his ears that had my curiosity revving. He didn't mind eye-balling me but he didn't want me to return the compliment.

I tried a little experiment. I took out my diary and began to read it with an all-consuming interest. I had my head buried in it for a full three minutes, then I snapped it up straight at him. Ha! Caught him.

He did another rapid about turn but this time I'd seen his face. It didn't mean anything to me. Male, white, clean-shaven, fat nose. I stared at his back and tried to estimate height and all that. He looked big enough.

Now I was boring holes in his shoulder blades, daring him to turn round again. I reckon he was on the verge of breaking when Jason returned to the fold.

He said, 'That's some interviewing technique.'

His smile was a mite nervy and his colour was up. He was trying to make out we'd just been kidding around. I wasn't having any of that. 'It's not a technique. Now, let's get back to where we were.'

Jason said, 'Wait till I get a Coke. Another drink?'

'That's technique. You're playing for time.'

He was trying to hold his grin together. After a while he gave up and started scratching his stubble. His rabbit eyes were everywhere, except on me.

Over his shoulder I saw another fashion victim

wander into the pub. He made straight for the first bloke at the bar. The newcomer, tall, gingery, said something to him. The seated punter said something back. Immediately the new bloke squinted across in our direction.

Jason said, 'I don't want to go on with this.'

'All right. Let's try something different. Suppose you tell me how Fez the Pill Pusher knows your name.'

He didn't want to go on with that either. Tough.

I said, 'Let's see if that silent technique works.' I went quiet but kept my eyes hard on him.

Maybe it might have worked. I'll never know. Thirty seconds into the silence my mobile shrilled. Damn and blast.

'Max?' It was Vic on Night Desk. Double damn and treble blast. 'Where are you?'

I told him where, reasoning that Dulwich was too far from anywhere for me to be of any use for whatever it was.

'That's great,' he said. 'We've just got a tip-off about a babysnatch from the Mayday down in Thornton Heath.'

I groaned. Off all the hospitals in all the metropolis, some nutter just had to pick on the Mayday.

'You're right next door to it,' said Vic with ill-concealed glee. 'You'll be there before Gary.'

Gary is the late-watch monkey.

I know an own-goal when I score one. I said, 'OK, what do you have on it?'

'I've just told you.'

So he didn't know the name/sex/age of the snatchee. Nor did he have anything on the snatcher. That was par for the course.

I said, 'I'm on my way,' and clicked off the mobile.

Jason had come alive again. 'What's the story?'

He offered to drive me there. I would have got there quicker but I'd had enough of his company for one night.

He was downcast. 'Come on, Max. Look, we'll sort out the Joni stuff later. Please let me go with you.'

I was feeling bloody-minded. 'No.'

He put on his hurt puppy look. It was wasted on me. I turned away and walked out.

I felt pretty bad about that later.

Chapter Twelve

As babysnatches go, the Mayday job wasn't in the same league as the Lindberg kidnapping. It wasn't even a babysnatch, unless you think a seven-year-old is a baby. But it still took the Old Bill until midnight to straighten it out. In the end it added up to just another domestic.

Here's how it goes. Some dingbat called Pickles takes the hump with his live-in after she boots him out. She then takes their younger kid who is a proper baby to hospital because he has appendicitis or a saucepan stuck to his bean or something. The elder son, the above-mentioned seven-year-old, goes along for the ride. Meanwhile the aggrieved dad is down the pub drinking it dry. After a dozen pints a pickled Pickles comes over all sentimental and staggers off to kiss and make up. The neighbours tell him she's at the hospital. He gets it into his sozzled skull she's done a runner with the kids. So off he toddles to the hospital. The mother character takes one look at him and tells him to get lost. A ding-dong ensues, in the course of which he grabs his elder son and legs it. That's all that happened.

The Law traced Pickles & son to the granny's gaff, down Lewisham, thumped him with a nightstick and sprung the kid. So everybody was happy, except for Pickles and his bump.

I was getting to be fairly happy myself. By this stage I'd made it back to the Elephant and Castle where there is a pub that has never heard of closing time. A couple of late duty hacks from the *Express* were keeping me company.

I was in no frantic hurry because this was one of those nights where Rosie felt she could live without me. I planned on giving it another hour before I got them to call me a taxi.

We were gainfully employed swopping meal receipts when my mobile let me know it hadn't forgotten me. I looked at my watch. It was an edge past two. What was it this time – a bomb, a mass murder, World War III?

Nothing so mundane. 'Hello, Max. Hope I haven't woken you. This is Gabriella Cardigan.'

I knew that as soon as she said hello. I told her it was OK, I was doing nothing anyway.

She asked, 'Is Jason with you?'

Er, well, no, actually.

Gabriella's voice went crackly at the edges. 'Where can he be? Have you seen him tonight? Have you heard from him?'

Let's deal with the ones I know the answer to. When last seen Jason was lingering over a coke in a pub in Dulwich. That was about nine-twenty.

'Which pub?'

I never forget the name of a bar. 'The Greenstone.'

She knew it. It was barely half a mile from the Cardigan mansion.

'Oh God. He should have been home hours ago,' Gabriella wailed.

I wasn't feeling very clever either. I'd just remembered the two iffy blokes at the bar. I didn't feel like telling her about them.

She said, 'What do I do?'

First of all you panic. But she'd already got to that stage. Next you find something useful to do.

I said, 'You ring round his friends. He's probably off with one of them. But maybe your husband could drive round to the Greenstone and see if Jason's car is still there. I'll do a few checks and phone you back.'

She wanted to know what checks. I had to spell it out. 'Police and ambulance. But that's just a long shot. I'm sure Jason's OK.'

Gabriella's voice was too high. 'I've already called his friends.'

I said, 'What about George?'

'George Kevlin?'

Yep, that George.

Gabriella said, 'I tried him earlier but he was out.'

'Give him another go. Jason's probably there.'

I didn't think so either but I wanted her off the line. She went.

I rang Ambulance Control which is about the only place in London you'll find any intelligent life at this time of night. Things were quiet so the duty man was happy to rattle through his log from nine o'clock. A stabbing in Sydenham. Right area, wrong time. A youth beaten witless in Poplar. Right time, wrong area. A road rage victim in the Blackwall Tunnel. Wrong age. Fire-bombing out Stonebridge Park. Wrong race. Biker and pillion passenger killed on the M25 at Potter's Bar. Wrong everything.

So Jason was not on the dead or critical list. At least not yet. I was beginning to wish I'd paid a lot more attention to those blokes in the bar. I was wishing a lot harder that I'd let Jason come with me.

I tried Dulwich nick and was told I had to speak to Scotland Yard's Press Bureau if I wanted information on anything. I said I was Chief Inspector Skelly's brother so maybe I'd just wake him up instead. That worked, though it didn't do me any good. No one with a pony-tail, an earring and an embryonic beard had figured in the night's carnage.

I switched off and soaked up some gin. My phone piped up again.

'Mister Chard. We haven't met. This is Wedge Cardigan.' He was calling from his car.

I said, 'Is Jason's car still at the pub?'

It was. So that ruled out a road accident.

Wedge had also kicked the guv'nor awake but he couldn't remember Jason even being in the bar. Terrific.

I said, 'I've checked with the police and the ambulance people. There's no reports of anybody fitting Jason's description.'

Wedge Cardigan said that was good. He'd tell his wife. She was rather distressed . . . especially after what had happened with Joni. Meanwhile, he was going to trawl around the streets just in case. And if I heard anything, perhaps I might give him a ring.

I took the number though I'd hit a dead end.

I helped myself to a Gordons and that must have done the trick for I started thinking. It went like this:

not everybody who winds up in hospital gets there in the business end of an ambulance. You get walking wounded and all sorts.

Back to the mobile. The nearest hospital to the Greenstone was East Dulwich. He wasn't there. Nor was he staining the sheets at King's College. What other hospitals did I know down thataway? But of course. The Mayday.

And that's where he lay. Or someone like him. They didn't have a name. Well, what shape was he in? The nursing sister said she could only disclose that to kith and kin. I told her I was ringing on behalf of Jason's doting mum who was too distraught to do the asking. Oh all right then, said the sister. He was admitted at ten-twelve. He was badly concussed but otherwise stable. I got her to run through the description again and it still matched.

I called Wedge Cardigan and told him to hotfoot it round to the Mayday. I left it up to him to break the tidings to Gabriella.

The next gin I really enjoyed.

I heard Jason's story the following morning by which time they'd moved him to a flash private hospital round the back of Dulwich Village. He told the yarn in one unbroken run. He was sitting up in bed and acting chipper but you could see he'd had a pretty good going over. This is why I didn't call him a liar. The fact that I was still feeling guilty probably also had something to do with it.

The way he told it, it went like this. He was crossing

the road from the pub when some eight-foot-tall geezer
he'd never seen before popped up out of the night and
demanded his watch and his wallet. Jason told him to
get stuffed. Not the smartest thing he's ever said.

Jason briefly remembered the stranger playing
squash with his head against a convenient brick wall.
After that it was all a blur.

He'd been found bloodied and staggering by an
unknown passing motorist who couldn't have been a
cabbie, for he did the decent thing and drove Jason to
hospital. And there you have the whole yarn.

There were a couple of points I might have picked
him up on if my conscience had been up to it. Such as,
if the unjolly giant was so covetous of Jason's watch and
his wallet, why was the watch still ticking there on the
bedside locker? Such as, why was he crossing the road
when his car was in the car park?

Also, though it is generally overlooked, muggers
have a rigid code of morals. They demand your goodies
and if you hand them over, they go away whistling a
merry tune. If you play the hero, they thump you or
knife you or brain you with a lump of pig iron. What
they don't do is beat you up and down the street.

I said, 'Did this bloke have ginger hair?'

Apparently it was dark at the time.

'Did he have a fat nose?'

It was still dark.

I said, 'In the pub there were two men watching us.
Maybe I should tell the police about them.'

Jason didn't think so. 'There was only one guy.'

I let him think I believed it. But he'd have to be a
hell of a lot better at lying if he ever wanted to be a hack.

I was on my way out when I ran aground against Wedge Cardigan. I introduced myself. He turned on a wraparound smile and shook me warmly by the hand. I think he liked me.

He said he wished to express his 'sincere gratitude'. I blushed becomingly and said it was nothing.

He looked at me keenly and asked, 'Are you married, Max?'

Eh? I didn't know he was *that* grateful.

I said that so far the Angel of Death had given me a miss.

Next he wanted to know if I'd a girlfriend. I owned up to that one.

'Good,' he beamed. 'Gabriella and I would like you to join us for dinner on Saturday evening – you and your girlfriend.'

I came back to the office to find several shades of trouble lying in wait. The first sign was a yellow Post-it note stuck to my computer screen. 'Please pop in and see me. Thanx. A. Greer.'

A. Greer, otherwise known as Alf, used to do forward planning on News Desk. He was embarrassingly good at it. So much so that they had to kick him off the Desk because he was showing the rest of them up.

They gave him another fifteen hundred, a cubbyhole of his own, half a secretary and a title. Readers' Ombudsman.

If ever you write to a newspaper, claiming you have been misquoted, misrepresented or otherwise stitched up, the chances are your letter will go to the Ombudsman.

His role is to investigate complaints and find a

happy solution. He is there to champion *your* rights. And if you believe that you probably believe our horoscopes too.

This note from Alf signified that somebody had been griping about me. I couldn't for the life of me work out why anyone would do a thing like that.

I strolled off to his den with a clear conscience and a blood pressure of 120 over 80.

'Ah. Max.'

'How's it going Alf?'

He ducked his shiny head and started rummaging around a pile of papers on the desk. After a while he resurfaced.

'Do you know a Mister F. Pegg?'

'Felix? What does he want?'

Alf said, 'He says you . . . where is it, oh yes, here we are, "interrogated, intimidated and harrassed" him.'

'Is that it?'

'No. He says you misrepresented yourself and that he was unaware that you were a reporter.'

I said, 'What did he think I was – a Jehovah's Witness?'

Alf read the letter through. 'He doesn't say. But he claims you also attributed quotes to him which were untrue and without substance.'

I sat myself down. 'Which quotes?'

All of them.

I offered Alf a cigarette. 'OK. Let's go over them. He told me he walks his dog in the park every morning. He told me Joni had a green paisley-patterned scarf round her throat. He told me it was an ugly crime. He told me she was smiling. Now unless he was lying on all of that, our quotes are accurate.'

'There are other quotes,' said Alf the nitpicker.

'I got them from Pegg. He's pissed off because the police gave him a bad time for talking to me.'

'So you're saying there's no grounds for complaint?'

'Not quite. There are five thousand grounds for complaint.'

Alf batted his eyelids so fast his specs slid down his nose. 'What?'

I explained. 'Pegg found the body. That means he thinks he's entitled to the five thou reward the Editor put up. For one reason or another he hasn't got it. It's probably held up in Accounts. Once he gets his mitts on the cheque, Pegg will forget his complaints. I'd give Accounts a buzz if I were you.'

A little matchlight of hope gleamed in Alf's watery eyes. This was one mess he didn't have to clean up.

He showed me out the door, a fatherly hand on my shoulder. 'Thanks, Max. Maybe we'll have a pint later.'

Fat chance. Alf never buys his round.

Back to my corner. Post-it notes had been breeding all across the screen in my absence. There had been two urgent calls from a Det. Sgt. Mortown. I recognized his number as Dulwich nick, which meant he was one of Chief Inspector Skelly's clones. Whatever he wanted to say to me was something I didn't want to hear. So I pretended I never got the messages.

There had also been a call from a Cheryl somebody on an 01273 number. That's Brighton. The only people I know in Brighton are American Express. That triggered another sudden bout of amnesia.

The most recent message was one I couldn't ignore: *Tony Belker wants U to call ASAP.* His mobile number was thoughtfully appended in case I'd lost it.

Dinesh, who sits by my right hand, had taken the message. I asked him what he'd told Belker.

'I said you were away from your desk but you'd be back in five minutes,' he said airily.

There are times when Dinesh does not deserve to live.

I pulled the phone towards me but didn't dial right away. I needed a bright idea to keep the Beast at bay. The simple solution was to tell Belker I had thought long and hard about his kind offer and had come to the conclusion I preferred to remain a crime hack.

But you don't look a gift elephant in the mouth. Belker would go spare if I told him to stuff it. I think I'd worked out how this whole thing had happened. Angela Whipple, for no very good reason, had suddenly become bad news. Belker had picked on me as a replacement. If I refused him I would frustrate his grand stratagem. And a foiled Belker is a dangerous Belker.

He would then conclude I had an attitude problem, for that is how he brands anyone who dares disagree with him. The next stage would be to declare M. Chard a non-person. And right after that he'd start scouring the gutters for my replacement.

Either way I ceased to be a crime hack. My only hope was that a dumber candidate might miraculously present himself.

I punched out Belker's number with a leaden finger.

'Max!'

Oh God, he still loved me.

I scraped together some stuff about my being caught up in the Poelma case and not having a chance to get back to him.

He pushed that away. 'Yes, sure. Now, you've made up your mind?'

I said, 'To tell the truth, Tony, I never expected it.' Well, that was true.

Belker turned patronizing. 'You looked gobsmacked when I suggested it. But I know you. You'll take to it like a duck to water.'

I'm not a great duck man and the appeal of water has somehow passed me by. But I had to sound enthusiastic.

I said, 'It's a fantastic offer. It's one hell of a job.' That was true too.

'So the answer's yes?'

I fudged it. 'There's just a couple of points I'd like cleared up first.'

He thought I was talking about the money. 'Don't worry. We can sort that all out later. I think you'll love the package.'

I tried to say 'Great!' but the word got snagged in my teeth.

He didn't notice. He said, 'There's just one minor glitch.'

Glitch? I liked the sound of that.

Belker said, 'I'm stuck on this Galaxy Awards business for the rest of the week, and after that I'm off to Kenya for a short break.'

Kenya. With a bit of luck he'd get shot by big game poachers.

'But,' he rolled on, 'I'll get the contract drawn up today and we'll sort out the fine detail in a fortnight. OK?'

I said that was just wonderful. And he agreed.

I put down the phone and wept silently.

Dinesh plonked a coffee on my desk.

'Did you get Belker?' he asked.

I looked at his bright chipmunk's face with murder in my heart. If they did make me News Editor, I knew whom I would pick as my deputy. Dinesh.

That would teach him.

As soon as I could I ploughed down to the Stone dive bar for an urgent pick-me-up. I needed it.

Frankie Frost was in his usual corner fondling a large and hideous cuddly toy. Sometimes you don't want to ask.

I bought him a pint and started warbling on about the price of drink. That's usually a good one to get him started.

He didn't fall for it. He perched the cuddly toy bang in front of me on the bar. It was a panda or something like that.

'Yours for a tenner,' he offered.

'You'll give me a tenner to take it off you?'

Frankie was outraged. 'No way. I paid fifteen quid for this thing.'

I was careful not to ask why. I said, 'That reminds me, you owe me from Maastricht.'

'I haven't done my exes yet,' he lied.

'I reckon it's a couple of hundred.'

'Bollocks. I owe you a hundred top whack. Anyway, what do you think of this?' He stuck his finger into the Panda's belly.

I said, 'Two hundred.'

He was not to be diverted. 'Want to know why I bought it?'

I gave in. Last night at the Royal Albert Hall, Britain's great middleweight hope Rocky Ellson had had the stuffing knocked out of him by somebody else. In the course of his pasting, Rocky had both his eyes blacked. Are you following this so far? We move on to today when Frankie was sent to take a snap of our heroic loser. Now when monkeys take a non-action pic of a sportsman they always feel the need to press a prop into his paws. Look at the sports pages of any tabloid and you'll see what I mean.

The big question always is which prop? This is where Frankie put his lateral brain to work. Rocky, he thought. What goes with Rocky? Why, Rocky Racoon. Just like in the Beatles' song. And the genius of it was that a racoon has two big black eyes, just like Rocky himself. So Frankie shot off to a toy shop for his prop. They were clean out of racoons, but how about this nice panda?

What the hell, said Frankie, handing over fifteen quid in exchange for the fat panda and a receipt for twenty quid.

Tomorrow this very panda would appear on our back page, only the caption would say it was a racoon. You don't get many David Attenboroughs reading our sports pages.

Back to right now. Frankie was still vainly trying to offload the stupid panda on me.

I suggested he stick it in his car boot, along with all his other props, like the battered teddy bear which has graced more pix of motorway crashes than you'd believe.

Frankie mourned, 'No room.'

I believed him. Besides the famous teddy, he's got a wreath of plastic flowers, a bouquet of the same, an empty champagne bottle, a child's shoe, sundry balls of sundry shapes, and, for some inexplicable reason, a string of cameras.

The night lawyer wandered in, fresh from his latest debacle in the courts and Frankie turned his sales pitch on him. Only now the price had gone up.

'Yours for fifteen quid,' he offered.

The night lawyer squinted at it through his bifocals. 'Fifteen, eh?'

'Yep. Only fifteen. It cost me twenty.'

Frankie even had the receipt to prove it.

Chapter Thirteen

I cleared off to Battersea to tell Rosie about the Cardigans' dinner invite. I broke the news gently.

'If you've got a thousand pounds, you can join me for dinner on Saturday night.'

She wanted to know where first, why later. She liked the sound of the venue anyway. Even Rosie, who has never knowingly read a newspaper, has heard of Wedge Cardigan and his uncountable millions. She moved on to the why bit.

'Why do I need a thousand pounds?'

'Because I owe Gabriella Cardigan two grand and I've spent half of it.'

'Why?'

'Because I was broke.'

Rosie clicked her tongue at me. 'I mean why do you owe her two thousand pounds?'

'Because that's her going rate.'

Rosie can be very thin skinned sometimes. This was one of those times. The smoky blue eyes turned cold and her nose went pointy. I checked around. It was all right. The ice bucket was still in the kitchen.

'Why do you owe her two thousand pounds?' She repeated. Her voice had lost its huskiness too.

So I owned up, reciting the whole nonsensical saga. She wasn't quite convinced.

'What does she look like, Gabriella Cardigan?'

I sidestepped. 'You'll see tomorrow night. Providing you come up with a grand in the meantime.'

'Is she pretty?'

'Wedge Cardigan thinks so.'

Rosie said, 'What about you?'

'No, he doesn't fancy me at all.'

She blew smoke out her nostrils. 'Right. You can go on your own, if you're just going to eff about.'

And so I behaved myself for a solid half hour until she'd run out of puff. I even nodded and tried to look intelligent while she pondered aloud what to wear for the soirée. I never knew she had that many clothes.

She must have made her mind up for she eventually went quiet. I prodded her gently. 'And don't forget the money.'

She'd already forgotten that. She said, 'So I've got to lend you a thousand?'

'Just for a couple of days. I'll pay you back.'

'How?'

I looked at her with eyes radiating a cool blue honesty.

'I've got a whole wodge of exes coming my way.'

The phone burbled as soon as I sat down at my desk.

'What did the alsatian say when it limped into the Wild West saloon?'

I know all of Mac's jokes. ' "Ah'm a-lookin' fo' the man who shot my paw." '

'Ach, have I already told you that one?'

Several times. It was a smidgeon after nine-thirty. Too early for Mac. Maybe he'd been up all night.

I said, 'What are you doing out of bed at this time of the morning?'

'I've got a wee tip for you. You know your man Felix Pegg?'

'What about him.'

'Skelly's lifted him again. How about that, heh?'

'For the Joni Poelma killing?'

Mac was scornful. 'Naw, for riding his bike without lights. What do you think?'

I said I made it a rule never to think before ten o'clock. But just out of interest, why had they fingered his collar again?

Mac said, 'I've given you a wee tip already. Here's a big one. He had her handbag.'

So that's where they'd found it. I said, 'Half a second, Skelly let it slip a couple of nights ago that they'd found her bag. But then he let Pegg go. What's changed?'

Mac is a racist who thinks all Englishmen are thick, not just the cops. He patiently explained. 'They found the bag last week. It was in his dustbin, OK? But it was empty. Nothing in it. Pegg told them that's the way it was when he pinched it.'

'But?'

'But they gave his place another going over and they found the stuff that was in it.'

'Aha.'

'Aha indeed. He had it shoved down the back of the fireplace and they never thought of looking in there the first time.'

Somehow that didn't surprise me.

I said, 'So what did they find?'

'I'm still waiting to hear that myself. Give us an hour or two.'

'Are they going to charge Pegg?'

'What – with murder?'

I sighed. 'No, with riding his bike without lights.'

Mac told me to go play with the traffic.

My guilty conscience was still digging its spurs in, so I rang the Cardigan mansion to ask after Jason's welfare. I got Gabriella who cooed down the line at me. I tried to picture her. But a picture of Rosie sprung to mind instead and I thought better of it.

Gabriella said they were all *so* looking forward to our dinner engagement. Oh, and that reminded her: was there any type of food which we didn't like?

I was tempted to say anything green. I just said, 'No. Porterhouse, sirloin, fillet, any of those things. I'll eat the lot.'

'What about your girlfriend? Rosie, isn't it?'

Rosie it is. 'She'll eat anything too,' I said generously.

Gabriella said, 'Really?'

'Well the only way I can get her to eat veal is to tell her it's pork.'

Gabriella trilled. 'Not veal then.'

I had to remind her that I was calling about Jason. She provided a brisk bulletin. The beamish boy was up and about, still a trace tender in the head department, but she'd heard him practising the guitar this very morn, so it couldn't be that bad.

I said I was glad to hear it. And I was. The sooner he recovered the sooner I could give him the third degree again.

Gabriella said, 'I've heard so much about Rosie.'

'And she's heard a lot about you.'

'All good I hope?'

I said, 'Nearly all. I also told her that you had bunged me a couple of thousand to look after Jason. I'll give it back to you tonight.'

Gabriella took over all serious. 'No, Max. The money is a gift. I am very grateful for all you are doing for Jason.'

Like leaving him to get battered brainless. I thought that but I didn't say it.

She said, 'You may not know it, but he was on the brink of giving up on his media studies course. But since you've been helping him, he's really keen again. Now he's got his heart set on becoming a journalist. That's all thanks to you.'

I said, 'In the end you won't thank me.'

More mirth from her end. Gabriella was a girl who liked to laugh. But then if I had her money I'd probably be chortling all the time.

I shook her off the phone and rang Press Bureau to see what was happening in the world. They had no idea. I asked specifically whether there were any moves in the Joni investigation. Nope. Either they knew about Pegg's lifting and were just being bloody minded, or Skelly had neglected to tell them. My money was on the second option. I left Press Bureau to return to their slumbers.

Sometime around eleven, when the Crazy Gang

were in morning conference, and all was peaceful and happy in the Newsroom, my phone chittered.

It was front hall reception. 'Mister Chard? There is a caller here for you.'

'Male or female?'

Neither. It was the Old Bill. A Det. Sgt. Mortown. The same geezer who'd been after me yesterday.

I said, 'Tell him I'm busy.'

'Perhaps you should tell him.'

The receptionist, may she fall off her chair and hurt her brain, promptly handed the phone over to Mortown.

'Mister Chard?'

I grudgingly acknowledged it was I.

'I wonder, could I have a few minutes of your time?'

'Why?'

'Just one or two things that Mister Skelly wants cleared up.'

As long as it's not his complexion. I said, 'What things?'

DS Mortown said it would be better if we discussed them face to face.

I was about to ask better for whom, but this could go on all day. In the end I folded and said I'd be down in a minute. I took the milk train lift and by the time it had hit the bottom, there were about 200 people on board. Me and 199 red-blooded secretaries all pressing themselves against me.

I found Mortown lurking amid the rubber plants which clutter up the front hall. He was wearing one of those blue fat-arsed double-breasteds that make Tony Blair look such a dweeb. As I got closer I recognized his fat face. He was one of the plods I'd seen keeping Skelly company in the bar down in Dulwich.

I lit a cigarette, taking care not to offer him one. This was my manor here.

'What do you want?'

Mortown pulled a notebook from his pocket and crinkled a low brow in what passed for concentration.

'You told Mister Skelly that Miss Poelma was involved with a drug dealer.'

I said, 'No. I told him there was a pusher hanging around the Silver Lino club.'

'It's the same thing.'

'It's not. She could have been scoring drugs all over the place. She might even have been selling stuff herself.'

Mortown wasn't programmed for free thinking. He went on to the next question, the one that this was all about.

'Mister Skelly wants to know who your sources are.'

'I'll bet he does.'

He chewed his lip for a moment. 'Well?'

'I made it all up. Skelly said so himself. Remember? And you may also remember he told me drugs weren't involved.'

Mortown remembered but he didn't say anything.

I said, 'Now Skelly's found out that Joni was doing drugs and he's pissed off because I knew before he did.'

'Who are your sources?'

They get stupider by the minute. I said, 'That's none of your business.'

'We could make it our business.'

I love a bad cliché. 'And what exactly does that mean?'

Mortown squared his jaw. 'We could apply for the seizure of your notes. We could have your press pass withdrawn.'

'Bollocks. You could have my Scotland Yard pass withdrawn. My proper press pass is issued by the National Union of Journalists and you can't touch it.'

'But we could seize your notes.'

'Only if you could prove to a judge that I was witholding information pertinent to a murder inquiry. You can't prove that, so you're just wasting my time.'

Mortown, bless his furry little brain, wasn't giving in that easily. 'We could make things unpleasant for you.'

'You already are.'

'We could refuse to give your newspaper information. We could have you followed to see who you talk to.'

I said, 'And I suppose you could bug my phone.'

He didn't deny it.

I said, 'What you're threatening is harassment. But you know that.'

A fat grin. 'You call it what you want.'

This had gone far enough. I pulled out my tape-recorder and let him see it was still running. He didn't go pale but the grin melted away.

I said, 'So let's you and me go upstairs and play this back to our lawyer to see what I can sue you with.'

Mortown did an about turn and cannoned into a conveniently located rubber tree.

I said into the tape, 'This interview concluded at

eleven-forty-five ay em on February twenty-seven when Detective Sergeant Mortown left the room with his tail between his legs.'

The Old Bill don't have the monopoly on clichés.

Back to my corner where a couple of agency stories required a bit of beefing up. The first one didn't stand a chance. The twelve-year-old son of a vicar had just been lifted breaking and entering in Muswell Hill. It had taken two panda cars, a dog handler, a motorbike cop and maybe an armed response unit to apprehend the desperado. They cuffed him and led him off to the nick, him in tears, them mightily chuffed with themselves. It was only when they got him in the interview room and were limbering up with the truncheons that they learned the ghastly truth: the house which the kid had been trying to bust into was his own. He'd locked himself out. So they took off the cuffs and chucked him out again.

The vicar forgot all that stuff about turning the other cheek and was giving the Old Bill hell. The fact that he had been thrice burgled by genuine villains – all of whom had so far gone unnicked – lent added vim to his vitriol. For their part, the Law were saying nothing.

So the whole yarn was there. But it didn't have the pizzazz to make it a national story. I tickled it up anyway and winged it back to News Desk.

The second agency piece was a meatier affair altogether. It was a suicide with just the right ingredients to set our readers up nicely for the day. The basics of it were humdrum. Up in Middlesbrough a girl called

Gwendoline gives a bloke called Gerry the elbow. Instead of getting legless, he thinks it would be much more fun to top himself. The exit point he chooses is the tenth-floor balcony of a ten-floor block. And off he jumps to his doom. Routine stuff, you'll agree.

Ah, but I haven't told you what she bought him for his birthday, three weeks before giving him the heave-ho. She got him a mobile phone. And guess what he did as he clambered over the balcony. That's right. He rang her. Then he told her what he was about to do. He had a final message for her. And as he plummetted south at thirty-two feet per second per second, he relayed the message. Or most of it anyway.

He got as far as, 'Gwendoline, I love—' before the concrete came up and smacked him. I suppose if she'd been called Jane or Jo, he could have got the whole message out.

Rosie says I'm a cold-blooded son of a something or other because I can trot out stories like that with nary a thought for the bloke who now resembles little more than a splodge of grafitti. All I can say is the unlamented bloke was a million more times cold blooded in inflicting his suicide on his ex. Anyways, I'm just a hack.

The Defence rests.

It is not wealth that beguiles. It is the trappings thereof.

Gabriella Cardigan had told me she would send a car to pick us up and ferry us to dinner. Naurally I didn't expect an X-reg Escort with a wonky headlamp. (And indeed, it turned out to be an R-reg Daimler.) But that wasn't what beguiled me most.

What Gabriella forgot to mention was Benedict. Benedict zinged on Rosie's doorbell while I was snorting a pre-prandial gin. She was elsewhere, hunting down a delinquent earring. I opened the door.

There was a bod in a tight-fitting jacket standing on the welcome mat. 'Good evening, sir. I am Benedict.'

He must have sussed my bewilderment for he added, 'Mister Cardigan requested that I collect you.'

I'd never had my very own chauffeur. I goggled for a moment and then remembered my manners. 'Come in, Benedict. And call me Max.'

He said, 'Thank you, sir.' And in he came.

I pointed at a chair and invited him to sit down. He sat. Stiffly, with his hands on his knees. Maybe he didn't want cat hairs all over his nice blue uniform.

Rosie obviously hadn't heard the bell go. She came blowing into the lounge, half-in, half-out of her frock. She got as far as, 'Have you seen my . . .?' before she spotted Benedict. She stopped dead, her mouth wide open.

I said, 'Say hello to Benedict. Benedict is our driver for this evening.'

Rosie yelped and shot back into the bedroom.

Benedict said, 'Perhaps it would be more convenient if I waited in the car, sir?'

I told him not to mind Rosie. She often did dog impressions on strangers. I offered him tea, coffee, orange juice. He said, 'That is very kind, but no thank you, sir.'

He was a pink-faced bloke, about the same age as me, but a stone heavier. He had solemn grey eyes and a solemn grey voice. He didn't look as if he knew any good jokes.

After a while I tired of staring at him and I switched on CeeFax for the Premiership results. Out of the corner of my eye I saw Benedict sit up a fraction straighter. He was looking at the scores too.

He said, 'Ah!'

That was the first time he'd said anything without tacking 'sir' on the end. I guessed that meant he was excited. I looked at the screen. It read: 'Liverpool 3, Arsenal nil.'

I said, 'I heard a bit of it on the radio. They said it should have been five nil.'

'Really?' There was light in yonder eyes.

I said, 'Are you a Liverpool man?'

Benedict gave a shy little smile. 'No. I tend to support Newcastle.'

Why all this glee then? I got there, even as I thought about it. 'But you can't stand Arsenal.'

The smile broadened.

I said, 'Join the club.'

After that we forgot clean about yelping Rosie and everything else while we tore Arsenal to shreds. We had a pop at their chop-'em-down back four, their skanky forwards, their gormless midfield. By now Benedict had dropped all that 'sir' stuff. There's nothing like a mutual hatred of Arsenal to turn absolute strangers into bosom buddies.

We could have gone on like this for another hour or two but Rosie wafted into view, looking like Rosella, Queen of the Gyppos. She was arrayed in something with a fair bit of blue and green and yellow all over it. A chunk of the same material was threaded through her blue-black curls. The effect was pretty awesome. Even Benedict looked dazzled.

Rosie apologized for yelping and all that and for being almost twenty minutes behind schedule. We hadn't noticed.

We set forth into the night in fine form. Benedict wanted to stick us in the back of the Daimler but I insisted on sitting up front with my new-found friend. He probably thought I wanted to carry on slagging off Arsenal, and I did just that for the first couple of miles.

We were cruising down Streatham Hill when I changed the record. 'Joni's death must have come as a terrible shock to the family.'

Benedict said it was. Even little Oliver was all cut up about it. Oliver, I remembered, was the three-year-old.

I said, 'Joni wasn't with the family all that long, but Gabriella seemed very fond of her.'

I'd got that right too. Benedict said, 'Yes, and Mister Cardigan was very taken with her. I think they went out of their way to make Joni feel at home.'

I said that was nice of them.

A lout in a double-decker bus pulled out slap in front of the Daimler. Benedict didn't even tut-tut. He just checked his mirror and squeezed the brakes. I flung a glance into the back. Rosie was sitting there with her nose in the air, pretending this was how she usually got about. We rolled on.

I said, 'I don't suppose Jason and Joni got to know each other, what with him being away at university.'

A soft chuckle from our chauffeur. 'I'm not so sure . . .'

I pretended I didn't hear that. I said, 'He's a nice kid, Jason.'

Benedict felt the same.

I asked, 'He's not a secret Arsenal fan, is he?' I didn't really care. I just wanted to remind Benedict that he and I were members of the same Brotherhood.

Jason, he opined, wasn't all that hot about football. Music was his passion.

I said, 'Maybe I'm getting old: his idea of music and mine are somewhat different. He wanted me to go to the Silver Lino.'

'Yes. He often goes there.'

I acted sort of absent-minded. 'Joni liked clubs too, didn't she?'

'Yes. Jason used to take her.'

'I suppose he was just showing her the town?'

Another chuckle from Benedict. 'Well, she was a pretty girl.'

And Jason had all his chromosomes in the right order.

I said, 'He must miss her a lot.'

Benedict thought about that one. He said, 'Jason is a very deep lad. He, ah, . . .'

He left it there. It was OK. He'd said enough.

I got back into Arsenal-bashing mode and the miles slipped by until the White House reared up in front of us.

Chapter Fourteen

Gabriella Cardigan wheeked open the front door. I was disappointed. I was expecting Jeeves at least.

She and Rosie took a good gander at each other. I'd already seen Rosie so I ogled Gabriella. She was wearing a little black number except it wasn't black. It was a blue the colour of outer space. There was a sprinkling of silver round her neck and more silver dangling from where her ears were hiding themselves. I was looking pretty nifty myself, but I don't think either of them noticed me.

After a moment, Gabriella switched on a million megawatt smile and bade us welcome to her humble abode. We were crossing the threshold when Jason scorched up grinning like a fool. He was still a shade purplish around the eyes but otherwise in the pink.

The last time I'd come through these doors I'd been too intent on Gabriella's jeans to take in the surroundings. I wanted to have a proper look this time but there wasn't much hope of that, what with Jason slapping me on the shoulder and everyone except me firing off questions all at once.

We were hustled through into a drawing room which you could hold a medium-size rock concert in. The walls were sort of peachy-apricoty and there were no ceiling lights, just a whole stack of lamps of various sizes, so the ambience was one of muted luxury. The facing wall featured a fireplace carved from a great chunk of ripe Stilton, and above it was a square acre of art which might have featured yachts' sails or sharks' fins or maybe they were just triangles. The Cardigans seemed to have cornered the market in fat sofas. They were all over the shop and they were all sporting identical mushroom covers. It was a safe bet the household didn't include a couple of Red Setters. My eye flickered onwards and came to rest on a cherry-wood sideboard, bowed down under decanters and bottles of this and that. I'd taken in enough of the scenery.

We parked ourselves in an open square of sofas fronting on to the fireplace in which a giant sequoia or somesuch blazed cheerily. A square table, made from the same stuff as the fireplace took up the centre. It was low enough to afford me an uninterrupted view of Gabriella Cardigan's legs. Her frock ran out of material a good two inches above the knee. My gaze ranged from her legs to the decanters and back again. It was a nice view.

So far we were minus one of the company. Wedge Cardigan was nowhere in sight. I was sorely missing him because Wedge, I reckoned, was the man who un-corked the decanters.

Off to my left Romany Rose was chirruping away to Gabriella and vice versa. A stranger might have thought they were lifelong chums who hadn't seen each other for at least a day. Jason was gawping at Rosie in a way which was not polite but was understandable. After a while he remembered me. He wanted to know how things were going with the Joni story and I told him they weren't. But just out of mischief I said the Drugs Squad were planning to turn over the Silver Lino and all who bopped therein. He nodded gravely and dried up.

The big creamy door swung open and in stalked Wedge Cardigan, lamplight glinting off his specs. He seemed surprised to see us. I stood up and introduced Rosie. Big smiles all round. Wedge plumped himself down on the sofa beside her and reprised the same rigmarole of questions we'd already answered.

I was getting worried. He'd been in the room the best part of a minute and he still hadn't plied us with liquor. I sat there looking thirsty. He didn't catch it but Gabriella did.

'Wedge,' she scolded. 'Don't you think we'd all like a drink?'

He dripped out a goofy smile and off he loped decanterwards.

'Honestly,' Gabriella confided to Rosie, 'I always have to remind him.'

Rosie said, 'Max is just the same.' Which is a foul and slanderous lie.

Over by the sideboard, Wedge rattled off the menu, starting with Martini, Cinzano, Campari and similar low octane stuff. Eventually he got down to the gin and three of us said yes. That left Jason who'd vanished and reappeared with a can of Bud, and his dad who wasn't drinking anything. A bad sign.

'Slimline tonic, darling,' Gabriella reminded as he slopped gin into crystal glasses.

Personally I prefer the fatline version, but right now I wasn't picky.

My gin arrived, confirming my worst fears. The glass was only half full and the business half also contained a young iceberg, a chunk of lemon and a so-far unspecified amount of tonic. Take that little lot out and there's not enough gin to keep a grown man happy.

Also, I do not like drinking gin from crystal glasses in other people's houses. The thing is they still look full long after you've licked them dry. You usually have to clutch your throat before your host gets the message.

I took a sip. Yep. Wedge had shortchanged me on the gin. A little cloud centred over my end of the sofa. It threatened to be a long and awful night. But help was at hand.

'Dad,' said Jason. 'Max likes a *proper* drink.'

'Eh?' from Cardigan senior.

'Never mind. I'll do it,' said Jason.

He prised the glass from my clenched fingers, toted it to the drinks corner and filled it to the brim with neat Gordons. A warm happy glow suffused my person.

Gabriella watched the cabaret through amused green eyes. 'So, it's true that reporters are fond of drink?'

'I'll say,' piped up Rosie, who is no mean shakes at putting it away herself.

'And what else is true? That reporters always misquote you?'

I said, 'All that. And we invade your privacy, steal pix off your mantelpiece and spell your name wrong.'

Wedge Cardigan took this in as if I was serious. He said, 'Still, it must be a very interesting job.'

I shrugged. 'I expect yours is just as interesting.' This was an out and out lie but he was providing the drink.

Wedge brayed a laugh. 'I don't think so. Unless you find the minutiae of business interesting. It was rather more rewarding when it was research-led.'

I had to take his word for that.

Jason did the translation. 'Dad started as a research chemist but now he runs the company so he doesn't have time for lab work anymore.'

Gabriella said, 'We hoped Jason would follow Wedge into the business, but . . .'

'But he takes more after his mother,' said Dad.

A small silence fell.

I said brightly, 'And now he wants to be a journo. Did he get that from his mum?'

'No.' Simultaneously from Gabriella and Wedge. They didn't elaborate, but Gabriella smartly switched the conversation round to Rosie. The two male Cardigans were content to listen.

I asked Wedge, 'What exactly do you make?'

'Pharmaceuticals.'

'And what do they do?'

Jason joined in. 'They cure asthma.'

Father and son both laughed at this. I looked suitably bemused.

Wedge Cardigan explained, 'When Jason was very young, just after his mother died, he developed a form of asthma. It did not respond to the usual proprietary drugs and after some research I came up with an alternative.'

'Quadroloxin,' from Jason.

'It was reasonably successful in commercial terms

and I began developing other, ah, products,' Wedge continued. 'They met with varying degrees of success and, ah, and I eventually launched my own company, Intraphilyn.'

I said, 'So what are you working on now?'

Wedge Cardigan flopped a hand. 'All sorts of things. We're working on a process to break down lindane. But we also research osteoporosis, anti-convulsants, a range of treatments.'

I said, 'Anything for the kidneys?'

Maybe he deliberately misunderstood me. He puffed out a laugh and pointed at my glass, 'Do you mean the liver?'

No. I meant the kidneys. But I didn't push it.

The conversation flickered around the usual gamut of bloodless topics until the big door opened and a girl with frizzy hair poked her head round it. She didn't say anything.

Gabriella said, 'Thank you, Agnes.'

The head vanished.

'Well,' said Gabriella, 'if everyone's ready we can go in.'

I could have done with another helping of gin but the rest of them were looking peckish. We went in.

The dining room was out of scale to the rest of the place. There was a round wooden table with enough space for eight people top whack. Maybe they had a king-size banquetting hall elsewhere. The motif here was intimate, with pinkish beech walls that matched the table. There were a couple of fat silver candlesticks, a corner lamp and that was it for the lighting. You get trattoria like this up in Hampstead.

I had Gabriella to my right, Wedge to my left, with Rosie and Jason completing the circle. The girl called Agnes steamed in and started dishing up. The first course was a green and yellow Swiss roll affair with a puddle of green sauce. My superkeen senses detected there wasn't any meat in there.

Jason asked, 'Red or white?'

I was tempted to say both, but I let him pour me a decent ration of something called Maligny. Across the table, Wedge Cardigan suddenly fell off the wagon and asked for white too.

'Cheers everyone,' said Gabriella, tucking into the red. And the noshing commenced.

Between forkfuls the conversation centred on me. This is something that happens to hacks at strange dinner parties. People always want to know the inside track on (a) all the Royals, (b) half the luvvies and (c) the odd politico. I duly obliged with stories of drugs, debaucheries and assorted devilry. They were suitably aghast.

If I repeated any of these yarns in public, I'd probably be executed for slander. The terrible thing is they were all true.

Meanwhile as I was carelessly rubbishing the great and the good I was also observing the Cardigans. They seemed a reasonably happy little band, comfortable together. There was no undertow of tension. Or none that I could pick up. But Jason wasn't saying much.

We got off me and on to things in general. As is the way with these aimless conversations, the women present knuckled down to beefing about the men present.

Gabriella said Wedge lived in a world of his own, never noticed when she got her curls clipped, was the worst driver this side of Naples, and so on. But she tempered it all with much affectionate shaking of the head. Wedge for his part put on a soppy smirk. That's where Jason got it from.

Rosie, not to be outdone, told scandalous tales of my drinking, spending and staying out half the night. I thought it was time I played too.

I said, 'Rosie snores.'

That raised the decibel level a few hundred degrees.

The Swiss roll thing vanished and something full of scallops took its place. There was different wine for that, which was a pity, because I was just getting used to the first one.

I concentrated on the scallops because the item on the agenda right now was keeping fit, and I didn't have much to contribute to that.

Gabriella was rabbitting on about her amazing aerobic centre, somewhere up in Covent Garden. 'Why,' she gushed, 'don't you give it a try?'

I swallowed my wine a shade sharpish. Happily the invite was addressed to Rosie.

'I'd love to,' said she. 'I need to flatten my tummy.'

I growled a silent growl. There are many things about Rosie that thrill me to the marrow. Way up there among the best of them is her little tummy. It is not flat, and that's the joy of it.

Ask any man in the world whether he'd prefer his beloved to have a tum you could iron shirts on, and he'll tell you to sober up. Men should have flat bits. Women should have bumps and curves. Anything else just isn't natural.

The debris of the scallops was wheeled out and other dishes came and went. So far we'd talked about every topic known to man, except for the one thing that had brought us all together: the murder of Joni Poelma.

A couple of bottles of Burgundy appeared just as Agnes rolled in with the main course. Beef Wellington. Proper grub at last.

Gabriella was right there with me. She put her hand on mine and said, 'I thought you'd like this, Max.'

I caught the full blast of her eyes. She didn't mind a bit of flirting, did our Gabriella. I was all set to return the compliment but I remembered Rosie just in time. Sure enough, there was a 'Don't you dare' look in her smoky-blue gaze.

After a while we'd polished off everything and back we waddled to the drawing room with our little round tums. It was somewhere about here that Wedge Cardigan somewhat shyly confessed he'd taken up watercolours. Painting them, that is.

Rosie, who can flirt with the best of them, said, 'Reeeeely. I'd love to see them.'

He took a bit of pushing but eventually he led her off to see his etchings. Jason went too. Maybe he just liked looking at Rosie. Maybe he didn't want to be with me.

So that left Gabriella Cardigan and me all alone together on adjoining sofas, she sipping brandy, and I demolishing the Gordons.

She tilted her head back on the cushions and I had a perfect profile shot of her breasts. The dark blue stuff of her frock had the same effect as cashmere. Gabriella knew it.

She said, 'So, Max. What do you think of our family?'

'Oliver and Ceri, I haven't met. The rest of you seem hunky dory.'

'Well Oliver and Ceri are "hunky dory" too.'

I lit a cigarette and waited. I knew there was a stack of other questions lurking behind the green eyes.

The next one was predictable. 'And I was right about Jason, wasn't I? He's a good kid.'

I didn't answer that. I said, 'That reminds me: I owe you two grand.' I pulled a chunky envelope out of my pocket and plonked it right down on the table.

Gabriella was hurt. 'Please, Max. We've already gone through this. I know you'd rather not have him in your way, but it means a lot to us.'

I said, 'It means two grand?'

It didn't faze her. 'It means more. Jason's got a sense of direction again and . . . well, you don't quite understand.'

I lifted my right eyebrow half an inch.

Gabriella sighed and tinkered with her earring. She said, 'Jason didn't have anyone to call mother until Wedge and I got together nine years ago. His mother died shortly after he was born.'

'How?'

'What?' She knew what I meant.

'How did she die?'

'It was very tragic. Post-natal depression.'

'Suicide?'

She nodded a yes.

I said, 'Pills?'

She darted me a sharp little look. It was pills.

Gabriella moistened her lips with brandy. She said, 'Her parents offered to bring up Jason, but Wedge wanted to keep him. They are very close. Wedge did his best, hiring nannies and so on, but really, Jason lost out emotionally.'

'And then you came along?'

She said, 'And then I came along. But that wasn't until much later. I was working for Wedge and gradually we got to know each other. And then, after a while . . .'

'You became Missus Cardigan.'

She floated a laugh. 'It wasn't quite that simple. From the start, Wedge made it clear that Jason was very much part of him.'

'Love me, love my son?'

Gabriella frowned. 'You can be very cynical, Max.'

That was the third time she'd called me Max.

She said, 'But there was an element of truth in that. I knew that whatever plans Wedge made, Jason would be part of them. If Jason and I hadn't hit it off, well, we would never have married. I have no illusions about that.'

'But you did hit it off.'

Her eyes went all misty with memories. 'The first time I met Jason, he was about twelve. He was tall, like his father, but very, very shy. Even now he tends to retreat into himself and I have to coax him out.'

She sampled the brandy again. 'He was terribly thin, with the most expressive eyes. He was like a frightened animal. You just wanted to give him a cuddle.'

That must have been nice for Jason. I said, 'It was mother love at first sight?'

Gabriella put on a pretend frown. 'There you go, being cynical again. I felt instantly protective towards him, but it took Jason the best part of a year to trust me. The first time he called me Mum, I just cried.'

This was all very touching. But.

Gabriella still had the floor. She said, 'I know what you're thinking. You think I was attracted to Wedge by his wealth.'

Well it wasn't his looks anyway.

She said, 'He was *reasonably* well off when we met, but he was ploughing almost all the profits back into the company. It didn't really take off until a few years after we married.

'I left Intraphilyn – and a very well paid job – because I don't think husbands and wives should work together. I set up my fitness centre to give me independence. And I'm very proud of its success. What I'm saying, Max, is I didn't marry Wedge for money.'

I said, 'I believe you.'

She slotted a sidelong glance but went on, 'But what we're really talking about is Jason. I made sacrifices, you know. A great many sacrifices. Wedge and I put off starting a family of our own until we were certain that Jason felt secure. I regard him as my son, just as Oliver is my son.'

I said, 'What does this have to do with two grand?'

An impatient flick of the head. 'I'm trying to explain to you that Jason has had a traumatic time of it. He has never been able to settle for long at one thing. We were surprised when he suddenly said he wanted to become a journalist, but we supported him fully.

'Then, as I told you, he changed his mind halfway

through his first year on the media course and he was about to give up. When you came to the house that morning, I thought you might be able to revive his enthusiasm. And you did.'

She paused and fired a flinty glance at me. 'Now, wasn't that worth two thousand pounds, Max?'

'Not to me it isn't.'

'What is your price, then?'

I said, 'I'll settle for another gin.'

She thought I was kidding. But she made free with the Gordons anyway. As she handed me a glass she stuffed the two grand back in my pocket. She curled up on the sofa again. Her mood had changed and so had the subject.

She said, 'So, tell me. Do you think he can make it as a journalist?'

'Probably. He's bright enough. But first he has to unlearn all this guff they teach him at hack school.'

'That's why I wanted you to show him what it was really like.'

This was just going in circles. I said, 'He's young for his age. Has he any girlfriends?'

That was an easy one. 'Not what you'd call serious.'

I said, 'What about Joni?'

Gabriella gave me a cool green look. 'I thought you'd ask that. You have a suspicious mind.'

'So?'

'Joni was a couple of years older than him and, let's just say rather more worldly-wise.'

'Is that a yes or a no?'

Gabriella sighed. 'They were *friends*, Max. That's all. He may have taken her to the club a couple of times.

And maybe he fancied her a little. But, as I said, Joni was more mature. She had other boyfriends.'

'Like George?'

'George who?'

I said, 'Let's try George Kevlin for a start.'

Gabriella weighed it up. 'I shouldn't think so. He's not much older than Jason. Anyway, Joni never confided in me about who she was seeing.'

'Or who was keeping her supplied with Ecstasy?'

'Hardly. All I knew was that she had taken drugs in the past. She didn't make any secret of it.'

I said, 'What about Jason?'

'Jason? How do you mean?'

I said, 'Did Joni turn him on to Ecstasy? Or was it the other way round?'

Gabriella put her glass down on the marble table with a deliberate chink. She said, 'Let's get this absolutely straight, Max. Jason is my son. If I thought he was involved in drugs, I'd do my best to straighten him out. But the last thing I would do is tell anyone else.'

Well that's one way of not answering a question.

She wasn't finished. She said, 'You're determined to tie Joni's death with the drug scene. Maybe that's true. But Jason's not on drugs. I'd know if he was.'

'And if you knew, you wouldn't tell me anyway.'

Gabriella had forgotten to smile. She said, 'Now you're not being cynical. You're just being plain rude.'

'Who's being rude?' This from Rosie, who breezed in towing a couple of Cardigans.

Gabriella didn't miss a stitch. 'Max is. He's refusing to accept expenses for looking after Jason.'

Wedge Cardigan said, 'Expenses?'

Gabriella's voice was honeyed. 'Never you mind, darling. It's just a little arrangement I made with Max and now he's reneging on the arrangement.'

'Oh,' said Wedge without inflection.

But Jason was sharp to it. He asked, 'Do you mean, you're not going to help any more?' His eyes were round and doleful.

I looked at Gabriella and she looked at me, her smile quizzical.

Damn. I said, 'Nope. We're sticking together until I teach you all I know, which shouldn't take long.'

Chuckles all around.

From then on we were back to the usual tame topics until I caught Wedge Cardigan strangling a yawn. I could take a hint. Besides I was feeling much the same.

'Right, Rosie. It's time we went home.'

She didn't argue. Jason went off to roust Benedict and the rest of us rolled out into the hall. I made a big production out of saying goodbye and the assorted Cardigans entered into the spirit of things. In the midst of all this I smartly pulled the envelope of fifty-pound notes from my pocket and lodged it just out of sight behind a horse sculpture affair on the hall table.

We cruised off in the Daimler with many a goodbye wave. As we exited the driveway, I sat back, confident that Gabriella would soon find her two grand.

Providing Agnes didn't trouser it first.

Chapter Fifteen

Sunday. I feel the same way about Sundays as Omar Khayyam did about New Years. Omar Khayyam the poet, that is, not the kebab joint. The way the thinking man's drinking man saw it:

> Now the New Year, reviving old desires,
> The thoughtful soul to solitude retires.

This thoughtful soul likes to retire on Sundays to contemplate the sports pages. And afterwards, if I'm up to it, I do a trawl through the tabloids to see what my mates have been inventing. The *People* splashed on a newly married rock star who had gone back to his ex-missus for an auld-lang-syne bit of nonsense the night before he married his new soon-to-be ex-missus. The *News of the Screws* had an inside page lead on two teams of villains picking the same night to turn over a stately home. When Gang A bumped into Gang B in the library a right old rumpus ensued, with the A mob flattening the B mob and getting flattened themselves in the process. Awakened by the barney, the gardener called the Old Bill. Now teams A and B were languishing in

Brixton's remand wing, apart from those members who were still in hospital.

The *Screws* also ran a page on a Royal aide and a headmaster getting lifted for a spot of the usual up on Hampstead Heath. And just in case its readers couldn't figure out what the two were up to in the shrubbery, the *Screws* helpfully spelt it out for them, stopping just short of drawing a diagram.

Over to the *Express* where the IRA had put a £2 million price tag on the head of its latest informer. IRA stories are great fun altogether, because you can write what you want and nobody's going to deny it. There are people in Fleet Street who've carved themselves reputations as terrorism specialists solely through being more inventive than the rest of us.

The *Mail on Sunday*'s crime man came up with a special exposé of a British arms company flogging weaponry to Myanmar, or what you and I call Burma. There were photocopies of End User certificates, grainy snaps of sinister Mr Fixits and about 2,000 words filling the spaces in between. I read at least twenty words.

The *Mirror* had turned over a lottery winner who was spending his hard earned cash on his very own torture chamber, complete with a couple of Madams Whiplash.

That was it for the tabloids. I don't buy the *Sunday Sport*. A man has got to draw the line somewhere.

I moved on to the heavies, not because there was anything in them worth reading. I just wanted to keep Rosie at bay. She was in her standard post-dinner party mode, champing to open an inquest into the events of last night. Frankly I'd had my fill of the Cardigans for a while so I stuck my head in the *Sunday Times* and pretended to read.

'Max?' She doesn't give up easily.

'Umph?'

'Remember we're going out this afternoon?'

I'd forgotten. Whatever it was, it had nothing to do with the Cardigans. It was safe to pull my head out of the *Sunday Times*. But I was still a tad wary.

'Where?'

Rosie said, 'Herbie Marks. The flat warming party.'

'Oh yes.' How could I forget. Old Skid Marks is one of our luvvie reporters and as such should be shunned by decent society. But until last year he was a proper hack and he still has a lot of credits. Besides, Skid's notoriously generous with his drink.

I looked out the window. It was the average pissy grey day you get at the fag end of February. Yep, a party would brighten things up. I put down the *Sunday Times*.

Rosie said, 'It's just a sweater and jeans affair, isn't it?'

It might be for her. I take more pride in my appearance.

'Yes. Sweater and jeans.'

Rosie was thumbing through the colour supplements. 'So that thing I wore last night would be too dressy?'

'Definitely.'

She said, 'You never told me if you liked it.'

I still didn't see it coming. I said, 'It was terrific. You looked knock out.'

Her voice was ever so casual. 'You'll never guess what Gabriella Cardigan did last night.'

My radar woke up. I grabbed the *Sunday Times* and plunged back into its folds. I didn't give a toss what Gabriella Cardigan did. I didn't care if I never knew.

Of course sooner or later she'd corner me and I'd get the whole bit. But right now I was considerably more interested in a two-page spread on the Common Agricultural Policy and its implications for Britain's dairy farmers.

The party got going at three, but we didn't show until it was gone four. I make it a point of honour never to turn up until things have got past the sober stage.

Skid's place was in Fulham, not far from my own drum. Showbiz hacks earn a lot more than the rest of us, largely because they moonlight as ghost writers for every sad thespian and rocker who thinks he/she/it has a yarn worth inflicting on the unsuspecting public. Skid's a dab hand at ghosting. He gets his victims to parade every skeleton in their closet, sexual, criminal or otherwise. The result is the books then tend to get serialized in the *Star* or the *Sun*. The alleged author, and Skid, pick up a bundle from that, and everyone is satisfied, particularly the pathetic actor/rocker who believes his book has been serialized because he's such a fascinating human being.

Skid's fortunes were evident from the size of his flat. The door was opened by Lisanne, his girlfriend, a real luvvie who inhabits the wilder shores of reality. She sprayed me with kisses for she's like that. I eventually fought her off and pushed on through to the action. The centre of it all was a big room, or maybe it was two rooms knocked into one. There were sixty or seventy people already in there, whopping back Skid's drink. I was helping myself to a Gordons when the Wildebeest butted up and began explaining how he recently got the tin tack from the *Sun*. The story that had been doing the rounds was he rolled back to the office after an even livelier lunch than usual and threw up over the News Editor. This, the Wildebeest said, was a vile slur on his famous ability to hold his drink, and if he found out who was putting it about, he'd rip his head off. No. What really happened was he came back from the aforesaid lunch and found himself taken short. Whereupon he relieved himself on an adjacent potted palm, behind which the News Editor was standing.

Having set the record straight, the Wildebeest slouched off, his reputation intact. I was happy for him. Even so, I made a mental note to steer clear of potted palms when he was around.

Jodie, a secretary on showbiz, came up, linked an arm in mine and made big blue eyes at me. If ever Rosie and I go belly up, Jodie is top of the list of girls I'd like to know better. But right now she was taking her life in her hands. Mine too. I gently disentangled her and sought out safer company.

There was a group of us hanging round in the corner and admiring Skid's record collection – that's another perk of the trade – when a new face popped up.

'Wotcher, Max,' said Neil Milltain.

Milltain is in the same lark as me, that is he's a crime hack. But we don't particularly hit it off. He's too secret squirrelly for my liking. Therefore I generally just say hello and that's it.

But today I felt a sudden pressing need to talk to Milltain at length and in private. For Milltain is the chief crime man on the *Mail*, the one who is all set to fold his notebook and go off globe-trotting.

The truth is I was feeling a touch desperate. If Belker got his way, I would cease to be a crime reporter on the *Gazette*. If Belker didn't get his way, I would still cease to be crime reporter on the *Gazette*. But I wanted to stay what I was. At the moment, the only chance of me carrying on as a hack was if I switched papers. And the *Mail* would soon be looking for such as me. Hence my sudden interest in Milltain.

I edged him out to a corner by the window, checked there was no one snogging in the curtains, and opened up.

'What's this I hear about you taking a year off?'

'It's true,' said Milltain. That's a first for him.

I sucked my gin. 'So who's taking your slot?'

Milltain looked crafty. 'They've got a few people in mind, but they haven't decided yet. Why? Are you interested?'

'Me?' I put on a 'you've-got-to-be-joking' smile.

He wasn't fooled. 'They could do worse.'

Gee, thanks Neil.

I said, 'The *Mail* couldn't afford me.'

His turn to smile. 'I don't know. How much are you on? I'm on sixty.'

That's a lie for a start. I pretended I believed him.

'A fraction more than me. But our exes are better.'

Milltain demurred. 'I'm on two-fifty a week, and that's before I go out of town.'

Another whopper. I stayed polite. 'Not bad. But your News Desk is a bugger to work for.'

'They're OK. They've got no time for people who argue the toss over every job.'

That means you've got to suck up to them. Not my forte.

Milltain said, 'I've had no problems. They've even said they'll keep the job open for me.'

A third porkie. As soon as he quit hacking, he'd become Neil Who?, just like anybody else who gets out of newspapers.

I said, 'Who's in the frame?'

Nobody famous, or the way he told it nobody of his multitudinous talents anyway.

I asked, 'When does the new guy take over?'

'April. That's when I'm off.'

This was my cue to ask him all about his trip so he could bore me rigid for the next hour with tall tales of tall ships. I steered him back on course.

'They'd better appoint someone soon.'

Milltain shrugged. It didn't concern him anymore. But he said, 'They've got a new policy at the *Mail*. No more head-hunting.'

'How come?'

'It's Geany's idea. He reckons that if anyone wants to work at the *Mail*, they should chase the *Mail* and not the other way around.'

Geany is the News Editor. He is not the most beloved man down Kensington way. When the time comes for him to get the chop, they'll be dancing in the streets.

I said, 'So Geany wants the new crime man to butter him up?'

Milltain got conspiratorial. He moved closer so I could smell his breath. He'd just eaten five cloves of garlic. He said, 'If you want me to put in a word, Max . . .'

'Thanks Neil, but I'm OK at the *Gazette.*'

'I'm serious. It's a good number.'

I said, 'I'm serious too.'

He moved back and I could inhale again. He dished me a patronizing smile and said, 'Oh well, it's worth thinking about.'

We left it there. Milltain launched into telling me his plan to sail the seven seas over, but would you believe it, I'd just run out of drink. I sloped off, promising to be back soon. Somehow or other I clean forgot.

The rest of the party went merrily enough and I made all the right noises. But my mind was elsewhere. It was tearing at the ends of a particularly knotty problem, to wit: could I lower myself to write to the imbecile Geany, begging him for a job.

After a couple of hours and a ferocious amount of gin, I'd made my decision. I could.

On Monday Jason showed up freshly scrubbed and in something which approximated a suit. He had also shaved. If he'd only chopped off the ponytail and slung out the earring he might have looked all right. I collected him from reception and signed him through security.

'What story are you on today?' he asked before we'd even hit the lift.

'Just bits and bobs at the moment. Nothing interesting.'

I had lunch planned with a bloke from Customs but I didn't want Jason along. The question was how to dump him. Then I remembered Angela Whipple's open invitation for him to sit in on News Desk.

I said, 'But I thought you might like to see how the Desk operates, you know, how they choose which stories to run and which reporters to bollock.'

Jason said, 'Safe.'

That, I vaguely remembered, meant super or something similar.

Angie was already in morning conference but I negotiated it with Nige, her deputy, and he welcomed Jason with bright insincerity. They found him a slot where the Regional News Editor used to sit before the last round of redundancies.

I returned to my corner and began dialling friends and enemies. The last I saw of Jason he was staggering under a tray of coffee. They teach 'em fast on News Desk.

I shot off for my lunch date at Doggett's Cap and Badge which is handy for the Customs people. Its one snag is it's bang opposite the *Express* and I didn't want any of my mates there sniffing around. Fortunately these days the *Express* keeps its hacks chained to the treadmill and the only people I knew were a bunch of layabouts from its News Desk. They pretended not to see me which was fine by me.

My Customs contact was in thirsty form and I let him knock it back for an hour until he warmed up. He offered a useful little yarn about the Essex Old Bill screwing up a surveillance job off West Mersea. The scenario was this: a cabin cruiser stuffed with Moroccan gold was making a drop. Also on board were four tearaways tooled up with guns, stun grenades and, for all I know, bazookas. But here's the catch. There were only three tearaways aboard. The fourth was an undercover Customs guy.

Plan A was to let the cabin cruiser make the drop and not interfere. When it got off round the headland again, there was a Customs boat waiting to nick it. Meanwhile the cannabis would be safely ashore and en route to Mr Big, whose identity no one knew.

What *he* didn't know was the drugs had a bleeper attached and somewhere way up in the sky, a satellite spy was tracking it. When it got to wherever it was going, Customs and police would march in and collar the lot of them. Simple enough.

But not simple enough for Essex constabulary. Just as the cabin cruiser made its rendezvous with a smaller version of itself, some woodentop on the shore switched on an arc lamp. Wholesale panic out there on the briny deep. The big cabin cruiser scuttled off into the night. Its baby brother dumped the whole lot overboard. So when they reeled in the little boat there was nothing on board except for two innocent villains. No Mr Big. No drugs. No case.

Meanwhile, out at sea, the cabin cruiser crew scratched their head for about three seconds and worked out they'd been tumbled. One of them was not the respectable crook he'd painted himself. They were in the act of turfing the undercover guy to the lobsters when the Customs boat loomed up and persuaded them this might not look good on their CVs.

The story was all there. I just had to ring Essex

police for a 'no comment', and that would be it. Another exclusive page lead for what, say twenty-five quid. Or sixty-five, as my exes would later reflect.

Seeing we were on the subject of drugs, I asked my pal who was shifting Ecstasy into Britain. Much of it, he said, was home grown, knocked up in back rooms and attics. Most of the rest came from Holland. Surprise, surprise.

I told him about my various suspicions involving Joni Poelma and he said, yes, the Drugs Intelligence Unit had been sniffing around. And? And nothing. They'd accessed her NatWest bank account and it was all kosher. She'd no previous, but that didn't mean anything, because the Dutch anti-drugs lot only get interested in Dutch druggies if Britain or somebody else wants them turned over. And even then their heart isn't in it. So that got me nowhere.

But under the heading of Useless Information, he told me that kids were prepared to pay way above the going rate to buy Ecstasy tabs which were known killers. I said, 'Oh really' and we talked about football instead. We swallowed another glass or so and then he went off to play detective.

I stopped by the City Golf Club, which is not a golf club, but a place where hacks gather and practise putting it back. I rang the story in from there because I wanted to keep a healthy distance between me and the office. It wasn't just because of Jason.

Ollie, a mate from the *Mirror*, was in the Golf Club, savouring the bright lights. The *Mirror* are stuck way out Canary Wharf which is an even more God-forsaken slice of Docklands than the place the *Gazette* calls home. You don't often see *Mirror* hacks sampling civilization.

Ollie had been up at the High Court where some girl with a voice like a mosquito was suing her ex-agent over her crashed career as a singer. It was all terminally boring, but she'd nice boobs, which was why the *Mirror* bothered to cover the case.

I got out the Bensons and Ollie got in the Gordons.

He looked at me straight. 'What's this I hear about you going after the crime job on the *Mail?*'

Bugger Neil Milltain and his big garlicky mouth.

I said, 'Me? Not interested. I wouldn't work for the *Mail* for twice the money.'

Ollie and I go a long, long way back. He's never stiffed me or done me a mischief. But in newspapers there are some things, many things you don't tell your best friend.

He said, 'If you can work with Belker you can work with anybody.'

There's a certain degree of truth in that. Even so, I was giving nothing away. I dredged up the true story of how the Wildebeest got fired from the *Sun* and we forgot all about the *Mail* as the afternoon deepened into a lurch down memory lane and tales of drunken atrocities too outrageous even for *Private Eye* to sneak on.

We had to cut short the reminiscences because Mrs Ollie walked in and she's not a hack so she wouldn't appreciate yarns like that. I cleared off hoping I'd convinced Ollie I wasn't after the *Mail* job. I hoped that. But I wouldn't bet on it.

Back at the gulag, Jason was still beavering away with the coffee tray. I kept my head down, knocked out a couple of stories and even made a start on one week's exes. After inventing three days of lunches and meetings with special contacts I was feeling virtuous enough to slide down to the Stone for a fast one.

Around seven my tender heart got the better of me and I rang Desk to invite Jason down for a snort.

Nige said, 'Jason? No, he's gone off home. He said he was sorry he missed you but he'll catch up with you tomorrow.'

Tomorrow was a long ways away. I returned to my drinking cronies.

Later, much later, I was back in my own flat and watching the rugby I'd taped from Sunday when my mobile cut in.

'Max.'

'Vic.'

'I've got an odd one here.'

I said, 'So I've heard.'

It went past him. He said, 'We need an urgent featurette. About four or five hundred words.'

Featurette! And we're supposed to be the guardians of the Queen's English.

'What do you want these words to be about?'

'Ecstasy. We've got a kid, a young bloke, who's in intensive care after taking it. But I've got Louise writing up the newser. What I need from you is a piece on the agony and the ecstasy. I need it in fifteen minutes if it's going to make the fourth edition. OK?'

I said OK. Vic didn't say thank you, Max, that's awfully nice of you.

I lit a Bensons and poured myself a glass just to get the grey cells on stream. Features are easy-peasy. You

don't have to fiddle around looking for a snappy intro.
But old habits die hard. I started off thinking about how
much a tab of Ecstasy costs. The going rate was around
fifteen quid. What else costs fifteen quid? A litre of gin?
No, wrong image. Four-and-a-bit packets of Bensons?
That didn't work either. Bugger. Nothing costs fifteen
quid.

My restless eye prowled the room. It took in the
bookcase, the video, the stereo. Got it! I started writing.

It costs no more than the price of the latest pop CD.

They call it the hug drug or E or just Pills. Or
Ecstasy.

For only £15 a tab, youngsters are promised the
trip of a lifetime.

But for many, it is a one-way ticket to tragedy.

And last night as another teenage tripper lay
fighting for his life in intensive care, the true cost
was exposed.

Now parents and anti-drug campaigners are
demanding tough Government action to halt the
agony of Ecstasy.

An undercover detective said:'There are scores
of makeshift labs in attics and spare rooms all over
Britain.

'They are churning out death.'

And crime syndicates operating under the pro-
tection of Holland's soft stance on drugs are flooding
British discos with the killer pills.

Dozens of young thrill-seekers have already died
chasing an instant high.

Countless others are suffering side effects, from paranoia to irreversible kidney damage.

A campaigner said: 'They are not getting the message that drugs kill.'

The back street labs stamp their own tawdry brand image on the pills.

Some feature doves, or hearts or flowers.

But a drugbuster warned: 'There is nothing innocent about them.'

And when a particular Ecstasy mix turns out to be a killer, it only stimulates demand.

A senior detective admitted: 'The teen ravers are prepared to pay more for brands that have cost the lives of their pals.

'It's like playing Russian Roulette with all the chambers loaded.'

This is only about half of the whole thing, but you get the general idea. I also mixed in a few quotes from my pathologist chum, Paul Grasmith, only he appeared as an unnamed expert on drug abuse.

I dictated it all to Copy, wrapping it up in three minutes under Vic's stipulated fifteen.

Anybody reasonably human would have been grateful. Vic just said, 'I haven't read it yet. Where can I get you if I have any queries?'

I said, 'Why don't you try the number you called last time?'

'Oh.'

He wanted me off the line. I dragged my heels.

'How's this kid doing anyway?'

'The one in intensive care?'

No, Vic, the one in Medicine Hat, Alberta.

'I don't know, do I? Pretty bad.'

'Got a name for him? An age?'

Vic clucked his fat tongue. 'Hold a minute.'

I held on, listening to his pudgy fingers popping the story up on the screen.

He said with unconcealed triumph. 'No. No name.'

'Well, where did it happen then?'

Vic is not one of nature's speed readers. He got there eventually. 'South London. Dulwich.'

I took a deep breath and asked very carefully, 'Was the kid at a club?'

He had to read it all over again. 'No, he'd just come out of a disco. The Silver Lino.'

I exploded, 'Jesus Christ, Vic! You've got a story.'

'Whumf?'

'That's the same club Joni Poelma was in the night she vanished.'

'So?'

'Joni was shot through with Ecstasy.'

Somewhere in the black cave which Vic calls a brain a lonely candle flickered.

'Bloody hell.'

Such was his gratitude he made me write the sodding thing. When I was done I called him back and got him to promise he'd let me know as soon as they got a name.

I sat back with a new glass and a fresh pack of Bensons and thought about things. I thought about giving Jason a call. I thought about getting Mac on the case to see if he could come up with a name. Then I thought what the hell. I turned the rugby back on.

It was nudging two in the morning and I was in my pit when Vic rang back.

'Remember the kid in hospital? Well he's snuffed it.'

In his off hours Vic works for the Samaritans.

'You've got a name?'

'Hold it. Yes. He's twenty, lives at Merrilees Park, Dulwich and he's called Aubrey George Kevlin.'

'He calls himself George,' I said automatically.

'How do you know?'

'I know. That's all.'

Vic rang off. If I'd really pushed it, I could have scrambled a story together in time for the London final. But that's got a print run of only 50,000. The story was better than that and so far nobody else had a sniff of it.

I sat up in bed and scratched my chin. Well, well, well. So the mysterious George, probable ex-boyfriend of the ex-Joni had tripped out.

Somehow I was less surprised than I ought to be.

Chapter Sixteen

Tuesday morning, and I had an urgent overpowering desire to talk to Jason. That was the day he didn't show. I asked around News Desk but they'd no idea, so no change there.

Maybe he was off at hack school or maybe he was keeping out of the way, in which case if I phoned Maison Cardigan, Gabriella would spin me some pretty lie.

So far I was not enjoying Tuesday, and I don't just blame Jason. The chief culprit was the geezer who knocks up shoes for Cherie Blair.

Last night, while I was slogging my head off, she was out enjoying herself at the ballet or the opera or one of those things. All very nice for her, I'm sure.

Or it was until the moment she stepped out into the night and her heel snapped, thereby decanting her into an unsuspecting gutter. While she lay sprawled in a puddle, the gibbering horde of monkeys did the decent thing and went pop-pop-pop.

The upshot was every single tabloid turfed out its front page splash and replated with a stonking great snaps of her, legs akimbo. CHERIE'S FALL FROM GRACE (*Express*), DIVA CHERIE TAKES A DIVE (*Mail*), CHERIE-OH! (*Sun*) and so forth. Normally I don't mind this sort of nonsense. It keeps the subs out of the bar. But I do object when it means proper stories get spiked or otherwise butchered. And this is what had happened to my stuff on George Whosis. It was pegged as a single column on five, and of my instant featurette, there was nary a word.

But hacks get used to such wanton vandalism and after a thirty-minute sulk I was back to normal. I briefed Angela Whipple that there was a possibility – I didn't put it any stronger – that George was Joni's mystery lover. She whooped with glee for until then her news schedule was a bit anaemic.

Next I phoned Mac and asked him to find out if Chief Inspector Skelly was showing any interest in George. He came back ten minutes later and said no. That meant I had to do some proper foot-in-the-door hacking. Outside my window it was chucking it down. The prospect of lurching around Dulwich in the rain and cold did not appeal. What I needed was my very own driver.

I went across to Monkey Desk and told the head keeper I had a cracker of a job which needed a good photographer. He was all out of those but he loaned me Frankie Frost instead.

Frankie threw a major moody which was OK by me because it meant I didn't have to listen to him witter on. We shuttled off towards Dulwich in his office jam jar in silence. I closed my eyes so I wouldn't hear the usual abuse from other road users.

He didn't open up until we were belting through Dulwich Village. 'What's this all about, then?'

Monkeys can't think and drive at the same time. I said, 'Pull into yonder pub and I'll tell you.'

I kept it simple. He washed it down with a pint of

lager top and delivered his considered opinion. 'What a load of balls. Is this your dumb idea?'

I was deeply offended. 'No. We've got Angela Whipple to thank for this.'

Frankie said various rude things about Angie and I went along with it because you've got to humour monkeys.

'So where do we go now?' he asked.

Number 18 Merrilees Park was a big drum. Not in the same league as the Cardigans' spread, but generous enough. It was one of those modern jobs with twee mullioned windows to make it look old. It wasn't fooling anybody. I got fed up waiting for Frankie to drape himself in cameras so I walked up the path and thumbed the big brass bell.

Silence for two minutes. I gave it another go and the door opened right away to reveal a red faced geezer with sandy hair and an orange sweater. Maybe he was colour-blind.

I said, 'Mr Kevlin? My name is Max Chard. I'm from the *Gazette*—'

'Piss off,' said he, and banged the door.

I slopped back through the puddles. At least Frankie was smiling. 'No luck?' he asked happily.

I just growled and pulled out my notebook. In big clear letters I wrote the following:

Dear Mr Kevlin,
　　　I very much regret if I have added to your great distress today. That was not my intention.
　　　The *Gazette* is presently campaigning for tougher action against drugs.

We have spoken to other parents who have suffered the same tragic loss which you and your wife now face.

If at some time you feel that you can speak to me about George, my card is attached.

I will quite understand if the pain is too great for you to talk about it.

Once again, my sincere apologies, and my deepest sympathy.

I just signed it Max. Frankie read it over my shoulder. 'Are we running an anti-drugs campaign?'

I gave him a look.

'Oh.'

I folded the note round my card and trudged up the drive. Pop. Into the letterbox it went. Back to the car.

'It'll never work,' said Frankie.

I have a touching faith in me. 'I'll bet you I get quotes out of him today.'

'You haven't a chance and I'm not hanging about while you wait. Let's get back to the office.'

'Hold your horses, Frankie. First I'm going to show you the woman of your wildest fantasies.'

'Who?'

'Wait till we get there. You will not believe it.'

On the way to the Cardigans' place I talked up Gabriella's charms until she came across as a Venus de Milo only with both her arms still tacked on at the shoulders. Frankie was slavering by the time we reached the White House.

I said, 'Are you ready?'

He gave a soft moan. He was ready.

I said, 'This woman will knock your eyes out.'

I hit the bell and waited, with Frankie panting away to my left.

The door swung open, and there, clutching a can of furniture polish, stood Agnes and her frizzy hair.

From my left I heard a gulp.

I said, 'Ah. Is Missus Cardigan in?'

'No. But Mister Cardigan is.'

Frankie said to me, 'I thought you said—'

I cut in before Agnes brained him with the furniture polish: 'May we speak to him please? Tell him it's Max.'

Agnes padded off. Frankie curled his lip, 'Some babe.'

'That wasn't the one I was talking about.'

'Huh.'

He's got no right to complain. Agnes was about three miles better than his usual rascals.

We waited for her return. But next on the scene was Wedge Cardigan. He looked down his bony nose at me and flicked through his memory bank.

'Max,' he said after a moment. 'Won't you come in?'

I wiped my feet carefully on the mat and made sure Frankie did the same.

Cardigan said, 'Coffee?'

I could think of better ideas but I said that would do nicely. We trailed through to the kitchen where Gabriella had entertained me on Day One. En route I was asking myself where she was, where Jason was and what Wedge Cardigan was doing at home instead of making millions. Maybe he and Agnes had a thing going on. No.

Not for Wedge the dainty porcelain. He hauled out

three man-sized mugs and started brewing. He said, 'Gabriella's at her aerobics studio. She'll be sorry she missed you.'

I heard Frankie snort.

I said, 'Is Jason back at college?'

No. He was off seeing a friend. Oh well, Wedge would have to do.

I took the mug from him and said, 'It's Jason's friends I wanted to talk about. Or one of them anyway. George Kevlin.'

Behind his square specs Cardigan's eyes went blank. He was thinking.

'George,' he said. I think he'd got him.

I said, 'Perhaps you haven't heard, but George died last night.'

'No!'

That's right, Wedge. I just said it for a joke.

I said, 'It was drugs. Ecstasy.'

He swung his square head back and forth. 'When will they ever learn?'

I didn't feel like making a guess. I said, 'Were he and Jason close pals?'

A nod. Then an afterthought. 'Not so much recently, but they used to be quite close.'

I said, 'And George was Joni's boyfriend.'

'Was he really?'

'And Joni was on Ecstasy too.'

'Good God!'

I said, 'I thought you knew.'

Wedge Cardigan looked aghast. 'She was on drugs? And she was caring for our children. I had absolutely no

idea. That is—' he hunted around for a word,
'—shocking.'

I lit a cigarette and pulsed out smoke. I glanced
at Frankie. He was otherwise engaged, scouting out
photographs to nick. There weren't any.

Cardigan was pondering in that analytical way of
his. He said, 'How do you know Joni was taking drugs?'

I felt like saying, 'Because your wife told me.' I got
scientific instead. 'There were indicators present in the
autopsy.'

'Which indicators?'

'Renal damage.'

'That would tend to suggest consistent or prolonged
use.'

I said, 'So now the police are looking for her supplier.'

Cardigan was following his own track. 'Was it a factor
in Joni's death?'

'No. That was just your average murder. But it might
be wrapped up with drugs.'

He'd been standing all this while. He sat himself
down across the breakfast bar. 'Drugs. She never gave
me that impression, but then I don't suppose I knew her
particularly well.'

'How did you come to hire Joni? An advert or
something?'

Cardigan said, 'No, she worked at Gabriella's studio
before she came here. Our previous au pair was
returning to Portugal.'

Which explained how Gabriella knew her better.

He swilled his coffee for a moment and then he gave
me a sharp square-eyed look. 'What has this to do with
Jason?'

He was making all the right connections.

'Jason?' I looked bemused.

Wedge Cardigan said, 'You wanted to see him.'

I waved a careless hand. 'Just to tell him about George. I was in the area anyway.'

He said, 'You're not suggesting that Jason is involved in drugs?'

Perish the thought. I laughed it off.

Cardigan said, 'I'll tell him about George. He'll be terribly upset. I'd better ring Bill. That's George's father.'

I needed him to do that right now. The problem was I didn't want him to suss what I was up to. I said, 'Maybe you'd better call Mister Kevlin soon. I spoke to the neighbours and they said he was going out soon.'

'Oh yes. Probably picking up the girls.'

Whatever that meant.

Wedge Cardigan sat on with his coffee. I flicked an eye at the chromed wall clock. It was ticking on for ten-fifty. I said, 'The neighbours reckoned he'd be leaving about eleven.'

He looked at his own watch. 'Oh. I'd better get him now.'

I suppose that was our cue to drink up and clear off. I stayed put. I said, 'May Frankie use your bathroom?'

They both said, 'Eh?'

I gave Frankie a tight glower. He twigged.

'Yes, may I use your bathroom?' he echoed.

'Of course. Turn right down the hall and it's second on the left.'

Frankie went. Cardigan consulted his watch again. I looked away. He swivelled his stool, unhooked the wall phone with one hand and ran a bony finger down a list of numbers pinned up beside it. He began dialling. I tried to look invisible.

After a couple of moments. 'Bill? This is Wedge Cardigan. I've just heard the sad news about George . . .'

Some words from the other end.

Cardigan again, 'Neither Gabriella nor Jason know yet. But they'll be very deeply upset. I cannot tell you how sorry I am, it really is an unimaginable tragedy.'

Many more words from Bill Kevlin. Wedge kept nodding his head and going 'Uh-huh.'

I had to push it in the right direction. I got out my notebook and scribbled in big caps JONI WAS USING ECSTASY TOO. I slid the notebook over the counter until it was in his direct line of sight. He read it and frowned. I sat back to see if it worked.

Time for Cardigan to talk. 'How is Sonia taking it? Do the girls know?'

Bill had a lot to say for himself.

Over to Wedge again. 'Yes, it is ghastly. One would think by now—'

Back to Bill.

And then Wedge. 'I know, it seems so many young people—'

Oh shut up, Bill.

Frankie tooled back into the kitchen and lifted an eyebrow in question. I was about to mouth 'no' when Wedge said, 'It's truly dreadful. Only this morning I learned that Joni – you remember our au pair? – that she was ah, heavily involved with drugs.'

God Bless you Wedge. Even across the breakfast bar I could hear Bill Kevlin's tinny voice go into overdrive. Wedge slipped into his 'uh-huh' routine again. He listened for maybe another minute and then he tailed off the conversation with a burst of deepest sympathies and so on. He put down the phone.

I said without looking at him. 'I imagine Mister Kevlin must be badly broken up.'

'Indeed.'

Wedge didn't sound too chipper himself. I glanced up and he was sporting a sourish expression. It was directed at me.

I said, 'Perhaps I shouldn't have mentioned that thing about Joni.'

'Yes. I'm afraid that rather upset him. Not to put too fine a point on it, he blames Joni for introducing George to drugs.'

'Really? He said that?'

'Well, it was worse than that, actually. He said Joni was a tramp and if George had not met her, he'd be alive today.'

I had a story.

Wedge was still talking. 'He said he had to stop George seeing Joni, because he and Sonia – that's his wife – felt she was a bad influence on him. I feel responsible.'

I was all sympathy. 'But you didn't know she was on drugs. Did Mister Kevlin?'

'I don't know. I'm not sure. They just thought she was using him.'

'And feeding him drugs?'

'Possibly. Certainly he was very angry when I mentioned Joni.'

That would do nicely. All I needed now were the minor details. I said, 'What does Mister Kevlin do?'

'Do? He's ah, he's got his own company. Construction.'

'What – building houses?'

Wedge thought so.

I said, 'Was George his only child?'

'No, there are the twins. Twin girls.'

He didn't know their names but they were about fourteen or fifteen. I had all I wanted. It was Frankie's turn now.

He said, 'We don't want to bother Mister Kevlin. Would you have any snaps of George? You know, seeing him and Jason were mates.'

Wedge looked uncertain. 'I don't know, and I am rather busy.'

Frankie played it just right. 'Oh, that's OK then, if you're too busy. It's just I didn't want to go banging on their door and upsetting them.'

A resigned sigh. 'I'll have a look.'

Frankie and I sat on in the kitchen, smoking and not talking. Five minutes went by. We were getting worried. At least Frankie was, I already had my stuff. But if we got a pic as well, the story would get a better show in the paper.

Wedge returned with two snaps. One showed George, half face in tennis whites. The other was straight on, sitting at a table with a bunch of blokes, among whom was Jason. It was a night shot and George had red eyes from the camera flash. It didn't matter. We've got the gear to clean that up.

Frankie took both pix and thanked Wedge nicely. We were anxious to wrap it up. I made all the right goodbye noises and we were out the door before Wedge could change his mind.

Back in the car, Frankie was mad keen to tear back to the office but I argued we deserved a drink. I didn't have to argue too hard.

So there we were in a pub, tipping a glass back and patting ourselves on the back. I said, 'That's another bet you owe me.'

'How?'

'I bet you I'd get words out of Bill Kevlin this morning.'

Frankie started splitting hairs. 'No, you got the words off Cardigan so it doesn't count. Anyway, I didn't bet.'

Some you can't win. I said, 'But you do owe me two hundred quid from Holland.'

'Oh all right.'

And to my utter stupefaction Frankie pulled out a Filofax sized wallet and counted out £200 in used tenners. They were possibly the grubbiest notes I'd ever seen in my life, but they were real.

I recounted them just to make sure and ordered in another round to celebrate. My mobile cheeped. Angie.

'How're you getting on with the Ecstasy kid?'

I said, 'I've got a belter. His dad blames Joni Poelma for turning him on.'

'No!'

'Yes. If my son had never met her, he'd still be alive today. Unquote.'

'He told you that?'

'And more. And we've got snaps.'

'Brilliant. Super job, Max. Let's have it straight away.'

Not so fast, Angie. I said, 'I've got a couple of check

calls to make first and then I'll ring the story in on my way back.'

'No. I want you to stay there, just in case.'

'Just in case what?'

Angie wasn't sure. All she knew was she wanted me to hang around Dulwich until she decided she no longer wanted me to hang around Dulwich. This happens all the time. What it means is News Desk is scared witless somebody else might pick up something you don't have.

I did my best. 'I've got the story in the bag. Nothing else is happening.'

It didn't work. 'Well give it an hour anyway and then check in.'

I clicked off the mobile and did a bit of swearing. I could see the way the day was going. In an hour's time I'd call her and she'd tell me to give it another hour, and so on and so on. I did some more swearing.

At least Frankie was happy. He'd phoned the Monkey Desk and they told him to hurry home with his snaps. Off he went before there was a chance of me getting him to buy a round.

I set up one for myself and presently I got things back in perspective. After all, I'd two hundred quid in my hip pocket and a tasty story in my head. Tuesday was turning out to be not such a bad day.

Just as I was beginning to lighten up, I heard a phlegmy 'Um-Hum' in my right ear. I swung about and there slap in front of me was the side of beef which Chief Inspector Tom Skelly uses as a face. I recoiled. It was only natural.

He said, 'Hello, Max.' His chops were split in a semblance of a smile.

This was strong gin.

'Hello,' I said warily. I looked around. There was a pair of dipsticks in the corner who probably belonged to him.

Skelly waved a fiver at the barkeep. 'A large Grouse please. Can I get you anything Max?'

This was all wrong. Skelly doesn't buy hacks drinks. Not unless he's up to something.

'A gin, thanks.'

'And a large gin,' he told the barman.

This was doubly wrong. Off to the side I saw the two defectives sidle out. Now there was just Skelly and me.

I hoisted my glass and peeled off a sort of smile. 'Cheers.'

'Skol,' said he.

There followed a full minute of silence. It was up to him to break it. He cleared his throat and said, 'I hear Dee Ess Mortown was a bit out of order with you.'

DS Mortown? Oh yes, the Plod who came barging into our reception, threatening to put the mockers on me.

I said, 'I expect he was only following orders.'

Skelly pretended he was amused. 'He's a keen lad, Mortown. Gets a bit too keen at times.'

This was damn near an apology. Surely he didn't think I was really going to do him for harrassment?

Skelly said, 'I had a word with him. He won't step out of line again.'

'Good.'

We swigged away in silence, broken only by the occasional throat clearing stage right. He was building up to something but he'd still a way to go. His glass was empty. Thirsty game, this sleuthing.

It grieved me, but we drinkers have to observe the social niceties. I said, 'Same again?'

'Don't mind if I do.'

When two men buy each other drink a bond is forged. You may not want it, but that's the way it happens.

Skelly leaned his hulk against the bar so that he was side on to me. 'It's a messy case, this one.'

He didn't even caution me he was talking off the record. I flung a speculative glance his way. His hard-boiled eyes were fixed on his glass.

I said without tone, 'You heard about this kid George Kevlin?'

A nod. 'Was he the George you mentioned?'

That's right.

Skelly pumped out a sigh. 'I still can't see what drugs have to do with Joni Poelma's murder.'

This was getting just too weird. He sounded like he wanted me to hold his little hand and show him the path to truth and justice.

Decency, or more likely vanity, got the better of me. I said, 'Joni was steeped in Ecstasy. She was popping it all the time.'

'OK, but it didn't kill her.'

'I know. She was killed by some bloke wrapping a Paisley-patterned scarf around her neck. That did the real damage.'

Skelly said, 'So what I'm asking is where do drugs come into it?'

My turn to sigh. 'Maybe Joni was a pusher, or maybe

224

she was a user who didn't pay her whack. All I'm saying is you've got an apparently motiveless murder. But just say the motive has something to do with drugs.'

He soaked this up slowly. 'And you say there's a dealer down the Silver Lino?'

'A skinny bloke. Calls himself Fez. Your drug boys ought to know him.'

Skelly asked, 'You reckon he was supplying Joni?'

'It's possible. It's also possible that Fez supplied George Kevlin with the Ecstasy that killed him.'

A long pause. We both stared at the optics and thought about it. I don't know about him, but it sounded all right to me.

He said, 'Maybe it's time I had a word with this Fez. What does he look like?'

Skelly was really pushing it. But what the hell. I told him. He didn't write it down. He just listened carefully and repeated what I said. Then he said, 'I think I'll give the disco a visit tonight.'

I said, 'Just one other thing. Get George Kevlin's dad to tell you about Joni. He says she got him on to drugs.'

The boiled eyes jumped. 'Does he now?'

That was enough helpful hints from me for one day. It was time he evened the score.

I asked, 'Are you still holding Felix Pegg?'

A negative shake.

'Does that mean he's clear?'

Skelly said, 'I don't know. Probably. He nicked her bag, but don't quote me.'

'But that was after somebody else topped her?'

'Yeah.'

'So is there any other likely lad on the horizon?'

'No.' He said that into his chin. I think he was embarrassed.

I finally figured out what was going on. Somebody upstairs was kicking Skelly's fat bum and he was desperate. So desperate he was even pumping me for info.

I asked, 'Nothing from forensic?'

Bugger all. It was a Marks and Sparks scarf and they'd sold about fifty million of them. There was nothing under her fingernails, no prints on her bag, no stray hairs.

I said, 'What was in her bag?'

Just the usual nonsense. Tissues, breath freshener, eye make-up, that sort of thing. And twenty-seven quid that Felix Pegg had half-inched.

'And an address book?'

He gave me a hard look. 'Should there have been?'

'I don't know. Most people have an address book.'

He said, 'Most do. She didn't.'

I switched lines. 'Any idea where she might have been in the days between her going missing and turning up dead?'

A doleful shake. 'She was killed three or four days before she was found.'

That was a new one. I said, 'What, her body was lying there all that time?'

Skelly turned scornful. 'Course it wasn't. It was rolled into the park the night before Pegg found her.'

'Rolled?'

'Yeah. There's a gap in the railings just there. Vandals. It looks like the killer drove to the park and rolled her down the slope.'

'You found marks on the grass or something?'

'Something like that. Another drink?'

I hesitated only for a flicker of a second. 'No thanks, Tom. I'd better be going.'

He seemed a shade disappointed. 'Well, maybe next time.'

'Sure thing.'

I was turning away when he touched me lightly on the arm. 'Look, I'm trusting you not to turn me over on this. Know what I mean?'

I knew. 'Don't worry. It's all off the record.'

He said, 'Thanks, Max.' He said it as if he meant it.

'That's OK.'

I wandered out into the rain. This is a funny old job sometimes.

Chapter Seventeen

Way after four Angela Whipple eventually decided she'd wasted enough of my precious time.

'Call it a day, Max. I don't think you're going to get any more down there.'

I could have told her that hours ago, but what's the use. I said, 'There's not much point in me coming back to the office now.'

Angie got the hint. 'All right, you might as well go home.'

Before she could ring off I got her to put me through to Dinesh to see who or what had been calling me in my absence. Nobody who couldn't wait until another day. Except one.

Dinesh said, 'And a guy called Neil rang. He didn't give his second name. He said you'd know him and what it was about.'

It was an 836 number. The *Mail* is an 836 number. Yep, I knew what it was about.

'When did he call?'

'A couple of hours ago.'

It was still too early to ring back. I didn't want to sound too keen and also I wanted to chew this over. I bagged a taxi and pointed it in the direction of Battersea.

The driver was a taciturn type, for which I was hugely grateful. We burbled along through the rush hour with him carving up God-fearing road users and me pondering deeply.

We were rounding the Elephant when I reckoned I'd delayed it long enough. I called the number.

'Neil Milltain,' announced a bright voice.

I made it sound as if I really wasn't all that interested in talking to him. 'Hi, Neil. It's Max Chard. Sorry I didn't get back to you sooner. What can I do for you?'

He was pleased with himself, but that's nothing new. 'You could buy me a pint.'

I acted the wide-eyed innocent. 'Is that all? I thought you might need my help with a story. Again.'

Scornful laugh from his end. 'Me need *your* help? Dream on, Max. But I've done something for *you*.'

'Oh yes?' I said without much interest.

He lowered his voice. 'I've had a quiet word with Lucas Geany and told him you might be just the man for the crime job.'

I went through the motions. 'I told you, Neil. I like it at the *Gazette*.'

He ignored that. 'And Geany said he'd like to hear from you.'

'Does he think I got you to put in a word?'

'No.' The lies people tell.

I said, 'Look, I know you think you're doing me a favour, but it doesn't appeal.'

He didn't believe me. 'You're kidding yourself, Max. Let's face it, the *Gazette*'s gutter press.'

'And the *Mail*?'

He got on his high horse. 'We're a legit paper. It would be a real move up for you.'

'So's a trip up Everest. But I don't feel like going there either.'

'Look, Geany is interested. Just give him a call anyway and listen to what he has to say.'

'I'll think about it.'

'Well, don't think too long. He's going to make a decision soon.'

'I'll think about it,' I said again.

'All right. But don't forget – you owe me a pint.'

End of conversation.

The taxi sloughed on through the nether regions of Battersea.

'Hello, this is Max Chard of the *Daily Mail.*' It didn't sound right.

'I'm Max Chard, News Editor of the *Gazette.*'

That sounded even less right.

I wheeled up at Rosie's umpteen hours before my estimated time of arrival. She was most surprised to see me. But not half as much as I was at seeing her.

It wasn't her mere presence that rocked me back on my heels: it was the way she was got up. She was squeezed into something largely the same colour as the Aurora Borealis on fireworks' night. It started off as a swimsuit with a neckline that could never be accused of false modesty. It ended up as a pair of cycle shorts. It clung to her with a rare enthusiasm. Even in the privacy of her own room it looked indecent. I was strangely moved.

She darted me a warning look. 'You can forget that. I'm too busy.'

'I can help you get undressed.'

No, thank you. She didn't want to get undressed, and even if she did, she knew how to do that all by herself.

I slumped into a chair and watched as she paddled hither and thither in bare feet, as casual as you like. I think I might have let loose a low moan.

I said, 'Why the gift wrapping?'

'This?'

'What else?'

She said, 'I'm just off to Gabriella Cardigan's fitness centre.'

'You're a bit overdressed surely.'

'It's what everybody wears for aerobics.'

'You mean there'll be a whole bunch of women kitted up like you?'

She said, 'I expect so.'

I tried to picture it. A dozen women, maybe even more, all wearing nothing more than a sliver of Lycra, bobbing about and stretching this way and that.

I said, 'Can I come too?'

No, I couldn't. I'd just sit there leering at them, Rosie said. I promised I'd keep my eyes shut. It was still no.

She wandered off leaving me to feel sorry for myself. I poured a stiff gin instead and watched the news. ITN gave a big segment over to the Ecstasy Kid. They trotted out a psychologist, a former user and a drugs cop. But they hadn't got a word out of George's old man.

Rosie reappeared. She was now tooled up for going out. She'd taken care to dress as unprovocatively as possible, with a big black floppy sweater and jeans. Sometimes she forgets I've got X-ray vision.

I offered to splosh out a gin but she wagged her head no. She curled up demurely on the sofa, safely out of reach. Maybe she hadn't forgotten.

She said, 'I'm cutting out drink. At least during the week.'

This was all a bit radical, especially coming from her. A lesser man might have said, 'Ha bloody ha.' I just smiled sorrowfully.

She said, 'No, I'm serious. I want to lose about half a stone and get myself fit.'

I suggested we try exercising together. She made it clear she far preferred jigging about and pumping iron and all that. Anyways, she'd better be going. She went.

The world was instantly grey without her. Even the TV weather girl looked a mite frumpish tonight. I switched off. Rosie might be gone a good couple of hours and what was I to do in the meantime? Tuck into the gin? No. Drinking's like sex: it's better with somebody else.

I mooched around the flat kicking the chairs and generally feeling sorry for myself. Much more of this and I'd be a raving neurotic. Neurotic. That triggered something deep in my memory. I suddenly thought of Oscar. Oscar is one of our feature hacks and when he's not hacking out features, he's reading books. All sorts of books. He is ever anxious to impart his learning. This might be OK if he read the Kama Sutra and that sort of thing. But Oscar goes for stuff which you wouldn't even use to prop up a wonky table. For instance, he's currently rattling through the works of Sigmund Freud.

I know this because last week he collared me in the Stone and told me so. He was agape and agog about what Siggy had to say on neurosis – which is what presently made me think of Oscar. The way he told it, Freud said a surefire cure for neurosis was to get the neurotic to do something creative.

Which brings me back to the present. So what could I do that was creative? Way down there in my id or my alter ego a little voice hit on it: Expenses.

It was not the answer I really wanted but it was the best I could think of. Choking back a sigh, I rooted out a bunch of exes sheets and all the old bills I could find. I lodged my tongue between my teeth and got scribbling.

There are hacks I know who can knock out a week's exes as fast as I can write a story. I'm not one of them. I get bored too easily. I have to have little games built in to keep me going. This explains why the unremarkable surburb of Pinner, the insignificant town of Ware and the unlovely sprawl of Staines make so many guest appearances in my exes.

MONDAY: Dinner Ware

TUESDAY: Meal Staines

WEDNESDAY: Dinner Pinner.

I know. It's not laugh-a-minute stuff, but it keeps me entertained.

I was on my seventh week of exes and thinking that maybe neurosis was better than this when I heard the cheery clunk of Rosie's key in the door. I cast the sheets aside and reached for the gin.

She came in bright-eyed and pinkish around the gills. I pointed at the Gordons.

'No way. Verner says I've got to lay off it.'

'Who the hell is Verner?'

'He's my personal fitness coach,' said she primly.

Without even knowing the man I took an instant dislike to him.

I said, 'So tell me about it.'

She went at it head first, leaping like a hyperactive gazelle from one thing to another. She didn't take breath either. I got my decoding gear going and pieced the whole bit together in chronological order. The Krysto Studio, for such was it called, occupied the second and third floor of a new block in Long Acre. The second floor was given over to exercise bikes, boats and walkers, a gym with all manners of iron-pumping devices, and a place where the girls could frolic and leap about. Up the spiral staircase was a sauna, showers, and off to the right, a restaurant.

'A restaurant?' I was intrigued. 'I thought these were ladies who didn't lunch.'

She'd had a very nice meal, thank you. Chicory salad, washed down with an impertinent little carrot juice.

I said, 'You must be starving.'

'No,' she lied bravely.

'Well, what were the other women like?'

'Why do you want to know?'

'Just out of interest.'

'I'll bet.'

I gave up on that. 'Then tell me about Verner.'

Verner was his first name. He didn't seem to have a second one. He was the big cheese thereabouts. He was the one who ran his eyes over the girls' bodies and made the subtle distinction between what was a curve and what was a bump. It's a dirty job, but someone's got to do it.

Verner was living testimony to mind over fatty matter. A big geezer with muscles and sinews and all that. I was disliking the oik more by the minute.

Rosie thought he was terrific. He was working out her very own exercise and diet regime to get her back into shape.

I said sourly, 'I bet he wants you to trim your tum.'

'Yep. And my hips.'

I said, 'Verner's a perv.'

No. He was witty, charming, helpful, dedicated, handsome, considerate, clean-living. All the things I'm not.

I'd had enough of Verner. 'Anyways, I'm off to eat. Care to come and watch?'

She wobbled, but she said yes.

Just for badness I chose her favourite Indian nosherie where, as usual, we were greeted as the last of the big time scoffers.

Rashid paled when Rosie said no, nothing for her.

'What would you like to drink?'

Another zero. Rashid, a stricken man, turned his big black eyes on me.

I said, 'A couple of bottles of Cobra in a pint glass, a handful of poppadums – plain and spicy – a chunk of nan, chicken dhansak, bombay aloo, cauliflower bhaji, and, oh, all the rest.'

He was touched. He fled to fulfil my order and tell the guys out back about the crazy woman out front.

I ate slowly and with enormous relish. Rosie averted

her eyes and studied the gold tigers chasing each other round the restaurant walls.

I said, 'What about Gabriella? Was she there?'

She was back down Dulwich with her feet up. But guess what? She'd left a prezzie for Rosie.

Rosie fished it out of her purse. It looked like a credit card. I was underimpressed.

'It's my year's membership of the Krysto Studios. I can go there whenever I like. And it's free.'

'Zowie.'

She tossed her curls. 'If I was paying for it, this would cost two, maybe even three thousand pounds.'

Now I was impressed. 'What – sixty quid a week just to pedal a bike that doesn't go anywhere?'

'Sybil says it's the best money she's ever spent.'

'Sybil?'

Sybil was from Blackheath. Her chum, Kate, was from Greenwich. And they'd all had a chinwag as they chewed their chicory.

I said, 'I suppose they're a couple of heavyweights who need to lose a stone here and there?'

An emphatic no. 'They're slimmer than me. But they've been going to the studios for a few years, sometimes three times a week.'

'And they're skinny?'

'Slim,' she corrected. 'They've got marvellous figures.'

No they haven't. They've probably got flat tums.

Rosie suddenly let loose a throaty chuckle. 'The funny thing is they're really depressed about their weight.'

'So they should be.'

'No, you don't understand. You see, every time you go to the studios, you get weighed and measured and it's all entered up on your personal chart.'

'And?'

'And ever since they've been going, their weight has been coming down. But now it's started going up again. I mean, I'd love to be as slim as them, but they're panicking over ounces. I've got *pounds* too much.'

'Maybe their bodies have reached a plateau,' I said sagely.

A flounce of the curls. 'Verner says there's no such thing as a plateau. He says—'

I switched off. I'd had enough of Verner for a lifetime.

I ate only half the nan, and the bombay aloo was surplus to requirements. I coaxed Rosie, but she wouldn't bite. She even turned her nose up when Rashid weighed in with the mint chocs.

We tripped off home, me feeling like a barrage balloon and Rosie prancing along like one of those supermodel waifs you read about.

Back at the ranch I settled down with a gin, she with a glass of lemon tea. I wasn't worried. This time next week she'd have the bottle at her lips again.

We were talking away about nothing in particular when she said, 'Remember last week?'

'All seven days of it.'

'No, I mean Saturday, the night we went to the Cardigans.'

'It's enshrined in my memory.'

She said, 'All right. And remember on Sunday I tried

237

to tell you something that Gabriella Cardigan had done, but you wouldn't listen.'

I had a vague recollection along those lines.

Rosie said, 'It was when we were leaving, you know, out in the hall.'

'What about it?'

'Well, when you were saying cheerio to Wedge and Jason she gave me this.'

She dived into her handbag and pulled out a mitt stuffed with a bulging envelope. She didn't have to tell me what was making it bulge.

Two sodding grand.

Chapter Eighteen

I have a set routine about waking up in the morning. First of all I open my eyes slowly to check they can still focus. Then I move my head ever so gently from side to side. Sometimes this is not such a smart idea. And after that I switch on the radio to hear what's new with the world.

This particular morning I bypassed the eyelid fluttering and the head shaking. And I didn't particularly care how the world had been behaving itself in the night.

The only thing in my mind was Gabriella Cardigan's two grand. It didn't take Einstein to work out what had happened. She'd seen me stuff the money behind the horsey statue or she'd spotted it anyway. She'd sneaked it out, waited until I wasn't looking, and slapped it right back in Rosie's hot little hand.

Naturally I'd had a go at Rosie for being daft enough to take it, and she'd got stroppy and said it had nothing to do with her. In which case why had she accepted the money? A reasonable question in the circumstances. But Rosie somehow turned that one upside down so that it was my fault. Anyway, it was pointless beefing at Rosie so I gave up and started being nice again. I had to dispense an awful lot of niceness before she found it in her heart to forgive me.

But all that was last night. What was bothering the hell out of me right now was Gabriella Cardigan's pathological need to chuck fifty-quid notes at me. And nipping smartly at the heels of that conundrum was another one: how do I slip the much-travelled two grand back to her without her shipping it straight back to me?

I was lathering up in the shower when the answer came. Jason. I said it out loud, a daft thing to do because I promptly got a mouthful of shampoo. When I'd finished gargling Wash 'N' Go, I worked out the next move. I would lure Jason to some deserted spot, say Hampton's, and threaten to quit as his hack teacher unless he pocketted this here two grand and gave it back to Mumsy when the whole story was over. I liked that idea. All the dynamics hung together. Now all I had to do was to con him into a tête-à-tête. A matey phone call should do the trick.

But when I got to the office there wasn't any time for matey phone calls. I lay the blame squarely at the door of Chief Superintendent Havis Turkington, a man whose very existence had gone unnoticed by me until this morning. The background was that up in Scarborough, all the chief supers in the country had got together to practise their Masonic handshakes and drink drink. In between such high jinks, one or other of their number would make a daft speech about some element of law enforcing, though what they know about law enforcement could be written in big writing on the back of a seaside postcard.

Turkington's speciality was prostitution. He was all

for it. 'Open a brothel on every high street,' he declaimed. 'Licence every hooker in the land.' 'Give 'em compulsory free health checks.' All that and more.

Turkington, from Cornwall, an area not exactly renowned for its red-light districts, even had sheafs of figures to back up his argument. According to his sums, the taxman could pull in fifty million in taxes from the working girls. On top of that you could add the million quid a year which the Old Bill currently blows on har-rassing the ladies.

And – and here's the beauty of it – legalized prosti-tution would free X zillion bobbies who could then devote their energies to catching motorists with faulty tail lights and defective wipers, thereby rendering Britain a land fit for heroes.

Angela Whipple summoned me from my corner and flashed the PA story up on her screen. 'You'll love this one, Max.'

I didn't say anything.

She said, 'Right, so here's what we'll do. I want a big run on page five – get some rent-a-quote politicians and vice people – and see if you can dig us up somebody who'll give us a first person news feature piece.'

I said, 'Are we for it or agin it?'

'Against it. Definitely.'

'Just so as I know.'

I trudged back to my corner looking murderous. I'll write up any old bilge they heave at me, but what pissed me off about this one is Angie had refused to let me go to the chief supers' beano on the grounds that it wouldn't throw up any stories. I'd sobbed and begged. I'd prom-ised I'd deliver a page lead every day, but she wasn't having it. The real reason she wouldn't let me go was because she thought I'd be up there for five days, drinking and enjoying myself. Which was also coincidentally the real reason I wanted to go in the first place.

I whinged for a while to Dinesh until he started to whinge back about the stupid job they'd saddled him with. I made an excuse and started phoning.

The news story fell into place without trouble. I opened up with a maverick lawman stunning top cops with his plan for street-corner brothels. I followed on with his planned £50 million lay-as-you-earn tax. And after that I did the rounds of churchmen, MPs, the Police Federation and assorted nutters who were all queuing to quote. I rattled off five or six hundred words and then sat back to think who I could get for the first person piece.

The lazy way round this is to ring a university, any university, and offer somebody a stack of money to write a yard of tosh. There's no problem in finding someone because the universities, the red-brick jobs anyway, send us detailed lists of bods eager to talk about every subject under the sun, and some above it. All these lecturers labour under the tragic illusion they are also red-hot journalists. They are encouraged in their folly by daft newspapers like the *Guardian* and the *Independent* who hire them to fill their features pages. They're a terrific cure for insomnia.

I wanted somebody better. I thought of one right away. And just as I was nuzzling up to the idea, I got another brainwave. I reached for the phone and rang the Cardigans. Jason answered.

'Jason! It's Max. Are you busy?'

He wasn't sure.

'Listen, I've got a super story, one that's a lot of fun. Fancy coming along for a laugh?'

His enthusiasm got the better of him. 'When?'

'Right now. Get here as quick as you can.'

He wanted to know what it was. Not so fast. He'd know when he got here. But it was one he'd remember. I had him hooked.

Next I went over to the chief silverback of the Monkey Desk and got him to uncage Frankie. My excuse was I needed a snapper to do a vox pop on what people thought about this legalized legover lark.

I copped the usual 'What a load of balls' from Frankie. I wasn't bothered. He'd thank me later. But I wasn't going to tell him my real plan straight off. He might melt. Instead I dragged him down to the Stone, by way of the reception where I left a message for Jason to meet us in the bar.

Deke the hired hand poured us a couple of pints and that shut Frankie up. But only briefly.

'I hate these stupid vox pops,' said Frankie.

'Me too,' I said truthfully.

'Where are we going to do it?'

'Paddington.'

'Paddington? Bloody Paddington? Why there?'

Because the person I want to speak to lives in Paddington. But I didn't tell him that.

He bitched his way down another pint and I let him because it makes him happy. He was waiting for me to cue up a third when Jason scooted in.

'What's the story?' he demanded.

'Who's he?' said Frankie.

I answered the second question and ignored the first. Enough small talk. I slapped my glass down on the counter and said, 'Right, let's go.'

Frankie wanted us to take the tube, or better still, for me to pay for a taxi. I insisted he took his jam jar. His driving alone would make it an experience Jason wouldn't forget.

So off we roared, across pavements, over people's toes, through brick walls, all the usual. I thought it only fair to let Jason sit in the front.

'Whereabouts in Paddington?' Frankie yelled above the blare of horns.

'Stick it in the station car park. That's close enough.'

'Close enough to where?'

I still didn't tell him.

It was only when we were strolling down Praed Street that a stray thought hit Frankie. 'Hey, this is where all the hookers hang out.'

Precisely.

I stopped by the nearest phone box and began gathering up the cards pasted all over its walls.

Jason spoke for the first time since he got in the car. 'What are you doing?'

'I'm collecting call girls' call cards. What does it look like I'm doing?'

Over his shoulder I saw Frankie's unlovely face crack into a hideous grin.

'I get it. We're going to do a vox pop among prostitutes.'

I shook my head. 'Nothing so dull. What we're going to do is find ourselves a genuine hooker, hire her for an hour and get her to talk to us. And after that, Frankie, you're going to take pretty pictures of her.'

Frankie was beyond speech. Jason was just about as bad. Fortunately there was one of us whose brain operates north of the groin.

I said, 'OK, each of you grab a handful of these cards and we'll sort out who we want to talk to.'

Frankie's first idea was Rubber Rhoda.

'No. No kinks, no kooks, no freaks.'

'What about a French maid?' asked Jason.

'No fancy outfits. What we want is straight sex.'

This sounds hard to believe but there must have been sixty different cards in that box. When we'd finished sorting, there were only four who fitted the bill.

I rang the first, 'Exotic beauty fulfils your wildest fantasy.'

A voice purred at me, "Allo. I am Mai Tong. I foo fih yo widest fan ha seee.'

I put the phone down. Frankie was aghast. 'Wot's wrong with her, then?'

'We need somebody who speaks English for a start.'

'What about this one?' said Jason shoving a card in my face. It had big curly writing. I read, 'English Rose 44DD invites you to explore her hills and dales. Travel cheques accepted.'

'Yeah,' said Frankie. 'Give her a bell.'

English Rose sounded as if she'd been waiting all her life for me to call. And yes, she was free right now. I didn't tell her precisely why I wanted her because she would have thought I was a wierdo. I just took her address and rang off.

Frankie and Jason both needed hosing down by the

time we got to her door. I hit the bell and listened to it tinkle out 'Land of Hope and Glory'. English Rose was obviously after the tourist trade. Nothing happened. We listened to 'Land of Hope and Glory' all the way through again. I was on the point of saying something rude when the door swung open.

It was a moment before I could speak. 'Are you Rose?'

She simpered. 'That's me.'

I breathed again. For one terrible moment I'd thought she was Belker in drag. But it didn't solve the big problem. And big is too small a word for it. English Rose was the size of Moby Dick. She was also about as old. OK, I might get the quotes from her, but she'd make a godawful picture. We'd need a double page spread just to get her chin in shot.

I said, 'Erm.'

She took it in her stride. 'Are you boys looking for someone less mature?'

That's one way of putting it. Maybe her skin was as thick as the rest of her because she wasn't offended. She just rolled twenty degrees and yelled over her shoulder, 'Monika. There's three here for you.' Then back to us, 'Come in, boys.'

I held back. I wanted to see what this Monika looked like. She was in no hurry to show herself. We stood there smiling stupidly at Rose and waiting for Monika to put in an appearance.

Eventually a bored and accented voice, 'Jus' comink.'

And then there was Monika. Not the best piece of totty I've ever clapped eyes on. But at least she was the better side of forty and of ordinary human dimensions. She was tallish, dark haired and fitted out in a lime-green trouser suit. It didn't do much for her complexion and vice versa.

Monika measured us up through straight across ice-blue eyes. Frankie looked penniless, Jason looked gormless and I looked the answer to every maiden's prayer.

'Three, huh? You all want, or some of you want to watch?'

I heard Frankie's tongue hitting his boots. I said, 'Perhaps we'd better come in and talk about it.'

'OK.' She turned with a shrug and headed off into the nether regions. English Rose kindly let us squeeze by her. Frankie enjoyed that.

I led the way down a hallway that reeked of something halfway between Brut and Harpic. The walls were scratched and scored as if five thousand head of long-horn cattle had just passed this way.

And so to the boudoir. An anonymous pastel cube with a small square window screened off behind a smaller square of Royal MacTavish Hunting Tartan. The bed itself, a low slung job, was draped in something flowery. There was also a faded red divan and a mela-mine bedside table with one of those bubbly oil lamps. The only other decoration was a repro print of a girl with bright blue breasts admiring them in a pool.

Monika pointed at the divan, 'Sit down. Relax.'

I said, 'Hello, Monika. I'm Max, this is Jason and that's Frankie.'

She couldn't have cared less. She said, 'What do you want?'

'An hour of your time, but not for sex.'

Monika said, 'You want a massage?'

'Well, actually—'

But before I could explain, she was into her spiel and her many specialities. She rattled through the catechism in tones that reeked of cigarettes and boredom. I must lead a sheltered life because I didn't know what half the things were. She also detailed her sundry charges. Throughout she kept her gaze battened on me because I was the only one who looked able to afford her.

From her accent, I guessed that Monika came from somewhere well east of Dover, but her English was up to the job. When she was all through I said, 'We're not here for that: we just want to talk to you, and take your photograph.'

She reacted as if I'd said something hideously indecent. 'To *talk*?'

It took me a good four minutes of fast talking before I convinced her we were not a trio of crazed deviants. She was still a bit grim but she'd latched on.

She said, 'Two hundred pounds. Up front.'

I didn't have that much on me. 'Make it one-fifty, and we'll throw in a whole bunch of snaps.'

'Schnapps?'

'Photographs.'

'Oh.'

She drew circles with her toe on the rusty carpet. The gimlet gaze came up again. 'What about him?' That was meant for Jason.

I said, 'He's—'

'I've got thirty pounds,' said the cretin.

Monika said, 'Okay, one hundred and eighty. For half an hour. Money first.'

I hauled out the last of Frankie's grubby tenners, counted them and laid them on the bedside table. Jason chucked his nice crisp notes on to the pile. I placed my palm flat on top of them.

I said, 'This is what you get for an hour.'

She shook her head. 'Half an hour.'

I fetched a sheaf of the phone kiosk cards out of my pocket and said: 'An hour, or we go to see Stunning Tanya, or maybe the Biggest Boobs in Town, or Luscious Nymphet Emmanuela. It's a buyer's market, Monika. Take it or leave it.'

She took it. She began hauling off her trousers. 'You want the pictures first?'

The other two did, but I said balls to that. So I started on the questions. Her name was Monika with a 'k'. She was Czech and she was twenty-nine. The Czech bit I believed. And what did she think of the chief super's idea for licensed brothels? She was horrified. And why? Well, because . . . she floundered for a while before she came up with some waffle about the privacy of her clients.

It wasn't a bad line, especially when she mentioned closed-circuit TV surveillance. I didn't quite catch the drift of this, so she explained: 'On the streets, at the banks, the shops, everywhere, there are these video cameras. If you have a brothel, all the people goink to it will be photographed. Many customers are very shy. They don't want people to take pictures of them.'

Then she regaled us with what her clients got up to and I wasn't surprised that they were averse to having their snaps taken. Half the time I couldn't hear her, on account of the two halfwits panting on either side of me.

I got all I needed in half an hour. Any longer and Frankie would have self-combusted. He creaked himself upright and said winningly, 'All right, love. Get your gear off.'

She was up for it. Maybe twenty years back she'd had a gatefold in Bouncing Czechs magazine. The trouble was she thought she still had the equipment. This was going to need some fancy camerawork. But Frankie was undismayed.

I got busy mugging through my notes while Jason goggled and Frankie flashed. I suppose I glanced across at her from time to time. I'm only human. We still had ten minutes of the hour left when she announced, 'Enough.' She started putting on her kit again.

Frankie said, 'OK, I'll do a couple in the street with your clothes on.'

There's a first time for everything I suppose.

Monika was curiously unkeen to be snapped fully dressed, but old silver-tongued Frankie talked her into it. Back out on to Praed Street where he popped a roll or two. English Rose watched the proceedings with crinkled up eyes. Monika evidently had to be paid extra to smile.

I looked at my watch. It wasn't even two o'clock and we had the whole thing wrapped up. This called for a drink. I rounded up the other two and dragged them away.

Monika called after us, 'Send me my photographs.'

And English Rose, sporting a rubber smile, said, 'Come back soon.'

'Sure,' said Frankie. He may not have been kidding.

Every department in a newspaper hates every other department. News looks down on Showbiz. Features look down on News. Showbiz looks down on Fashion. Fashion looks down on City. And *everybody* looks down on the subs.

So when I got patched through to Features, the Dep. Feat. Ed. responded with his usual enthusiasm.

'An interview with a prostitute? *We* don't want it.'

Back to News Desk. 'Angie, Features are effing about.'

'Leave it to me.'

She went off to bully the Editor. So we had another drink. I gave her ten minutes and called Features.

'All right, let's have a look at it anyway,' said the Dep. Feat. Ed. 'But it sounds crap.'

'Well then, it won't be out of place on the Features pages.'

He couldn't think of a snappy comeback, which is why he's in Features and I'm in News.

I gave them near enough eight hundred words, and if I got a shade creative with Monika's quotes, it was only in the best interests of the story.

We piled back into Frankie's car and screamed off home. This time Jason didn't even notice the tide of slaughter. He was still too perked up by the sight of Monika in the raw. This was fine by me. It was just the way I wanted him.

In the office I perched him on News Desk where he
spent the rest of the day recounting his adventures to
Norbert, the Foreign Editor. Norbert got so excited he
bought the coffee.

I whiled away the afternoon doing nothing much
except keeping an eye on Jason, for I didn't want him
slipping off home before I could corner him. The only
other thing of note was a four o'clock phone call.

'Max!'

Damn.

'It's Tony Belker.'

And there was me thinking it was that Michelle
Pfeiffer again.

'I thought you were in Kenya.'

'I am.' He sounded tickled with himself.

'What's up? Is it monsoon season?'

No, the sun was shining or at least it had been before
it plopped over the horizon. Now it was a balmy evening
with waves lapping the beach and a soothing zephyr
rustling the palms.

Personally if I'd been there I'd be swigging a tall
glass of something and doing my best to pretend that
Alexander Graham Bell had not been invented.

He wanted to know if I'd had a look at the draft
contract yet. No, not yet. He said, 'Doesn't matter. I'll be
back next Wednesday and we'll get it signed, sealed and
delivered then. You're still looking forward to the job?'

I forced myself to say yes.

'Super. Next Wednesday then. And Max—'

'Yes?'

'I hope you've been getting in the right mindset.'

Er.

'I want you to have your ideas on stream from the word go.'

I said, quite truthfully, that I'd been doing a lot of thinking.

'Great. Can't wait to hear what you've got. Anyway, mustn't keep you. Just rang to touch base.'

I replaced the phone and lit a Bensons and counted off the days to Belker's return. There weren't enough of them. I'd been effing around long enough. With a sigh that came from my very soul, I picked up the phone again and dialled a number.

The geezer on the other end sounded pleased to hear me. He said, 'I was expecting your call.'

That was the only small talk. After that he consulted his diary, I pretended to consult mine. We hit on a time, a place.

He ended, 'Look forward to seeing you.'

I hung up with an even heavier sigh. I needed a drink.

I was back in the office long before knocking off time. From my corner I saw Jason reach for his coat. I got up and wandered over with an amiable smile pinned across my face.

'Well, how did you enjoy the Monika job?'

'It was mega. Thanks, Max.'

I said, 'Is that all I get?'

His brow went all crinkly.

I said, 'I was expecting a drink at least.'

'Oh, yes. Sure. Now?'

'Why not? Let's slip round to Hampton's and drink it dry.'

He was still looking worried. 'Well, I've no money. Or only a few pounds. I gave it all to Monika.'

My smile stayed where it was. 'No problem. They take plastic. And if you haven't got plastic, I do.'

You could see various thoughts chasing each other across his face. Chief among them was his burning desire to rush home and tell Mum and Dad all about Monika. They could wait.

I said, 'Besides, there's a couple of blokes I'd like you to meet. And Rosie'll be there.'

One of the lies worked. He said: 'OK.'

Hampton's was going through its early evening hush with gaggles of lawyers and knots of hacks manfully building up a head of steam. I returned the various salutations and marched straight through to the dining end. There was no one else there. Good.

Jason was perplexed. 'Where's the blokes you wanted me to see? Where's Rosie?'

'They'll be here any minute now. Let's sit.'

Babs wafted up behind me and grabbed me round the neck, pulling my head back on her pillows. She was in no hurry to let go and I suppose I didn't fight too hard.

She purred down at me, 'Have you got tired of Rosie yet?'

Deep amid her bosoms I wagged my head no. We both enjoyed that.

Jason said, 'I think I've got enough for a round.'

We ignored him. Babs said, 'Let me know when you do.'

I was hoping she'd ask me fifty more questions I could answer in the negative, but she unwrapped her arms and sighed. 'OK, what can I get you?'

Jason said, 'I'm not driving, so I suppose I could have a beer. Do you have Becks? Great, I'll have a Becks. Same for you, Max?'

Good God no. I have never let Becks cross my lips, or at least not since the day I read it was the favourite tipple of *Guardian* readers.

I stuck to Gordons and sent Babs away with a fond pat on the bottom. Sexual harrassment is compulsory in Hampton's.

Jason and I chewed the fat about Monika. He did just about all the talking. I waited until Babs had done the business before I got started.

I said, 'I want you to do me a favour. And it's got to be a secret.'

'Oh yes?'

I pulled the dog-eared envelope out of my pocket and slapped it down in front of him. 'This is your mum's money. I want you to take it for me.'

He sat back sharply. 'Uh-uh. Mum wanted you to have that. It's yours.'

I'd expected that. I said, 'Jason, we're mates. Aren't we?'

'It doesn't matter.'

'But we're mates?'

'Yes.'

I said, 'Right, well one thing about mates is they don't charge each other two grand.' I had to hush him up because he was all set to argue the toss.

I said, 'I took you under my wing in the first instance because it was a trade-off: the *Gazette* got an exclusive interview with your mum, and I got to show you the ropes. That was the deal your mum and I agreed.

'No. You can talk later. Anyway, your mum then goes and gets you to slip me this money. That wasn't what I agreed to. That was cheating. Besides, you and I get on well together. Rosie likes you too. She'd be really pissed off if I took all this money just for showing you around.'

I took a pull on my gin which gave him the chance to butt in. I didn't pay much attention.

I said, 'This is my cunning plan. I give you the money and then, say in a week or so, when you're back at hack school, you return it to your mum.'

The answer was no.

'All right, in which case I'm going to nip down to Harrods and buy you a couple of dozen pairs of Versace jeans which I'll dump on your doorstep. I'd say you were a thirty/thirty-two waist.'

'You wouldn't.'

'I would. Definitely no bigger than a thirty-two.'

Jason said, 'You know what I mean. You wouldn't do that.'

I leaned forward. 'I bet you a fiver that is precisely what I'll do. Want to bet?'

No. But he kicked up a din, arguing that I deserved the money – he called it moolah – for sharing my hack lore with him, for letting him see Monika with her boobs out, and generally for being an ace bloke. It was all very flattering but I was unmoved.

When he was done I slid the envelope across the table. 'Stick it in your pocket.'

A new line of argument suddenly hit him. He looked at me with his round soft eyes and he said, 'You're making me deceive Mum.'

I blinked.

He elaborated. 'I have never once lied to her, or deceived her. But if I do this, it's, well, it's just not right.'

Sometimes I forget other people have scruples. I'd have to think about this one. I puffed on a Bensons. In the meantime the least welcome bunce since the thirty pieces of silver lay untouched on the table between us.

'All right,' I said after a while. 'I don't want you to feel bad about it. Here's what we do. You *hold* the money for me for a couple of weeks while I have a serious think about it. If at the end of all that I still feel your mum should have it, I'll ask you to do the necessary. If not, I'll just ask for it back. OK?'

He spotted the flaw. 'Why should I hold the money until then?'

'Because I might lose it or something. I'd feel safer if it was with you.'

'But it still seems deceitful.'

'How? Because I'm asking you to look after it? What's wrong with that? You're just doing me a favour.'

He was still hedging. I got stern. 'Look, I've agreed to compromise by thinking it over. It's only fair you should compromise too.'

I should have hit on that earlier. Compromise is the natural antidote to scruple.

In the end he agreed but only after making me swear blind I would think really, *really* seriously about accepting it.

Now we'd got that out of the way I was anxious to move on to the interesting stuff. I didn't want us to be disturbed in the middle of it, so I yelled for Babs and got her to lay in a bottle of house red for me and a couple of doses of Becks for him.

I let her get well out of earshot before I started. 'So, when did your mum find out you were doing drugs?'

He sloshed Becks over his thumb. 'What?'

I said it again. I said it in the same way you would ask someone where they bought their suits.

He was slow to answer so I gave him a push. 'That night we were round at your place for dinner, she told me then.'

'She didn't!'

'She did.'

He wasn't drinking. He said, 'What did she say?'

I poured myself a measured ration of rusty red. 'Not a lot. Only that you were doing drugs. So when did she find out?'

'I don't believe you.'

'That's OK. I don't believe your big brown innocent eyes either. But I believe your mum.'

He was staring fixedly at me as if he expected my nose to start growing or something.

I said, 'So I asked her what you were popping, but she just said "the usual". What's the usual?'

'Why should Mum tell you that?'

'Well, we were talking about Joni, and I mentioned George and one thing sort of led to another, and that's when she came out with it.'

He went quiet and concentrated on getting the Becks in the glass this time. I just smoked and drank and waited.

He said without looking at me. 'I know what you're

doing, Max. You're putting me through the third degree – the same as you did that night down in the pub.'

We'd come to that one later. Right now I wanted to pin it down to the topic under discussion.

I said, 'Have you noticed anything funny about this conversation? All along you've been confirming what your mum told me.'

'What?'

Sometimes you have to join up the dots for them. I said, 'If your mum merely *suspected* you were on drugs, you would have stormed and stamped your foot and said balls. But you didn't.'

He was looking at me now. His voice was low. He said, 'All right, I've dabbled once or twice.'

'Yeah, and I occasionally have a drink.'

He slurped on his Becks. 'It's my own business.'

'Balls. It's also your mum's business, because you told her, and it's mine because she told me. Anyway, I don't want to have some hop head hanging around with me.'

He got defensive. 'I'm not on anything now.'

'But you were. I want to know what and when. And where you got it.'

He tried out a laugh for size. It sounded false.

I said, 'So tell me.'

He said, 'I want to use the toilet.'

'No way. That's the stunt you pulled last time. Besides, Hampton's don't like people shooting up heroin in their bogs.'

'It wasn't heroin.'

'That's a start. What was it then – Ecstasy, uppers, downers, acid, what?'

He got going at last. 'It was just stuff, the stuff every-body does.'

He saw my eyebrows go up.

'All right, it was E, a bit of skunk, maybe sometimes Billy Whizz, acid once or twice. Mostly it was just blow. That's it. Everybody's doing it. Everybody I know. But I never touched Charlie or skag.'

'Oh, that's all right then. Everything except cocaine and heroin. So now we know what you were popping or puffing, maybe you'd like to tell me about Joni.'

He hesitated. Then he said, 'I don't know about her.'

'Jason, I'm an expert at what I do. I know when people are taking the piss, and that's what you're doing right now. Let's hear it about Joni.'

He went schtum.

I said, 'OK. I'll tell you then. Joni was a right little popper too. Your mother told me that the first time I met her. She – your mum – was quite open about it. But that's because she wasn't supplying Joni. Therefore, my rapier intellect tells me that the only reason you won't talk about Joni is because you were her pusher.'

'I'm not a pusher.'

I shrugged. 'Maybe not. But you were her supplier.'

This time he didn't even try to deny it.

'And I reckon you were supplying George too.'

A spark of defiance. 'It wasn't like that.'

'What was it like then?'

He topped up his glass. I kept him locked in my sights.

He began hesitantly. 'It was ... it was more like doing a favour. Joni told me she did skunk in Holland and when she worked in Mum's place in Covent Garden she was able to score stuff around there. I said I could get some for her in Dulwich. Skunk was all she wanted. She gave me the money. But I wasn't making on it. I just picked it up for her.'

'From Fez.' That was a statement, not a question.

He nodded.

'And what about George? Did you do him favours too?'

This time the laugh was less shaky. 'George? Sometimes he used to pick it up for me.'

'And for Joni?'

Another nod.

I said, 'Let's get back to Fez. He and you seemed fairly matey that night we saw him.'

A smile with a sour edge. 'I was a good customer.'

'So why did he beat the holy hell out of you?'

That stopped him. I had to say it again.

'It wasn't Fez.'

'Sure. It was the National Front or the Dulwich Village Choral Society. Yes, I believe that.'

He said, 'It was your fault anyway.'

That was a new one. 'Me?'

He stuck his head down and talked into his glass. 'It was for talking to you.'

'Fez reckoned you were grassing on his little drugs scam?'

'Um-hum.'

I said, 'So how did he know who I was?'

'Because I told him – that night we saw him in Clutterbucks.'

Good God, the lad had the brains of a gnat. 'And why were you daft enough to tell him that?'

'He asked.'

I said, 'Let's stick this together. The Old Bill start leaning on people after I run stories about Joni's drug taking. Fez figures I'm getting my info from you, therefore he belts seven shades out of you.'

'It wasn't him.'

'All right, it was his mates.'

'Yes.'

I hadn't touched my glass for a least three minutes. I took a long swig. It hadn't improved with age.

I said, 'Did Fez top Joni?'

'Might have.'

'Jason, this isn't some minor incident which is just going to go away. The Law gets very mean about certain types of crime. One is parking on a double yellow, the other is murder. It's a close call, but murder is what really gets up their nose.'

He said, 'What are you saying?'

I took a breath. 'I'm saying the police are going to turn over everybody – including you – until they find out who wrapped a scarf around Joni's neck and throttled the life out of her.'

'It wasn't me.'

'I didn't say it was. But for all I know, the stuff you've been sitting on might have helped them find out who.'

He suddenly got worried. 'You're not going to tell them?'

I said, 'I should, but I won't.'

A flicker of gratitude.

I said, 'Now, have you anything else you've been hiding from me?'

Nothing else.

'Are you sure? Because if I find out you're still playing silly buggers, then that's it.'

He was sure.

We drank for a while in silence. There was something more he wasn't saying. I stayed very quiet just in case he changed his mind. I'd almost gone through another Bensons before I called time.

I said, 'All right. It's all out of the way now. That's the Spanish Inquisition over.'

He eased back and I realized he'd been holding himself tight throughout it.

I said, 'So let's talk of cheerier things. Another Becks?'

He said, 'Rosie's not coming, is she?'

'She's washing her hair tonight.'

A crooked smile. 'And the two blokes you said you wanted me to meet?'

'They're helping her.'

He said, 'You can be a right bastard, Max.'

I raised my glass to acknowledge the compliment.

He shook his head ruefully. 'I just can't understand why Mum told you.'

'She didn't.'

That jerked him back in his chair.

'She didn't?'

I said, 'What she told me was she was absolutely, *utterly*, one million per cent certain that you didn't do drugs.'

'Then . . .?'

'It's easy. There's not a parent in the land, from the Chief Commissioner upwards who can lay his hand on his heart and swear by all that's holy that his kid is not a secret popper.'

He was still confused.

I said, 'So the only parent who can be so openly certain is one who knows her kid *is* on drugs.'

It took a moment or two to sink in.

'You really are a bastard.'

This time he meant it.

Chapter Nineteen

I don't usually throw a sickie. It's unprofessional. No matter how grievous the hangover, I schlep off to the office and get on with it.

Today was different. Today I had the most ferocious imaginary toothache imaginable. I phoned News Desk to break the sorry news.

I cricked my jaw so that I could sound in agony. 'Hi, Angie. This is Max. I've got to see an emergency dentist. One of my molars is giving me gyp.'

I was going to say wisdom tooth, but I thought that was pushing it.

She had neither the time nor the sympathy to listen. 'Bloody hell, Max. There's a lot on at the Old Bailey.'

No there wasn't. She was just letting me know that this rampant absenteeism would not go unnoticed.

I said, 'I'll be in by lunchtime.'

'Oh all right then. As fast as you can.'

Next I made myself a pot of coffee and sat down with the morning's *Daily Mail*. I read every single news story in it, the showbiz piffle too. I even sampled half a dozen paragraphs of features. And when I was all done, I unearthed the *Mail* for the previous three days and swotted up on them too. When I was through I was world expert on which stories the *Mail* had run all week, what show each had got and who had written them. The coffee ran out just as I finished. I was ready to meet my fate.

We met in a boozer down Kensington High Street. That was his idea. I got there well ahead of time. I wanted to check it out to make sure there weren't any hacks from the *Standard* or the *Mail* in there for a swiftie. The place was devoid of riff-raff but I still felt uncomfortable. I collared a table a long way off the bar. It also gave me an oblique view of anybody coming in.

I was five minutes down my pint when Lucas Geany showed. He's a tall bloke and a slaphead long before his due. His glasses swivelled and picked me out. On went the smile. He came loping forward with his right hand stuck out.

'Max. Good to see you.'

'Drink, Lucas?'

'Too early for me. A Perrier.'

A Perrier. This did not augur well.

I rolled over to the counter and prodded the barman awake. As he fiddled around with ice tongs and the lemon slicer I ran over what I knew about Lucas Geany. There wasn't much. Like most news executives, his career as an on-the-road hack was distinguished by its mediocrity. I have met him at various parties and thrashes, but I bumped into him only once on the road. That was ages back, when he was a downtable hack on the *Sun*. He was riding shotgun on some flaky showbiz girl the *Sun* had bought up. The story was something to do with her bonking a once great footballer. Geany was not long on the *Sun* and I conned him into thinking I was from its Features department. I told him the office wanted him back, so off he went, leaving me to nick their exclusive. There must have been blood on the wall down Wapping when they found out.

And now here I was in my favourite two-piece, hoping that the man I'd conned might give me a job.

I returned with his foul drink and sat down again, shooting him a quick glance. I was trying to determine if he remembered the mischief I'd done him. Any proper hack would carry the memory to his grave, but News Desk people toss a cloak of selective amnesia over their days at the sharp end. And who can blame them?

'So, I hear you would like to join us,' he opened.

I can be patronizing too. I said, 'I heard your crime job is open and Neil said you might be interested.'

'I thought you were settled at the *Gazette*.'

'I am. Unless something better comes up.'

Geany didn't like the way this was going. A frown. He said, 'I want to move away from this old image of the foot-in-the-door crime man. That's way past its sell-by.'

So was his tie. I just smiled brightly. But not too brightly.

Geany said, 'We've got to look at the bigger picture. We want a crime man who can turn his hand to writing an instant feature. Someone who can deliver an exposé, as well as covering any breaking stories.'

Oh, is that all?

I said, 'The *Gazette*'s moving the same way. I've got the main Features page today.'

'Yes, I saw that.' That's all. He didn't think much of it.

I said, 'Any crime man is only as good as his sources.'

'Yes, but they've got to be the right sources. The

days of reporters in grubby macs meeting detectives in smoke-filled bars are gone.'

I was sorely tempted to say bollocks. Then the bloated image of Belker swam to mind and I remembered my predicament. I nodded sagely.

Geany said, 'Today's crime reporter should be on first name terms with judges, top coppers, lawyers, politicians. The decision makers.'

'It's got to be the right decision makers.'

He changed course. 'So why do you want to quit the *Gazette*? You've been there how long?'

'Eight years.'

He shook his shiny bonce sadly. 'Eight years? That's too long in one place. Unless you go on to News Desk.'

So far the man had insulted my methods, my sources, my drinking habits, my career, my feature, my clothes. I reminded myself he was a News exec. You've got to make allowances.

I said, 'Desk work requires a certain mentality.'

Like Americans and most women, Desk people lack irony detectors.

Geany said, 'I have some very promising people lined up. What do *you* have to offer the *Mail*?'

I went into my pitch. I'm not going to tell you what I said, because even now I wake in the night and go Yeuch. He listened to it without interruption. When I had sufficiently abased myself he said, 'I might as well tell you, a couple of people have spoken highly of you.'

I heard the unspoken but.

He went on, 'And I've taken on board what you've said.'

Another silent but.

He said, 'I'll get back to you, Max. I've a couple of other people to see first. But I should be able to tell you by the end of next week.'

The end of next week. Bugger. Belker was coming back midweek.

I said fine, I'd look forward to it.

He frowned at his watch and said, 'Sorry to cut this short, but I'd better be off.'

We put our smiles on again and shook hands. I watched the light bounce off his pointy dome as he headed for the door. I was kicking over several thoughts, chief of which was: did I really want to work for a man who hadn't the decency to buy his round?

I taxied to the office where all was quiet. I made the usual checks but it looked like the villains were taking a day off from their labours. In the absence of anything useful to do, I called up my memory bank and got it to replay last night's session with Jason. I ran through it a couple of times before I hit on something. It should have made me sit up as soon as he'd said it, but I was too busy bullying him at the time.

I whistled softly to myself and went in search of Morven. Morven is our health correspondent. The reason she got the job, I suppose, is she suffers from half the things in the medical encyclopaedia.

Morven holes out at a desk on the fringes of Features. You're never altogether sure if she's there because her desk is stacked four feet deep in Kleenex boxes.

Today I was in luck. She wasn't off ill.

'Hiya Max,' she said chirpily.

This is hardly her usual style. Maybe she'd been to Lourdes or something.

I rolled up a chair and moored it alongside her. 'I need your help.'

'Professional or otherwise?'

You can forget the otherwise. Skinny girls are not my speed.

I said, 'Tell me about Ecstasy.'

For answer she pointed at a book the size of a beer crate. 'It's all in there. Bring it back when you've finished.'

I nearly gave myself a hernia carting the thing all the way back to my corner. I then fortified myself with a cup of machine tea and started flicking through the pages. I spent an hour with my head in it.

Whoever wrote the book was not into user-friendly English, and every now and then I had to reach for Dinesh's dictionary to help me over a hard bit. I found Ecstasy easily enough and I also ran up against a whole string of cross references. I took notes as I went along, for under all the seven-syllable words there was some hot stuff. It even supplied all the slang names – speed, poppers, the works.

I closed the book with a crump and lit a Bensons. I couldn't see them, but I'm guessing my eyes were deep and troubled, my forehead was lined with thought. I was not happy. There were bits that were coming together. The only problem was they didn't make a lot of sense. Unless . . .

'How's your icky toot peg?' Angela Whipple.

'Behaving itself again.'

She hoisted herself up on my desk so we could both admire her legs.

'What was it – a loose filling?'

'Something like that.'

She said, 'They can be a real bugger.'

This sudden burst of sympathy threw me. I leaned back and took a good look at her. When I spoke to her a couple of hours back, she'd been a right old grouch. Now she had a smile loitering around the corners of her lips and it had nothing to do with our present conversation.

I said, 'You seem sparky today.'

'Me?' There was something giddy about the way she said it.

'So what have you been up to?'

'Nothing. I've just had a very pleasant lunch.'

That wasn't true. She was still sober.

I said, 'And the company was good?'

'*Very* good.' She was flexing a fully-grown grin now. There was something funny going on here.

'So whatever it is, you're not going to tell me?'

'That's right. But I'll tell you one thing.'

She leaned forward and put a cool hand on my cheek. I could smell Bilberry or Dewberry or something. She looked me in the eyes and said, 'You're all right, Max. You're OK.'

She got up and tottered away.

Late in the afternoon Neil Milltain called. I was expecting as much.

'Well? How did it go?'

I said, 'I thought you might tell me.'

Milltain said, 'I only had a brief word with Geany.

He seems to rate you, so I reckon you're in with a good chance.'

I threw away my last shred of self-respect. 'Geany said he's got some other people to talk to. Who're they?'

'There's only one who's any danger. He's on the *Independent*. He's got all the right credentials – public school and all that – but he doesn't have our contacts. I think you're probably there, Max.'

I made a last bid to restore my dignity. 'Maybe. Geany hasn't spelt out the package yet. If it's not good enough, I'm staying put.'

'It'll be good enough. You'll even have enough to buy me that pint you owe me.'

He rang off, the smug git.

The day trickled past. The only other item of note was I picked up £1,700 in exes and in a burst of reckless generosity I deposited all but a couple of hundred in the bank. There should have been bands playing and flags flying. But the bank didn't seem as moved by this largesse as it ought to be.

For some strange reason I didn't feel like knocking it back with my mates that night. I rumbled round to Rosie's instead. She wasn't there. Sometimes she can be downright thoughtless. Rosie, for some quaint reason of her own, has never supplied me with a key to her gaff – though she's got one to mine, so I slouched off to the pub on the corner and made merry with a couple of pints of Fosters.

After nearly half an hour of such hell-raising, I got

out the mobile and phoned her. This time she was home. She said, 'I want to see you.'

I said, 'Ditto.' But I got the impression she wanted to see me in a different way from how I wanted to see her.

She was wearing a long grey ribbed sweater thing. It was very fetching but it seemed to drain the blue out of her eyes. They were stone grey and serious.

I said, 'Hello my little chickadee,' and stuck my arms out.

She just gave me a wintry look. 'You're going to turn Jason over.' It was an accusation.

So this stuff about feminine intuition was true. I was standing there with my mouth open and my arms out. She swung around and trotted back into her flat. I followed.

'Why?' She demanded. She was standing. Her hands weren't on her hips, but they gave that impression.

I said, 'Where have you been?'

'Out. Why have you got it in for Jason?'

When in doubt, pour yourself a gin. I did. I offered her one too. She scorned it. Then I sat down, draped one knee over the other and admired my consumate skill at blending Schweppes and Gordons in just the right proportions. Really, I was treading water and trying to sort out why Rosie was acting up.

Light dawned. 'You've been to Gabriella's gym again.'

'The studios.'

'And Gabriella was there.'

She didn't answer, but I knew I'd got it right. And I also knew the rest of it. Jason had gone bleating to Mum after I'd given him a going over. She in turn had had a pop at Rosie. That was outside the rules.

I said. 'If she's got a problem, she should work it out on me.'

Rosie said, 'I'm on her side. I like Jason.'

'He likes you too.'

'Why are you giving him a hard time?'

I said, 'What did Gabriella say?'

'What did *you* say to Jason?'

'I can't talk to you like this. Sit down. Please.'

Rosie sat on the far end of the sofa. She said, 'I mean, Max, how can you be such a bugger to a nice kid like Jason?'

'You're right. He's the nicest drug pusher I know.'

'You're just making that up.'

'OK. I'm making it up. That's what he told me anyway.'

Rosie's eyes went big and round. 'He *told* you he was pushing drugs?'

'Yessiree. And his mum knows all about it. He was supplying Joni Poelma. Remember her? The one who got herself strangled?'

In the ensuing silence I unwrapped a fresh pack of Bensons and got puffing. She showed no inclination for speech so I kicked in.

'I'm surprised Gabriella didn't tell you the whole bit. Like why she's suddenly turned into our fairy god-mother.'

Rosie said, 'Meaning?'

I got exasperated. 'For God's sake, Rosie. A woman you've never met before bungs you free membership of an exclusive gym, membership worth a couple of grand. Do you not wonder why?'

She said, 'Because she owns the studios and it didn't

cost her anything. Because she was grateful that you were looking after Jason.'

I said, 'That's the cover story.'

Her turn to be stroppy. 'There's always a cover story with you. Nothing is ever straightforward. For once in your life, can't you accept that there isn't some bloody conspiracy? She was just being generous.'

'I suppose the same goes for the two grand she keeps forcing on me?'

'Jesus Christ, there's no talking to you. The Cardigans have loads of money. And Gabriella said you've been bloody marvellous to Jason.'

'Not that bloody marvellous.'

She clicked her tongue and stood up. She went over to the corner and poured herself a beefy gin. This must be getting to her.

I said, 'Gabriella's narked because of two things. First, I won't take her hush money.'

'What's the second?'

'I got Jason to cough to selling Joni drugs.'

Rosie said, 'Tell me exactly what Jason told you.'

I gave her a precis, tacking on the line about him being beaten up by Fez's cronies. She was thoughtful after that. I had another gin, smoked another cigarette.

She said, 'You said the two thousand was hush money.'

'Yep.'

'But when she gave it to you, you had no idea Jason was involved in drugs so how could it be hush money?'

True. I'd a slight problem with that one myself. I said, 'Maybe it was a sweetener, just to make sure I didn't look too closely at Jason.'

Rosie said, 'Or it might have been a genuine gift.'

That was also just about possible.

I said, 'But when I gave it back to her, she should have stopped there. Instead she forced it back on me. Why? Because she wanted me to stay sweet.'

Rosie said, 'So does this mean you're going to expose Jason as a pusher?'

'That depends.'

'On what?'

'On Joni Poelma. I've said all along that she was topped because of some drugs link. If it turns out it had something to do with Jason's little deals, then yes. I'll blow the lot.'

'Are you saying he might have killed her?'

It took me a couple of seconds before I answered. Even then I hedged my bets. 'Maybe.'

She looked at me and her eyes were still grey. 'If you think Jason's capable of murder then you're even more warped than I thought you were.'

'So he's innocent, because he's a nice kid, and he's got big brown eyes, and a goofy smile. Is that it?'

She didn't say anything. But that was it.

I said, 'And naturally, such a sweet, goofy, brown-eyed guy couldn't be a drug pusher either.'

She said, 'Oh shut up.'

I shrugged. I finished my gin. I even washed the glass. Then I put on my Burberry again and went out. We didn't say goodbye.

Back at my own flat the ansaphone was blinking. I played it back. Whoever had rung hadn't left a message. He/she had just listened in silence for ten seconds and hung up. I rang 1471. It told me that the caller had withheld their number. So that was a fat help.

The phone trilled about an hour later. I said, 'Hello.'

There was a moment of indecision at the other end. Then, 'Max Chard?' A man's voice, gruff and indistinct. But not that indistinct.

'Who's speaking?'

'Leave Jason Cardigan alone.'

'Are you threatening me?'

He put the phone down. I stood there with the receiver in my hand. I didn't need to call 1471. I already knew his number.

It was Wedge Cardigan.

Friday I was due a day off. Plan A involved me tacking down to Regent Street to prospect for shirts and that sort of thing. After all, I'd money to spend, and this time it was rightfully mine. Besides, Rosie hadn't called and I needed cheering up.

But as I ploughed through the day's acre of newsprint with the radio on for company the news cut in. Item three was: *'Police in Essex have issued a warning over a particularly dangerous form of Ecstasy after two teenagers collapsed at an all night party.*

'The warning follows the death last week of a twenty-year-old London man . . .'

That was George. I'd clean forgotten about him. On impulse I grabbed the phone and gave Dulwich nick a call. I got through to the incident room.

'Mister Skelly, please.'

'Who's calling?'

'Just tell him it's Max. He'll know.'

'One moment, Mister Chard,' said the brightest cop in London.

'Hello?' Skelly himself. Wary.

What the hell, I went for it. 'Hello, Tom. Fancy a pint and a pie?'

'Why?'

Because I pine for your sparkling repartee, your smooth urbanity, your duck-egg eyes.

'Because I thought we might have a bit of a chat.'

'What about?'

This was tougher than I thought. I said, 'The last time we talked you helped me and maybe I helped you. You also told me to keep it under my hat. I haven't printed a line of it, have I?'

'No.' Grudgingly.

'Well, then, how about it?'

'Make it eleven-thirty in the Coterie. That's the wine bar near the nick.'

'I know it.'

I got there to find Skelly already in residence, a glass before him with maybe a teaspoonful of Grouse in the bottom.

I said hello and without pausing rustled up a large G&T and a matching Grouse. Skelly said, 'What have you got?'

I poured tonic and didn't rush it. I said, 'Fez was supplying Joni and George.'

He forgot himself. 'Fez has legged it.'

I tucked that one away. I said, 'He was pushing the whole range – acid, Ecstasy, cannabis. The works.'

'How do you know?'

I said, 'I've been talking to a few kids. None of them will talk on the record. Seems Fez gives a right spanking to anybody who talks.'

Skelly looked at me sharply.

'Like Jason Cardigan?'

I said quickly, 'No. That was a domestic. He'd nicked some other bloke's girl.'

'And you believe that?'

'Sure. Why not?'

Skelly purred a laugh. Somebody had been telling tales.

He said, 'You were right about Joni and George. Them being girlfriend-boyfriend, I mean.'

So it was George's old man. I said, 'Did his dad know where George was getting the stuff?'

'No,' he lied.

I said, 'What about Fez – has he got form?'

Skelly put down his glass and said, 'You're just pumping me for information.'

Good grief, the man must be a detective or something.

I said, 'It's a fair cop, guv. You've got me banged to rights.'

He digested this and went quiet. He was thinking in there.

After a moment he said, 'All right, you did me a favour. Not a big one, but it helped.'

I waited for it.

Skelly said, 'You went out to Genk, didn't you? What was Joni Poelma's house like?'

Eh? Maybe the drink was getting to him. I answered

anyway. 'Just an ordinary place, three-up, two-down. It might have been a council house.'

He said, 'So nothing fancy?'

'Plain and simple.'

Skelly emptied his glass. 'I suspected as much.'

I furrowed my brow. It's hard to follow the thinking process of your average Plod.

He shouted for more drink. We were still talking anyway.

I said, 'What's the house got to do with it?'

A fat smug smile. 'You reckon Joni was buying drugs off Fez?'

That's about the size of it.

The smile got fatter. 'Just say Fez was buying drugs off her.'

He knew something. I played the dumb stooge role. 'Why do you think that?'

He didn't answer right away. He fished out a pana-tella and slid the wrapper off all by himself. I lit it for him. From behind a cloud of blue smoke he said, 'This is one hundred and one per cent off the record.'

I nodded.

He said, 'If you use any of it, I'm in it up to here.'

I couldn't see up to where exactly because of the smoke, but I nodded again.

He said, 'How do you think a kid living in a council house gets to have nearly a hundred thousand Dutch guilders in her local bank?'

'Wow.'

'And her sister – the one the French drugs squad are holding – she'd three times as much in half a dozen different accounts.'

'So they were in it together?'

He shrugged, 'What do you think?'

I followed this down the line. 'And Fez topped her because he owed her?'

A nod.

I said, 'Why did he hang on to the body for a week?'

'We'll know when we catch him.'

I didn't say anything. I figured we were in for a long wait.

Chapter Twenty

You have to be in just the right mood when you go shirt shopping, otherwise you end up blowing fifty quid on something that hangs about in the back of the wardrobe looking as if it sneaked in when you had your back turned. I wasn't in the mood anymore.

If this were a normal day off I could phone Rosie and persuade her to pack away her crayons and join me in sinking drink. I rang through to my ansaphone but she hadn't called, which meant she was still throwing a moody. She can be a right stroppy little strumpet at times.

So what to do? This is pathetic but true. I went to the office. I suppose the general idea was to root out a drinking mate or two. A forlorn hope. Some TV after-noon-quiz-show smarm ball had done a runner with an actress half his age and twice his chest measurement. Half a dozen hacks were on the case. Monkeys too were scattered to the four corners of the metropolis.

There was nothing else for it. I'd hit Hampton's. I was breezing through Newsroom when Angela Whipple gave me a shout. No doubt she had some old bilge from Horseferry Road Magistrates Court that she wanted me to tickle up. I plodded Deskwards with a glower which was meant to say, 'I'm on a day off. Give it to somebody else.'

She read it five yards off. 'It's all right. It's not a story. I just thought I'd buy you a drink.'

My first reaction was why. She saw that too.

'It's something I want a quick word about,' she said. Big smile, eyes wide and candid. She was up to no good.

I said, 'All right.'

I had to hang around waiting while she briefed her idiot deputies, made two phone calls, got her coat on and then slipped away to powder her snoot. She finally reappeared not looking very much older. 'OK?'

We walked straight past the Stone and round the corner to a run-down boozer which I use only as a last resort. She bought them in. We perched the drinks on a ledge glued to a pillar. Right, I thought, now what's all this about.

She was in no hurry to tell me. First of all she found herself a stool which she dragged across from the far corner of the bar. Next she went and hung her coat up. After that, she remembered her mobile, so she had to go and get that out of her coat. I tried to pretend she wasn't with me.

'Well,' she said when she was roosted back up on the stool, 'and what are you doing in the office on your day off?'

I said, 'Expenses.'

She wasn't listening. She said, 'I've been hearing things about you.' The smile was coquettish.

'They're all true.'

Her eyebrow crooked. 'Especially the story about the *Daily Mail*?'

Here is a word of advice to those who value their privacy: don't ever become a tabloid hack.

I lit a cigarette. 'And what story is that?'

'Come on, Max. We've known each other long enough.'

'I'm not with you, Angie.'

'Not for long, I hear.'

I sighed. 'Look, Lucas Geany gave me a call and said he'd like to talk to me about the *Mail* crime job. That's all.'

She shook her head. 'That's not what I heard. What I heard was that you approached the *Mail*. And Geany has already seen you. Right?'

I suppose I could have lied but it wasn't worth the effort. Anyway she wanted to do the talking.

'It's a good job. Good money too.'

I said, 'I don't know. It was only a preliminary discussion. I just wanted to see how Geany came across.'

'And?' There was mischief in her eyes.

'And what? I talked to him for a couple of minutes. We didn't go into details.'

She put her hand on my arm and said earnestly, 'Go for it, Max.'

It's bad enough when Desk people tell you how to write a story. When they tell you what to do with your life, that's abusing things.

I said, 'If there's a good enough deal on the table and if I think Geany and I can hit it off, then I might be interested. Otherwise, I'm staying put.'

She laughed. 'Don't try to snow me, Max. From what I hear, they're keen. And don't worry about Geany. You'll have no trouble getting on with the *Mail* Desk.'

I was getting a bit pissed off by now. All Angie wanted was to get me out of the *Gazette* so that I didn't nick her stupid job. I remembered yesterday and her cryptic 'You're all right, Max.' Somebody at the *Mail* must have grassed and that's why she was so cutesy.

I said, 'You want to know what I really feel?'

'Sure. Fire away.'

'I'm going to stick with the *Gazette*. I don't rate Geany and the job isn't all it's cracked up to be.'

This was said just to scare her. It was a spectacular failure.

I felt the hand on my arm again. She put her face right up close to mine and gave me the full treatment with her eyes.

'You'll love it. I *know* you will. Any decent News Editor would be glad to have you.'

I said, 'Except you.'

That stopped her. She busied herself chucking back wine. Then she said, 'I'm thinking of your future.'

And your present. Now I was really narked. I said, 'Forget it. But you could do me a favour.'

'Ask it.'

'Whoever you've got as a snoop at the *Mail*, tell him I think Geany is a baldy waste of space. Tell him to spread it around. I don't care what they're paying, I'm not taking the job. Now, I've got exes to do. I'd better be going.'

I left the glass though it was still half full and headed straight for the door. Angie shouted after me. 'You'll take the job.'

At the door I was so wound up I nearly knocked an incoming punter skew-whiff. We snarled at each other.

I stomped back to the office in a vile bate. It was a combination of things. Bloody Jason, bloody Gabriella, bloody Rosie, bloody Skelly, bloody Angela Whipple.

The sensible thing was to roll off to Hampton's and lay into it, but I wasn't fit company for man or beast. I mooched around drinking plastic tea and trying to talk myself down. After three cups of it the bromide began to take effect but I still didn't feel up to conversation and that's precisely what Dinesh was offering.

I grunted and eddied off to the library monitor. There was no real plan. I just wanted to be alone. I pressed the buttons and up flashed the menu. Now, what did I want to look at? Nothing really, but seeing I was here I keyed in POELMA, JONI, and tagged on ALL CUTTINGS. The computer told me it had seventy-four listed. I reckoned that reading through that little lot would get me back to my civilized self.

I started with the most recent and worked back. I split the screen so that I could have four stories showing on it simultaneously. There was nothing new, apart from a heap of wondrous inventions by my tabloid brethren. After half an hour, I'd read through all but four and I hadn't found anything. I was just about to switch off, but, sad obsessive that I am, I called up cuttings three and four. The left side of the screen showed the *Sun*'s first splash on her disappearance. The right side featured our own front page. I looked at them for maybe fifteen seconds before I saw it.

'Jesus!' I said.

I looked at them again. There it was in black and white. I pressed the PRINT button and ran off two copies. Just this once the printer forgot it hated me and the copies came shuttling out of it so clear you could actually read them. I lit a cigarette and smoked it all the way through, all the while staring at the two front pages, but I'm not sure that I was seeing them.

I switched off the machine and stood up. Now I deserved a drink. But before I could treat myself to a stiff one, I was distracted by the sound of shennanigans around News Desk. There was a war going on over there. Raised voices, angry words, vicious insults, the whole caboodle. I sat down again so that I could enjoy the bloodshed. Every other hack in the room was doing likewise. At the centre of the ruckus Angela Whipple was copping an earful from Goff, the Night Editor, a truly unspeakable man.

I listened awhile and pieced it together. The *Express* had bought up the jilted wife of the smarmy TV quiz-show host. The *Mirror* had snaps of the fugitive lovers. The *Sun* was sitting on the mum of the actress. And us? We had nothing. Hence the barney.

Goff was yelling, 'For Christ's sake, this is the splash. And you've got bugger all of a story. What sort of News Editor are you?'

Angie was standing up. She had knotted a daisy chain of paper clips and she was swinging it to and fro. She didn't seem all that bothered. She even had a trace of a smile. That, more than anything, had Goff frothing at the mouth.

He yelled, 'All you can do is stand there with a stupid grin on your fat face.'

Angie resorted to her feminine wiles. 'Go and stuff yourself,' she said sweetly.

Except she didn't say 'stuff'.

Goff was climbing the walls. Around him on the Back Bench the bunch of social lepers who call themselves subs were snarling and generally joining in the fun. On News Desk everybody else was keeping his head down. Angie had to face this one all on her todd.

Any other day of the week I'd be rooting for her, but I was still a touch embittered by her sneaky ploy to get me to quit. Therefore I didn't particularly care which of them lost.

Goff, his weasly mug all pinched and poisonous, roared, 'What did you say?'

Angie repeated it, this time adding that his toadying subs should go and stuff themselves too.

This was great theatre. In newspapers you don't usually get to see executives stabbing each other in the front.

Goff snarled, 'Right! Let's see the Editor.'

Angie mimicked him, 'Let's see the Editor. For God's sake grow up, you little fart.'

Hushed breaths all round. Night Editors are indeed noxious gas balls, but it's not a wise idea to remind them of it. For one lovely moment it looked as if Goff might have a coronary. He gargled air. He pointed a waxy finger at Angie, 'You, you're fired.'

Then he swung about and marched off to squeal to the Editor.

Angie stayed put. She glowered at Goff's Back Bench cronies. 'What are you bloody looking at?'

As of one, the snivelling underlings turned round and began mutilating reporters' stories.

We all waited, our eyes swivelling between a singularly unconcerned Angie and the big clock in the centre of the Newsroom. We were all thinking the same. Goff hadn't the power to fire Angie, but if he tells the Editor somebody should be fired, the Editor says, 'OK then' and fires them.

Almost ten minutes later the Editor's secretary came tip-tipping down the corridor and into the Newsroom. She went right up to Angie and whispered in her ear. We saw Angie nod her head yes. Back went the secretary to her den. Angie still hung around. She was reading stories and acting as if nothing had happened. I couldn't help myself. I was on her side.

Another five minutes ticked away and out popped the Editor's poppet again. Angie called, 'Two minutes.'

It was longer than that. Eventually she headed off towards the corridor. Her route took her past me. She said, 'Pop down to the Stone and set me up a large one. I'll be down in five minutes.'

No chance. I wanted to see the body being stretchered out.

Whatever they were saying in there in the Editor's office, they were taking their time to say it. We started reckoning the odds. The bets were that Angie was out on her backside. The Night Editor is way up there in the hierarchy, often second only to the Editor.

Goff emerged first wearing a yellow smile. The odds against Angie doubled. It was about here I started thinking of me. It was a chilling thought. I'd already been tapped to take her job. If she got the heave ho, I'd be appointed News Editor right now. I glanced across to her empty chair in the centre of News Desk. I tried not to picture me sitting in it ten minutes from now. Maybe I should have sloped off to the Stone after all.

Angie resurfaced. She wasn't in tears, but she wasn't smiling either. I beetled my brows at her. She said, 'Are you still here?'

I said, 'Do you still want that drink?'

She marched on, calling back over her shoulder. 'Later. I've got a paper to news edit.'

So she still had her job, for tonight anyway. I breathed again.

She had almost made it all the way to News Desk when she stopped, pivotted on a heel and came straight back to me. This time she was smiling.

She said, 'Silly me. I almost forgot – the Editor wants to see you.'

I said, 'Now?' It sounded hollow.

'Yep. Now.' And off she went again.

Oh God, this was it. I smoked a cigarette and pondered the options. There weren't any. The cigarette got all the way down to the filter and I still hadn't come up with anything. I rose slowly. I suppose I sighed as well. I shot a last glance at News Desk. Angie was back in her big black chair. She gave me a bright beam. It didn't help. Oh well, here goes.

I strode off through the Newsroom feeling about a hundred years old. Around me hacks jabbered into phones and battered hell out of keyboards. I didn't hear a thing.

It was quiet in the corridor leading up to the mock mahogany doors of the Editor's suite. It didn't feel like a newspaper. Petra, his secretary, her rear end to me, was stooped over stuffing bumf in a filing cabinet. Normally that's the sort of thing which brings light to the dark hours. Not today. She could have been buck naked and it still wouldn't have mattered.

I banged on the Editor's door. It sounded hollow too.

'Come,' said the Editor, a man of few words.

I entered and closed the door behind me. I didn't want anyone else to overhear what came next.

He was in shirt sleeves, brooding over a handful of page proofs littering his desk. He kept his bifocals focused on them for an unconscionably long minute. One of these days he should try a course in speed reading.

He looked up. 'Max.'

I owned up. 'Yes.'

'I've been meaning to have a word with you.' His gaze drifted back to the page proofs.

'Perhaps I should come back when you're less busy,' I said bravely.

'No. Now is fine.'

There was something bothering me. I couldn't place it at first. Then I got it. He hadn't asked me to sit down. Surely if he were about to make me up to News Editor he would park me in a chair, whistle up a glass of malt and treat me like his only son. Maybe he was going to fire me instead. A watery beam of hope flickered briefly in my darkness.

The bifocals were back on me. 'Tony Belker has already spoken to you of course?'

'Yes.'

'It's not about that.'

The watery beam got ideas above its station and started flooding my soul with light.

'Oh?'

The bifocals were suddenly accusing. 'Do you know Felix Pegg?'

Inside me brass bands were playing Dixie. I was slow to answer. 'I've met him.'

'Did you at any stage promise him a five thousand pound reward for finding that girl?'

I pursed up my lips and looked serious. 'Joni Poelma? As I recall, he asked me about the reward. He reads the *Gazette*.'

The Editor said, 'But you did not make any promises?'

'Me?' I trotted out a light laugh at so bizarre a suggestion.

'You see,' the Editor meandered on, 'the reward was for finding her alive. Dead didn't count.'

'Of course.'

A sigh from the big cheese. 'Unfortunately he seems to have got it into his head that he qualifies for the reward anyway. And he is most insistent that you promised it.'

I said, 'He's a very confused man.'

The Editor nodded his silvery bean. 'Perhaps you can straighten him out.'

Bugger.

The Editor said, 'I want you to go and see him tonight.'

I said, 'What about if we pay him a tip-off fee, say a couple of hundred? That might shut him up.'

'I am most averse to any payment. Our reward offer clearly stipulated that payment would be made only if the girl were found alive.'

Oh no it didn't. But I wasn't inclined to argue that right now.

I said, 'OK.'

'Good. Excellent. That's all, Max.'

The Editor returned to his page proofs. I turned to go. I had my back to him when he said, 'I believe you'll be seeing Tony next week?'

I did an about turn. 'Yes. Wednesday.'

'Um-hum.'

That was it. Nary another word passed. I found myself back out in the corridor with a scrambled egg where my brain used to be. The only coherent thought I could frame was 'Eh?'

Even later as I wallowed in a bumper gin I couldn't make any sense of it. Maybe I'd have to wait until Belker produced his accursed contract before the Editor deigned to smile and invite me to guzzle his scotch.

I could have stayed on in the Stone all night but for the unfinished business of Felix Pegg. I called him on the mobile. Yes, he was in residence, and yes, he wanted to see me. I cursed the man roundly, siphoned up the last millilitre of gin and made tracks.

The house in Sackville Road was in darkness. Maybe he'd gone off down the pub. I rattled the letterbox lightly. From way back in the house came the bronchial barks of Jack the Poodle. A yellow light gleamed through the grimy glass panel and presently a silhouette of Felix Pegg hove up.

'Who is it?' he yelled.

I resisted the temptation to play knock-down-Ginger.

'It's Max Chard.'

Much rattling of bolts and locks. The door opened a smidgeon. Then, when he was sure it was me and not the Big Bad Wolf in mufti, off came the security chain.

'I expected you earlier,' he complained.

I followed him down the gloomy hallway and into the room where we'd had our previous tête-à-tête.

He said, 'What about my five thousand pounds? Have you got it?'

I pulled out my Bensons. 'Do you mind?'

He probably did but he said OK. I took a long slow draw and asked, 'Are you by any chance familiar with the Press Code of Conduct?'

Fortunately he wasn't. He just repeated, 'What about the money?'

I said, 'Following representations by the Government and the Law Lords, it was agreed that newspapers would not in any way encourage, assist or otherwise promote financial rewards to criminals who seek pecuniary advantage from their misdemeanours.'

That threw him. I was having difficulty following it myself.

He said, 'What on earth are you talking about?'

I said, 'Put simply, we are not allowed to help criminals profit from their crimes.'

His moustache jumped halfway up his nose. 'Criminals? Crimes? What?'

I gave him a fake smile. 'It has been brought to our attention that you have twice been interviewed by the police in connection with the murder of Joni Poelma—'

'They've cleared me. I'd nothing to do with it.'

I rolled on as if he hadn't spoken '—and we have reason to believe you may be facing charges.'

Pegg's eyes were wild. 'You're mad. They've cleared me.'

I switched off the smile. I said sharply, 'What about the handbag?'

He mouthed the word back at me.

I said, 'You stole her bag. You also helped yourself to twenty-seven pounds that was inside it.'

He stood there clenching and unclenching his mitts. Jack was listening with his head cocked. I'm not sure he was getting all of this.

I said smoothly, 'Under the Code of Conduct we are forbidden to pay you. It would be unethical.'

Pegg was having trouble linking newspapers and ethics. I didn't blame him.

'But you promised me the money.'

'Mister Pegg, you were less than frank with me. You did not disclose you had just committed a crime. Indeed, when I mentioned the handbag, you gave me to understand you had not seen it.'

'It was just a bag,' he bleated.

'It was a serious crime. You interfered in a murder investigation.'

He whuffed through his moustache. He was adding all this up. It came to precisely minus five grand.

'Do you mean to say you're not going to pay me?'

'That's right.'

His face was about the same shade as the manilla walls. 'I'll sue you.'

'Go ahead. We'll sue you right back for criminal misrepresentation.'

'You – you—' whereupon he launched into an ear-scorching harangue of rude words. I remembered that

Pegg used to be a literary agent. By the sound of things, his clients must have been those new wave women writers.

I eyed him calmly as he built up speed. I wasn't bothered. It was just his way of admitting he was stuffed. After a while the list of swear words just got repetitive. I turned and walked out.

Now that Pegg was sorted I could get back to enjoying myself. My mobile had other ideas.

'Yes?' I said, carefully negotiating the dog turd chicane out on Sackville Street.

A woman with a voice hitherto unheard. 'Mister Chard? You don't know me. My name is Sonia Kevlin.'

I remembered. George's mum. I didn't say anything.

'You put your card through our letterbox after my son . . .'

'Yes.'

She wasn't finding it easy. 'You mentioned you were campaigning against . . . drugs . . .'

Her next words came in a rush. 'I really need to talk to someone. Perhaps . . .?'

I said, 'I'm in Dulwich now. I could be with you in half an hour.'

'Yes please, Mister Chard. I *do* want to talk about it.'

'And your husband?'

'Bill? He's not here this evening. But I would like to see you.'

So bang went my idea of a bender in Hampton's. I had to walk all the way to Merrilees Park. It was close on a mile.

Sonia Kevlin must have been hiding behind the door because she slung it open as soon as I banged the bell. She was in her latish forties but still in reasonable nick. Her blonde hair was too fluffed up and fancified. She was wearing a long red sweater over black leggings which were too young for her. Otherwise.

She gave me a tight smile. 'Come in.'

We ended up in a room with one of those glass-faced fireplaces glued into the wall. The other chief item of note was a whacking baby grand with fiddly looking music perched in its stand. I pushed a fat flowery cushion out of the way and settled down in a squidgy blue armchair. She had the sofa. She sat on the edge with her hands clasped round her knees.

I said, 'You want to talk about what happened?'

No she didn't. She wanted to talk about George. I got the whole bit from birth to death, not forgetting his motorbike accident and his A-levels. She accompanied the narrative with a fair sprinkling of tears. I just sat there with my brain ticking over. For some reason or other hacks often get mistaken for freelance psycho-therapists. People tell you the most amazing things.

So far Sonia hadn't said anything remotely amazing. It was time to nudge her in the right direction. I said, 'Your husband blames Joni.'

She said, 'Yes. George changed so much after meeting her. He was moody, truculent, you really couldn't speak to him. It was then we started thinking he was on drugs.'

'And Joni was supplying them?'

Another yes.

I said, 'But then she got murdered.'

297

Sonia's expression, her pose was just the same as before, but somehow there was a certain stiffness about her. I prodded, 'And you don't know who took over from Joni as the pusher?'

She squeezed up her lips and said nothing.

I said ever so softly, 'You do know?'

A half-hearted shake of the head.

I said, 'But you have a suspicion?'

She looked at me straight. 'This is not for your paper, Mister Chard.'

'You have my word.'

She inhaled noisily through her nostrils, then she said in a flat mechanical voice. 'The night after George died, Gabriella Cardigan phoned me to express her condolences. We have been friends a long time.'

I waited still as a rock.

Sonia said, 'Gabriella asked me, no, she *begged* me, not to involve Jason in it.'

I could hardly hear my own voice. 'Was he involved?'

She looked helpless. 'I don't know. We never thought of Jason in that way. He's always been such a nice, open boy.'

I said, 'But now?'

She unclasped her hands. 'I don't know.'

I hunched forward. 'Gabriella must have said more than that.'

'She did. She did. She said she wasn't certain that Jason was taking drugs but she had somehow found out that Joni took them. Gabriella suspected that Joni had got Jason involved, just the way we believe Joni got George involved.'

I said, 'You might be forgiven for feeling angry at Jason.'

A weary shrug. 'What's the use? If he was taking these dreadful things, he was just another foolish young-ster. You see, Mister Chard, we cannot blame George. But we do blame Joni.'

We sat on for another twenty minutes until Sonia reckoned she'd had enough therapy. In the meantimes I snaffled a bunch of snaps of George from the family album. And – joy of joys – there was even one of George and Joni together, with him looking like the git who kicks sand in people's faces and her looking like she could do with a square meal.

Sonia saw me to the door. 'Thank you, Mister Chard. You have been very kind.'

She didn't even ask me what I was going to write.

Heading back to the bright lights and feeling remarkably clear-headed for this time of night, I called up my ansa-phone. Nobody else had called it. Which meant that Rosie was still playing the injured party. I growled to myself. One of these days Rosie'll have to learn to say the word 'sorry'. My God, she's heard it enough times from me.

I rang her.

'Why haven't you phoned earlier?' she demanded.

Honestly. There's no reasoning with her. A lot of women are that way.

I said, 'What are you doing?'

She was doing nothing. I suggested we did it

together. She fliffed and flaffed about for a moment and then she said OK.

I told the taxi geezer to change direction. He glared at me in the rear-view mirror. I smiled back and made a mental note to undertip.

There are times when Rosie makes me feel like her bit of rough. This was one of those times. I can't remember just what she was wearing – I've got a vague recollection of a darkish trouser suit and one of those scoopy-necked vests that make you think you see more than you can.

She said, 'Missed you.' She kissed me first, which I suppose was her way of admitting she'd been a right old boot. I kissed her second, but my kiss was longer so they sort of evened up.

She said, 'What have you been up to today?'

I said, 'You don't want to know.'

She didn't either. She just wanted to go out, which I knew already because of the way she'd got herself togged up. That was fine with me.

We ambled off to Christsake's Club. It's not really called that. It's Krisjchak or something like that, only I've left out a z and a y and v and any other letter that gets you a ten in Scrabble. The guv'nor is a bloke from what used to be known as Yugoslavia, though you can never remember which part. Therefore it is not clever to talk politics. But they like drinkers.

We slung back bloody marys there until everybody else was paralytic and I began getting ideas. It used to be that vodka was an instant aphrodisiac. Maybe they've started diluting it or putting something in the tomato juice, but it's not that fast anymore.

Anyway, we lurched homeward, with Rosie bumping off lamp posts. All that dieting hadn't done her any favours. The good news was her tum was still where it ought to be and in fine shape.

I don't pray. God knows, I'd have to spend the first hour confessing to everything I've done in my working day. But that night, if I'd felt so inclined, I might later have raised my eyes to the apricot ceiling.

And just smiled.

Chapter Twenty-One

Another day. A different day. I got wakened with an honest cup of tea. It even had non-skinny milk in it. Still no sugar.

Rosie propped a pillow up behind her and sniffed her witches' brew. The radio was going hell for leather because some berk in an artic had jacknifed across the M11, thereby occasioning the sort of mayhem which Frankie scores on a daily basis.

I was feeling a trifle tender around the gills. I sipped slowly.

Rosie said, 'Sooner or later you'll have to talk about it.'

Talk? Right now I wasn't even up to think mode.

She said, 'It's all about Jason. Right?'

'Right.' I said that because it was less painful than saying no.

'You're still going for him, aren't you?'

We'd already been through all this. I tried to duck down under the duck down.

She tweaked back a corner of the duvet. 'Come on, Max. I'm not arguing with you.'

No. It takes two to argue. I lay there looking like the

Lady of Shalott, though I don't expect she had bristles poking out of her chin.

Rosie was talking to herself. 'So just say Jason was selling drugs to Joni.'

That wasn't even the half of it. But I didn't cut in.

She said, 'It would be different if we didn't know him.'

Yes. That's what all this grief was about. She knew him, therefore that made him OK. I growled. I couldn't help myself.

Rosie said, 'I just don't understand why you're so set upon crucifying him. It's not as if he's killed somebody or something.'

Which shows how little she knew.

She was just getting into her stride. She said, 'You've got the poor kid scared out of his wits.'

That one was way below the belt. I sat up straight and glared at her. 'Why is it always the hack's fault?'

She stuck her nose down in her cup.

I said, 'It was Jason who got drugs for Joni. It was Jason who coughed to that. It was Jason who lied about all sorts of other stuff. It was Jason who is up to his neck in mischief. So how come I cop the blame when I go to turn over the little twerp?'

Rosie said, 'He's not a little twerp.'

That wasn't the point and she knew it. I got out of bed. She stayed put.

She said, 'I'm sorry. I'm not blaming you. I'm just trying to understand how it doesn't bother you.'

I sat down heavily on the bed again and looked at her sourly. I said, 'Tell the truth: if you'd never met Jason would you feel this way?'

'No.'

'Precisely.'

She crinkled her brow. 'Precisely what?'

It wasn't that hard to follow. I explained it anyway. 'The only reason you're soft on him is because you know him.'

Her eyes were big and blue and serious. 'But Max, that's what I'm trying to say. I *do* know him, and I do like him. That's what makes this different.'

I curled a lip. 'For you anyway.'

'Yes,' her voice had zipped up the register, 'for me. And for anybody else. That's the natural thing. But you – you reporters – you're unnatural.'

Was that a criticism or a compliment?

She got her voice back down the keyboard. 'This is what I can't understand. How can you do him over when you know him?'

I said, 'That makes it easier.'

'Does it really?' Delivered without sarcasm.

'Yes.'

I got up to go. She said quietly, 'I just wanted to understand. That's all.'

'So now you know.'

She bobbed her head. 'Yes. Now I know. I suppose I knew all along. But I'm not blaming you.'

'That's demmed decent of you, old gel.'

'Please, Max.'

I looked at her. She put her cup down and held her arms out. She gave me three quarters of a smile. 'Come on.'

I felt like a stroppy two-year-old, but I came. The arms went around me and my face was full of her curls.

She kissed me and whispered things in my left ear. Then, in possibly the worst impression known to Man, she did a take-off of that guy in *Hill Street Blues*. 'And above all, be careful out there.'

I disengaged her arms and stood up. 'You got it.'

I had a vague game plan for the day ahead. The first bit was clear-cut. It involved me ringing News Desk and telling them I'd set up an exclusive interview with George Kevlin's mum. There was nothing else on the go so they'd jump at it. After that I'd sit down with a coffee and knock together the quotes I'd got from Sonia Kevlin last night. And when all that was done I'd do something about the bloody Cardigans. Though quite what I wasn't sure.

The first stage of the day's mission lifted off as planned. I got Nige on News Desk and he scribbled down the schedule line: Ecstasy Mum Tells of her Agony. He's never been accused of originality, has our Nige. He asked me if I wanted a monkey for snaps of Sonia but I said I didn't want to frighten her until after I'd got it all wrapped up.

'Okey dokey,' said he. 'By the way, have you heard about Angie?'

No. What about Angie?

'She's got the bullet.' He said this with a certain degree of glee. That was because he was figuring he was next in line for the big black chair. At my end of the phone I tried on a crooked smile.

I said, 'Is it definite?'

'Well, that's what she's hinted anyway.'

'What did she say?'

Nige had her exact quote on tap. 'She said, "My turn to buy the coffee lads. You'd better enjoy it. It's the last drink you get from me." '

That sounded definite enough. My crooked smile packed up and fled.

I said, 'That's all? She didn't say when she was going?'

'No. But Belker's flying back today. He's been out in Egypt or somewhere on a freebie but the Editor's suddenly called him back.'

I asked how he knew.

'Last night the Editor got Foreign Desk to book Belker on the first available plane to London. He should be in this afternoon. So it looks like they'll appoint a new News Editor today.'

I said, 'Who's up for it?'

Nige got all coy. He couldn't possibly guess. Smirk, smirk, smirk.

I put down the phone. If today the Editor lumbered me with the job, my first executive decision would be to bust Nige down to Night Desk. The thought gave me less satisfaction that it ought to.

I pushed Angie's present and my future into the pending file and I got down to translating Sonia Kevlin's quotes into hack-speak. It was coming along fine when my mobile went.

I picked it up like it was an unexploded shell. 'Hello?'

'Good morning, Max. A little snippet for you.' It was CI Skelly. I felt a sudden rush of deep affection for the man.

'Hi, Tom. Good to hear from you.' I really, really meant it.

I think my reckless emotion got through to him because his voice went gruff. 'Well, just thought you'd like to know: we've picked up Fez.'

They'd lifted him at Harwich and the betting was they copped him just before he legged it for Holland. He might have made it too if he hadn't got into a punch-up in some boozer. The Old Bill were called and in the ensuing jollity Fez stuck one of them with a butterfly knife. Twenty whacks of a nightstick later, Fez lost interest in the fun. They scraped up what was left of him and reassembled it in the local nick. That was when the desk officer did a CRO check and found out Fez was wanted by the big boys down south.

I said, 'Any charges yet?'

'He's looking at ABH, maybe grievous, carrying, resisting, and everything else.'

I tried again, 'Any charges involving the Joni Poelma case?'

A fat laugh. 'Plenty of time for that. I'm sending a couple of men up today. But don't write anything about it. I'll keep you posted on charges. I just thought you'd want to know – you were the one who put us on to him.'

I thanked Skelly nicely and off he went with his head in the clouds. I got back to work.

Just after eleven I had Sonia Kevlin's yarn knocked into shape and I whacked it through to Copy. I was fast running out of things to do, except for those things I didn't want to do. The only other safe item was a quick call to Sonia.

'A photograph? Why do you want a photograph of me?' She was already regretting talking to me.

I cursed myself. I should have prised a snap from her last night before she got her defences up. I went through a whole bottle of snake oil before she said yes.

Next I called Picture Desk and told them I needed a house-trained monkey for a delicate job. I eventually settled for Kim, who is a lady monkey, and in a certain light looks more like a lady than a monkey. I put down the phone. That was the last of the routine chores done and dusted.

I lit a cigarette and pulled at the options. By rights I should breeze into the office and await the clatter of cloven hooves. It didn't appeal.

The other choice was to tackle Jason. That didn't have much going for it either. But I had to pick one of them. In the end I flicked a coin: heads, the office; tails, Jason. It came up heads.

That decided me. Jason.

I called the Cardigan spread. After seven rings a woman with an unplaceable foreign accent came on and told me there was nobody at home. That was a lie for a start.

'Do you know where Jason might be?'

No, she didn't. But Mister Cardigan was at his office and Missus Cardigan at her studio.

So it had to be Gabriella.

I took a long time getting myself ready. I suppose I reckoned that if I lingered long enough some news story would break loose – gang warfare in the streets of Sarf London, a rooftop riot at Wormwood Scrubbs, a hijacking at Heathrow. Anything to get me out of going to Gabriella. But all London was on its best behaviour. I had nowhere else to go.

I shouldered into the Burberry and checked that the bleep, the mobile, the notebook, the pens, the contact book were where they ought to be. I thought about the tape-recorder. No. Too obvious. I left it where it was. At the door I waited a full minute just in case the phone decided to ring. It didn't.

It was just gone one o'clock on an early March after-noon. But it might have been mid-May. The sun was up there shining away to himself and people were smiling at each other. It even got through to me. I opted to hop on a bus, clean forgetting you can't smoke upstairs. Down in the streets, the girls were still in their close-season plumage. Faded greens, rusty yellows, bloodless reds. It looked like Fall in New England out there. I rode the bus all the way to Victoria and switched to the Tube. That's when all the colours seeped out of the day. I switched at Green Park and took the northbound Picca-dilly Line. It was only three stops. I wished it were more.

I resurfaced at Covent Garden. By now the sun had rolled into a big rubber cloud. I swung right on to Long Acre, away from the pretty part of the market. The pavements were knee deep in people pounding a path to the nearest pubs. I was moving against the tide.

I found the building which housed Krysto Studios and a whole bunch of sundry enterprises. I stopped just round the corner from it and got out my mobile. I hoped the batteries were fully loaded. I rang Tom Skelly. A DC dragged him back into the incident room, for Skelly was on his way to empty a Grouse bottle.

I told him what I was up to and he didn't sound particularly hot on the idea. Then I told him one or two other things. Skelly reluctantly agreed to delay his Grouse guzzling. We talked technical for a couple of minutes. And that was it. It was all set.

I strode into the foyer of the building. There was a Lincoln-green plate with the legend Krysto Studios and an arrow pointing up. I could have waited for the elevator but I took the stairs. There were twenty-two steps, all grey, all with little black rubber bumpers. They turned left and left and left again round the elevator shaft. On the street side there was a long window made up of small and square greenish panes of glass. It was like walking underwater.

The steps led on to a first-floor foyer and a grey melamine door. It had a copy of the Krysto Studios sign as featured downstairs, only minus the arrow. Beside the door was a magnetic strip thing where customers could slide their membership cards and gain entry. I just knocked on the door. There was a fizz sound. I prodded the door open and looking back at me with a chipper grin was a girl with streaked blonde hair.

'May I help you?'

I said, 'I would like to see Missus Cardigan.'

'Who shall I say is calling?'

'Max.'

The blonde-ish girl picked up a phone and chirruped into it. I couldn't hear what was said at the other end. She put down the phone and pointed at a door to my right. 'Please go in.'

I knocked at the same time as I pushed the door open. Directly ahead was Gabriella Cardigan. She was sitting behind a grey desk with her fingers forming a steeple. It was like the way a man sits. She had her head slightly tilted to one side. She was smiling as if she'd just thought of something funny.

'Max! I was expecting Jason. What brings you here?'

I said I was in the neighbourhood.

She unlaced her fingers and pointed at a green seat on my side of the desk. 'Make yourself comfortable.'

To my right there was a small table with a jug full of daffodils. I parked my mobile on it.

Gabriella Cardigan stood up and turned to a cupboard behind her. She had her back to me. 'I'm afraid I've little to offer in the way of refreshments. Oh, just a moment. Scotch all right?'

I nodded. She got out a glass and held it up to the light to make sure it was clean. I just looked at her back. She was wearing a soft-green blouse and a navy skirt. Maybe she'd chosen them to go with the office.

She turned around again and handed me the glass. 'Do you take water with it?'

Neat was fine.

She hadn't poured one for herself. She sat down and gave me a cool green look. There was still something secretly amusing her.

She said, 'My, my. You *do* look serious.'

'Mind if I smoke?'

She didn't have an ashtray so I had to use a saucer. I was in no rush to get going. I took in the office instead. For a woman's room it was strangely featureless. The only signs that somebody real worked here were the four snaps on her desk. One of her and Wedge in summer fig, one of Jason, another of the two younger kids, and a shot of the whole lot together. They were set sideways on so that anyone on my side of the desk could see what a happy little bunch they were. On the wall there was a poster-size pic of three girls in leotards miming that pose from the James Bond movie. The one in the middle was Gabriella. She was easily the sexiest. At the bottom of the pic Krysto Studios was spelt out in big letters, green on gold.

She saw me looking at it. 'How's Rosie?' she asked.

I said, 'Where does Krysto come from?'

'My maiden name is Christos. Krysto looks better. How's your drink?'

I prefer malt. But blends I can live with.

I let my gaze roam around the office before coming back to her. 'So tell me about Krysto.'

She leaned back in her chair. She lowered her lashes at me. Some girls just have to flirt. 'What do you want to know?'

'The whole story.'

'I'm flattered. Would you like me to show you around?'

'Maybe some other day.'

She got up and came round my side of the desk. She folded her arms under her breasts and leaned back against the lip of the desk. She was smiling down at me. 'I can't believe you really want to know all about Krysto.'

'I'll let you know when I've heard enough.'

She laughed. It came out like she was humouring me. Then she got going. 'This is my very own enterprise.

My savings launched it, my energies have made it what
it is. Does that sound egotistical?'

It sounded plain big-headed. But I wasn't inter-
rupting.

She turned away from me and walked slowly back
round her side of the desk, talking at the wall. 'Wedge
didn't take it seriously for a long time. He thought of it
as my little indulgence. You wouldn't know, but that's
one of the snags of having a wealthy husband.'

'You're right. I wouldn't know.'

Gabriella stitched a frown together. 'I'm quite
serious. When you're married to a wealthy man, society
expects you to do little more than join charity commit-
tees and go to Ascot. It's as if you lose your
independence, your identity.'

'And Krysto is your identity?'

A sudden snap in her eyes. 'You bet it is. It's mine.
It's important to me. It says I am independent.' She went
quiet.

I said, 'And it makes a lot of money.'

She didn't smile. 'Yes. But more to the point, Krysto
is exceptionally good at what it does.'

'Stripping fat ladies of excess baggage?'

'I think you'd be surprised at just how trim my
clients are.'

'Like Sybil from Blackheath and Kate from
Greenwich?'

Out came the smile again. 'Sybil? Kate? What do you
know about them?'

I took a pull on the whisky. 'Not a lot. Except they've
started putting on the beef.'

She gave a light shrug. 'It happens. Ounces come, ounces go. Have you had enough of Krysto yet?'

I said, 'Enough for now. Let's talk about Jason instead. Seen him recently?'

'Last night. And I'm expecting him shortly. Why?' The green eyes were guarded.

I looked steadily at her through a curlicue of smoke. 'You'd better make the most of it. He's not going to be around much longer.'

'What?'

I just threw it straight at her. 'Jason's for the slammer. This time next week he'll have little arrows all over his pyjamas.'

She was absolutely still.

I said, 'I'm glad you're not taking this hard. I don't have a clean handkerchief.'

Gabriella got up, went to the scotch bottle and poured herself a meaty one. She didn't offer me. She faced me again. 'What are you saying?'

I spelt it out flat. 'Jason's been flogging Ecstasy. He's killed his own mate.'

'There's no evidence.' So far she hadn't touched her scotch.

'There will be tonight. Even as we speak, two coppers are on their way to roast a bloke called Fez. If Fez coughs, they'll go easy on him. He knows the score. He'll cough that he supplied Jason and Jason sold it around.'

Her voice was low, too low. 'What will they do to Jason?'

I repeated, 'What will they do? They'll bang him up for supplying, thereby causing the death et cetera.'

She dropped her eyes and brushed an invisible speck off her desk. She was taking it in. I gave her all the time she needed.

In an even smaller voice she asked, 'Is this about Joni?'

I pretended I didn't hear her.

She said it louder.

I said, 'Not yet. There are still a couple of bits to be sorted.'

Her eyes were back on me. They were cold as the sea.

I sipped whisky and took it slow. 'The big problem is Joni's kidneys. They were shot to hell with drugs. If she hadn't been strangled, she'd probably have popped her clogs anyway.'

Gabriella said, 'Joni told me she'd stopped using Ecstasy.'

'Maybe she was telling the truth.'

She lifted the glass to her lips and looked at me over the rim. She really was a tasty woman.

She was putting it all together. It took her longer than I thought. Then she came out with it. 'You told the police about Jason.'

'If you want it that way, all right. But you told me.'

Gabriella slammed the glass down on the desk. A little golden bead plopped on to the sterile surface. 'Me? How?'

I said, 'You didn't pay me enough.'

She shook her blonde mop at me. 'Oh God. We're back to this bloody money. It was *not* a bribe.'

'I believe you.'

Gabriella went silent. I smoked and listened to the

cars and the vans fighting each other in the street outside. It was an ordinary day out there.

She got her voice back. 'Why did you tell the police that Jason was selling drugs to Joni?'

'They would have found out anyway. He admits it himself. He still hasn't owned up to giving George Kevlin the Ecstasy that killed him.'

'That's because he didn't do it.'

I said, 'And you know that for a fact?'

She caught the mocking edge. 'Yes, I *do* know that for a fact.'

Sometimes you almost want to laugh. 'Which is why you asked, no, *begged* Sonia Kevlin not to involve Jason.'

'You wouldn't understand.'

'No. I wouldn't.'

I lit a cigarette. She sat there with her head down, her finger squashing the little bead of whisky. She came back up. 'You're really out to prove Jason killed Joni. Why?'

I said, 'Where was he the weekend she vanished?'

She had it off pat. 'He was down in Sussex.'

'That's forty, fifty minutes from Dulwich. And where was Wedge?'

A smirk this time. 'In Milton Keynes at a conference. And Jason was in Sussex the whole weekend.'

I said, 'I reckon it's all down to Billy.'

'Billy?' Her eyes were wide. They caught the light coming in from the corner window. 'Billy who?'

'That's what everybody says. More of Billy later. Right now I want to talk about Day One of this whole thing – the day Joni turned up dead.'

Gabriella was watching me carefully, not sure where I was going with this.

I said, 'That's the day you did two strange things. You told me Joni popped Ecstasy. Even I thought that was a bit harsh. You were badmouthing your kiddies' nanny with her lying out there in the snow and her face turning blue.

'Then later Jason shows up with an envelope stuffed with fifty-quid notes. I stuck the two items together and the only conclusion I could hit on was you were slipping me two grand just so I wouldn't turn Jason over.'

She gave an impatient click of her tongue.

I held up my glass to show it was empty. She just nodded towards the cupboard. I poured myself a big one. I offered her a freshener. She shook her head no.

I got back to my seat and took a swig. I've tasted worse. Gabriella was sitting very still.

I said, 'You left out a bit in your history of the Krysto Studio. You left out Joni.'

She picked out the words carefully, 'Joni helped in the fitness salon. Only for a few months.'

'Then you roped her in as nanny for your kids?'

A nod.

'Even though she did drugs?'

Gabriella sparked. 'She *had* used drugs. But she told me she'd stopped. I've already told you that.'

I laughed. It was not the sort of laugh that hangs around long. I said, 'You told me a lot of things. Remember the night you had us down for dinner? That's when you told me Jason didn't do drugs, and if he did you would never ever tell anyone else.'

'So?'

'So why did you tell Sonia Kevlin to keep his name out of it? Until then she hadn't the faintest suspicion Jason might be involved.'

Gabriella's voice was almost plaintive. 'I couldn't be sure. I said it just in case.'

I lit another cigarette. 'And then we come to the bits you didn't talk about. Like Billy.'

She wasn't faking her bewilderment. 'Who the hell is Billy?'

I said, 'Out in Holland I met Joni's chum, Hanneke. I asked her if there were any boyfriends after George. She told me: "Joni said she was having much fun with Villi or Billy." '

Gabriella swished her hair. 'I don't know anyone called Billy.'

I ignored that. 'So then I get back and I start asking around and everybody says Billy who? Everybody except Jason.'

She blinked. 'Jason knows him?'

I said, 'Jason knows Billy. But the funny thing is he's not even aware he knows Billy.'

Her lips were tight. They were better the other way. Somewhere down the line she'd lost the control of this conversation. She didn't like that.

She tried to haul it back. 'I have absolutely no idea what you are talking about.'

I pulled out of my pocket the two print-offs of the front pages of the *Sun* and *Gazette* the day they reported Joni missing. I said, 'Here's an easy-to-enter spot the difference competition. See if you can spot it.'

I slid the pages across. Gabriella read the first few

paragraphs of each story and looked back up at me. She'd seen it all right.

She tried to bluff it anyway. 'What's this all about? Why do you want to destroy my son?'

I said, 'Yes, it's a shame about Jason. Take the drugs away and he's a nice kid.'

There was flint in the green. 'I've told you how much he means to me.'

I looked her full in eyes for maybe five long seconds. I said, 'He means two grand.'

She was good at rage. 'How dare you. How *dare* you.'

It didn't shake me. 'You've got a terrific act, Gabriella. You let the world know what a humdinger mum you are. You're the lioness, fighting tooth and claw to protect her little cub.'

She had both hands flat on the desk. She was breathing through her nose.

I said, 'But sometimes you cock it up. Like the time you bleated to me about all the sacrifices you had to make for Jason.'

She almost said something.

I hadn't finished. 'Like the time you told Sonia Kevlin that your little Jason might be hooked up with George's death. But the worst boo-boo was bunging me two grand.'

She was still silent.

I said, 'It fooled me for a while. I thought it was a bung to shut me up. It was only later I worked out it was a teaser, just to get me really interested.'

Her voice was straight out of the deep freeze. 'This is pointless. Would you please leave?'

I stayed in the chair. 'If you'd really been trying to

hush me up, you'd have dropped me twenty grand, just like you did with Joni.'

There was a little tight line either side of her mouth. 'What makes you think I gave her money.'

I said, 'Because in her local bank, back in Genk, Joni had over 100,000 guilders tucked away. That's nearly twenty grand.'

There was the slightest flicker of triumph. 'But you said – in your own paper – that Joni was dealing in drugs, and her sister had been caught smuggling them.'

I shook my head. 'There was one slight difference. Astrid, the big sister, had her stash in a string of accounts under different names. That's the way dealers do it. Joni's money was in her own name. That's not the way dealers do it.'

Gabriella sat back in the chair and swivelled it half towards the window, still keeping her eyes on mine.

'Why should I give Joni money?'

I smiled a smile that never touched the edges. 'Because of Billy.'

'Christ Almighty! Who *is* Billy?'

I pointed at the copies of the two front pages on the desk. 'Did you spot the difference, Gabriella?'

'No.' Tightly.

'You can do better than that. I can see it from here. In the *Gazette*'s snap, Joni is knocking on ten stone, maybe more. In the *Sun* she's not even eight stone. The difference is the *Sun*'s pic is only a month old. Ours was taken three, four months ago. So how come Joni turned into the incredible shrinking woman?'

'What has this to do with me?'

'You introduced her to Billy. And before you blow up – have you ever heard of Billy Whizz?'

Gabriella was getting there.

I said, 'That's what the kids on the street call it. It's the poppers' slang for amphetamine. We used to call it Speed. Look it up in your medical dictionary. It's got many strange uses. If you're dumb enough you can even use it as a slimming pill.'

She did her best. 'Joni told me she had taken Ecstasy.'

I leaned towards her. 'It's a good story, and you could nearly get away with it. Ecstasy is an amphetamine too. Which means it also zaps holes in your kidneys. And you knew that.'

She said primly, 'If Joni was taking amphetamines, it was without my knowledge.'

This time I laughed out loud. 'And I suppose Sybil from Blackheath and Kate from Greenwich have also been whacking it into them without your knowledge. But for some curious reason they jacked it in. Right after Joni's death.'

Gabriella put her hands back in a steeple. She said evenly, 'That is a very serious allegation.'

'Very. Extremely very. And I'm prepared to repeat it to the Old Bill.'

'They wouldn't believe a word of it.'

I tipped ash in the saucer. 'Don't bet on it Gabriella. Tom Skelly – you know, the fat cop – he and I go way back. All he has to do is run a drug test on Sybil and Kate and all the other Krysto cuties. They mightn't be on Billy Whizz any longer, but it's not the sort of stuff you swish out of your system overnight. And just say they find you've buggered up some other woman's kidneys.'

She swung her chair to and fro. It made a tiny squeaking as if there was some small animal trapped underneath. She swung back to me. 'I did not kill Joni.'

'Sure.'

There was more squeaking. She needed that extra shove. I said, 'I haven't told Skelly any of this so far. Maybe I'll just shoot down to Dulwich and fill him in.'

I stood up slowly. I even turned towards the door.

Gabriella said, 'Wait.'

I sat down again. More silence. I said, 'What am I waiting for?'

She was in profile to me. The blonde hair curled up underneath her ear and caressed her cheek. Her eyes held the light from the window. In another place, another time I could have thoughts about Gabriella. But not here. Not now.

She spoke softly. 'You said earlier I hadn't offered you enough.'

It was coming. I just nodded.

She turned full on me. There was a fragile smile hanging in there. 'I got you wrong, didn't I?'

'All the way.'

'You wouldn't really go to the police?'

I said, 'You're still getting me wrong.'

'And there's no alternative?'

I shrugged. 'Unless you can think of one.'

She held her hands up to admire her nails, the way women do. She looked at me through her fingers. 'I've been thinking for some time that the studio needs a press officer.'

'I'm a reporter.'

Her smile was more confident now. 'A press *adviser*,' she corrected. 'Nothing terribly arduous. The occasional piece of advice. That's all.'

I asked, 'Does it pay well.'

'Thirty a year?' It was a question.

I said deliberately. 'And all this press *adviser* would have to do is . . .?'

'Just advise.'

'How?'

A sprinkling of laughter. 'I'm sure you could think of something, Max. Are you interested?'

I said, 'And this press adviser forgets everything about Joni?'

That's where I nearly blew it. Her voice went sharp. 'Turn out your pockets.'

'What?'

'Turn out your pockets.'

I stood up and emptied my pockets one by one. The notebook, the bleep, my wallet, the rest of it. They made a heap beside the whisky glass.

She still wasn't satisfied. She came round the desk and frisked me all the way down from my lapels to my Loakes. There was nothing to find. She reached across for her glass and stayed on my side of the desk. She was a smidgeon too close. I tilted so I faced her square on.

She said, 'I was just checking, Max.'

'You thought I was wired for sound.'

'It happens.'

I didn't laugh. I said, 'Maybe I should have done that. For insurance.'

She thought she was back in control. 'You don't need insurance.'

I looked up at her. She was cradling her boobs again. I said, 'Joni didn't have insurance. Look what happened to her.'

'That was different. Do we have a deal?'

She had her hand out. It hung there in mid air, waiting for me to shake it.

I held back. 'Thirty thou a year?'

'That's the deal.'

I still didn't shake. 'For five years?'

'Three.'

I said, 'Call it four.'

She hesitated only a fraction. 'All right. Four years. Is it a deal?'

I took her hand and held it for longer than I needed to. She was trying to read my face. It was about as blank as I could get it. I said, 'It's a deal.'

Gabriella kept her hand in mine. I could see little darker flecks in her eyes. She held me in them for another few seconds. Then she leaned forward and kissed me on the forehead. I felt the folds of her hair against my face.

She sat up again. This time she was smiling. She said, 'I think this calls for a drink.'

She got up and sploshed whisky into both our glasses. We chinked them lightly together. She asked, 'What's the toast?'

I was smiling too. 'To friendship.'

She liked that. 'To friendship.'

We drank. After a while she said, 'Does Rosie know? I mean, have you told her any . . .?'

I laughed. 'Hell, no. Some things I keep to myself. What about Wedge – and Jason? Do they know?'

Her turn to laugh. 'They've no idea.'

I said, 'So we're safe.'

She stopped laughing. 'We?'

'Sure. Us. If the Law find out I'm suppressing evidence, I'd get banged up. End of Max Chard.'

She hadn't thought of it that way. She nodded slowly. 'But of course.'

So now we were co-conspirators. I said, 'If I talk, that's me finished. It's not like Joni.'

She tipped back her head and looked at me. 'How do you mean?'

I flopped a lazy wrist. 'Well, she got greedy, didn't she?'

'No. That wasn't it.'

Come on, Gabriella. Spit it out.

I said, 'So how was it?'

'You don't want to know.'

I shrugged. 'You're right. The way I'd guessed it was Joni's kidneys started acting up. She goes to her local GP in Holland and he asks her if she's popping anything funny. She says no. But she works out there's something iffy in the diet pills you're slipping her. Right so far?'

She didn't argue.

I said, 'Joni comes back to London and puts the bite on you for twenty grand. Then a month or so later she tries to squeeze you for more. You tell her to get lost. A struggle, as they say, ensues, in the course of which you wrap a scarf round her neck.'

That amused her. 'You don't know everything, Max.'

'What am I missing?'

'It doesn't matter.'

I said, 'It's a better scenario than the other one.'

She sounded detached from all this. 'Which is?'

'That you just got it into your head to strangle Joni for the hell of it.'

A paper-thin laugh. 'Oh dear, Max. You don't honestly believe that?'

'What else?'

She got up and walked a little way into the centre of the room before she turned to face me. I angled my chair round.

She said, 'What about euthanasia?'

I acted slow. 'I get it. Joni's kidneys packed in and you put her out of her misery.'

Gabriella sipped her whisky. Yep. That was her story.

I said, 'The only problem with that is the pathologist told me her kidneys had *not* packed in.'

'It was only a matter of time.'

'Unless she got treatment. That could have saved her.'

Gabriella didn't answer. She went round to the business end of the desk, pulled a chequebook out of the drawer and started scribbling. She pushed the cheque across the desk at me. She said, 'Your first monthly retainer.'

I almost snatched it off the desk. It was for two thousand five hundred, written in big curly letters. Even her signature was voluptuous.

I gave a fat grin, folded the cheque and stuffed it in my wallet. I said, 'So tell me the rest.'

Gabriella squeezed up a pout. 'There's nothing else. You were right about how she found out.'

I wasn't looking at her. I stuck on a puzzled frown. 'Why didn't you put her out of her misery when she first hit you for money?'

A weary sigh. 'She was perfectly happy with what I gave her. She didn't ask for any more, but then that night . . .'

I said, 'The night she went missing?'

Gabriella came back round to me and put her hand on my arm. 'She was in a state of collapse. I knew then she needed urgent medical treatment. But . . .'

'But she might have forgotten herself and blabbed?'

'I couldn't be sure.'

'And that would have put the kibosh on Krysto – your independence, your identity.'

A slow nod.

So help me, I put my hand on top of hers. I said very gently, 'It was a tough call. Did she struggle much?'

Gabriella's eyes had gone dark. 'I waited three days, but she wasn't getting any better. She was so weak. And she was sleeping . . .'

I patted her hand. 'It's OK. The police will never figure it out. Incidentally, why didn't you get rid of the body that night?'

A thin smile. 'I thought the longer she stayed missing the better. The police would start looking further and further afield.'

I gave an easy laugh. 'You're a hell of a woman, Gabriella. I'd better make sure I never get on the wrong side of you.'

I had the whole bit. Except for Jason.

I lit a Bensons. 'Shame about old Jason.'

'It's his own fault. He shouldn't have been selling drugs.' She didn't even notice the hypocrisy.

I said, 'Deep down, you don't like him very much, do you?'

'What do you think?'

I looked at the cigarette tip. 'Me? I reckon you meant it when you said you had to make a lot of sacrifices for him. You could have opened Krysto earlier. I suppose there were all sorts of things.'

She said, 'You can't begin to imagine. For years I had to vie with Jason for Wedge's attentions. That sounds crazy, doesn't it?'

No. Not crazy.

She had more to say. 'Even now he's like a little kid. He can't stick at anything. But he's always there demanding.'

I said, 'Is that why you bunged me the two grand – so I'd start suspecting him.'

She actually giggled. 'It's like you said. Ecstasy belongs to the amphetamine family. If the police started looking at Ecstasy they'd forget about other amphetamines.'

I said, 'And they'd also start looking at Jason.'

'So?'

'So they'd work out he was dealing and they'd throw him in the nick.'

She sat on the edge of the desk, her left leg swinging. 'Does it really matter?'

It does, Gabriella. It really matters.

I reached behind me and picked up the mobile. I said, 'Did you get all that, Tom?'

'Every word. Stay put. There's a car on the way. Don't let her do anything stupid.'

I said, 'She already has.' I switched off.

Gabriella jumped up off the desk. Her eyes were wide and shocked. 'Who was that?' she demanded. There was a big gap between each word.

'Tom Skelly. That's who.'

If I hadn't moved fast she would have caught me with the whisky bottle.

Chapter Twenty-Two

I spent an hour in Bow Street nick while DS Mortown and his DC got me to answer every stupid question they could think up. All that time I had only a mug of muddied tea for solace. And they snaffled my £2,500 cheque.

Gabriella meanwhile was heading south to Dulwich with her wrists cuffed. When last seen she was looking feisty. She'd gone right off me.

I eventually spilled out on to the street about a quarter to four and rang the office.

News Desk were their usual sweet selves. 'Where the hell have you been?'

I gave them the schedule line: Millionairess Held Over Joni Murder.

They wanted to know if we had the story all to ourselves. What do they take me for? Even before the Law had turned up to bag Gabriella I'd got on to Skelly and made him promise he wouldn't breathe a whisper to Press Bureau. We had it exclusive.

News Desk loved me again.

I found a bar that was less crowded than most. Even so, the assembled punters were doing their best to sound like the crowd scene from *Ben Hur*. It was hard to concentrate on my drink.

But every now and then my mind flashed up a shot of Jason with his big round eyes and Disney dog smile. There weren't going to be many smiles from here on in.

I was just warming up to my drink when my bleep triggered. PSE CALL TONY BELKER ASAP.

I said something rude which the barmaid pretended not to hear. I got her to drip me out another gin – scotch had somehow lost its charm – while I thought about it. There was nothing to think about. I'd stalled as long as I could. The end of the road loomed bang ahead. My only hope was a call from the *Mail*.

And it was right about then my mobile sounded. I answered warily. 'Yes?'

'Max.' It was Neil Milltain. Maybe, just maybe . . .

He said, 'Sorry old mate. I did my best.'

Damn.

He was rambling on. 'News Desk had nothing to do with it. Teresa – you know our Assistant Editor – thought the bloke from the *Independent* was right for the job. It's a bummer. But there you are.'

I muttered, 'Thanks for calling anyway.'

But he wouldn't go. He said, 'Lucas Geany was very keen to have you, but you've heard the news.'

No I hadn't. What news?

'Geany's been given the push.'

'What – fired?'

Milltain forgot about my plight. 'This morning. He's already out of the building. Can't say anybody's sorry to see him go. He always was a bit of a tosser.'

He remembered me and tailed off with a clutch of

empty apologies and murmurs of sympathy. They didn't do much for me.

That was it. There was nothing left. I rang Belker.

'Max! Great to hear from you. I need to see you as soon as you can make it. Where are you?'

I heard myself telling him I was cobbling together an exclusive splash and it might be another hour or two. He didn't sound too bothered.

'Fine. Fine. But we've got to get this sorted tonight.'

It took me a lot longer than usual to knock out the story. I had everything I needed in my head. But I suppose I was stretching out my road career to the very last second. God knows why. I certainly wasn't savouring those last few hours.

I cabbed it back to the office at sometime after six. Newsroom was going through its usual feeding frenzy, with hacks clattering away and subs yelling to make themselves sound important. I'm imagining that's the way it was anyway for I don't think I heard any of it.

Automatically my eyes honed in on News Desk. Angela Whipple was still there centre stage, still shouting at telephones. They hadn't told her yet. They really are bastards. As soon as she saw me she dropped the phone and came tripping across.

'Belker wants to see you,' she said.

'I know.'

She had two high spots of colour on her cheeks. 'You owe me a very, very big drink.'

My eyebrows semaphored, 'Why?'

She was right up close to me but she mouthed the words. 'The *Daily Mail* crime job.'

I said, 'Geany's been booted out.'

She laughed, 'I know. Now, off you go and see Belker. And the best of luck, Max.'

She returned to her chair, still grinning. She really had no idea. I blatted on Belker's door. The incredible hulk was squashed behind his desk. He jumped up with more speed than was wise for a man of his tonnage.

'Max. Let's go into the Editor's office.'

I tagged along behind.

The Editor was chin deep in the *Sporting Life*. 'Ah,' he said. He'd probably forgotten my name again.

Belker chipped up, 'I thought we might get this Desk situation unscrambled tonight.'

'Ah,' said the Editor again. He got up from his desk and trickled out a smile of sorts. 'Well, I think I'll leave that to you, Tony. You know all the ins and outs of it. See that Max has a drink.'

And off he went. Belker crouched on all fours in front of the drinks cabinet and started banging bottles around. 'Glenfiddich, Max?'

I said yes. I wasn't really thinking.

He poured me a big one, a tiddler for himself. He plopped ice cubes into them. 'There you go. Pull up a chair.'

Belker squeezed most of himself into the Editor's chair. He said, 'It's been a bit unfortunate, this delay. We should have had it buttoned up weeks ago.'

I took a snort. That's when I remembered I'd lost my appetite for scotch.

Belker shook his glass about. 'But that's the way it is in our game. Timing is everything.'

For the first time I looked directly at him. There was

something flaky here. For a start his eyes were ducking and diving.

I said, 'I was tied up with this Joni Poelma case.'

He wasn't listening. 'You've heard about the News Desk changes at the *Mail*?'

Too bloody right.

His skippy little eyes were now on the Editor's minibar. He told the minibar, 'That's the thing about good News Editors. They don't grow on trees.'

The minibar absorbed this in silence.

I replayed what he just said. What on earth was he waffling about? I tried to trap his eyes. They slid off towards the ceiling.

'Yes,' he said, 'it's like they say: if it ain't broken, don't fix it.'

That's when it hit me. Every cell in my body linked arms and started conga dancing. There weren't going to be any changes. Angie was still News Editor: I was still me.

Belker was yakking away to himself over there. Every now and then I caught a phrase 'horses for courses . . . diff'rent strokes for diff'rent folks' and similar babble.

I wasn't really listening. I was too busy telling my cells to pipe down so I could work out what had happened. It didn't take long. I could track it all the way down the line, from the time the Editor and Belker first plotted to give Angie the brown envelope.

The Editor, like most of his species, has the unshake-able conviction that his staff are a bunch of useless layabouts. He clings to that belief because he needs somebody to blame for our free-fall circulation. Every now and then he fires one deadbeat and hires a golden boy from somewhere else. Six months later, the whizz kid turns out to be just as bad as all the rest.

The only time the Editor thinks any of his troops are the business is when some other paper tries to poach one of them. And then he'll fight like a mad thing to keep the poachee aboard.

That's what had happened with Angie. The *Mail* planned to dump Geany and hire her to replace him. But when she told the Editor, he suddenly ditched his ploy to junk her and tossed her a whole heap of money to stay.

That left him with one problem. Me. I'd been promised the slot. And right now Belker was doing his slimy best to weasel out of it.

I wasn't going to make it easy. I said, 'What exactly are you saying, Tony?'

He gulped at his whisky. 'It's like I said. If you'd signed on the dotted line when I offered it to you, it would be all right.'

So he was trying to blame me. I looked at him steadily. 'I told you I wanted the News Editor job.'

His voice went all nasal. 'I know, I know. But . . . well, things have changed.'

I said, 'This is a real kick in the teeth.'

He put down his glass so that he could knead his paws together. 'I'm sorry, Max. But that's the way it is.'

I sipped at my whisky. I rolled it round my mouth and let my tastebuds frolic in it. Whisky is a wonderful drink. I said, 'So that's it. No title. No pay rise. Nothing.'

'Ah, not quite.' There was a stupid grin splitting his face and he was actually looking at me.

'Yes?'

He said, 'Angela tells me the *Mail* have been sounding you out.'

I put on my liar's face. 'Just an informal approach. We didn't talk terms.'

The smile got fatter. It said I wasn't fooling T. Belker, the sage of the sumo wrestlers. 'That's not what I heard. I heard they've made a definite offer.'

I couldn't tell a lie. I just ducked my nose back into the Glenfiddich.

Belker said, 'Well, as you know, we're already running way over budget. We can't match the *Mail*'s offer, but I think I can come up with a little something, if you're prepared to stay.'

'How much?'

I didn't need to ask. I'd already guessed precisely how much. Right down to the last zero.

Snap.

John Burns

Hack

Hack, the first novel in the Max Chard series,
is now available in Pan paperback, price £5.99.

What follows here is the first chapter.

Chapter One

Only one public-spirited citizen bothered to phone in and report the body, though at least a dozen must have seen the thing. Thirteen if you count whoever put it there.

I was just around the corner in Magpie Court when the tip-off came. Good as gold, Inspector McIvor gave me a bleep. It read: 'Maxwell lookalike found bobbing – Mac.' I called him back. He was in Hampton's, no doubt already blowing his twenty quid tip-off fee on a doxy or two. 'Good evening, you ageing lounge lizard,' I said sweetly. Mac loves it when I talk dirty. 'You rang?'

He said, 'Might have one for you. The river police have a corpse floating around in St Katharine's Dock. Could be a tourist, pushed in by one of our local muggers. Who knows?'

I was not exactly enthusiastic. 'Who knows, indeed. Might be a drunk who tripped and fell, might be a suicide, might be a heart case, a headcase, whatever. Might even be a police officer doing the world a favour.'

Mac said, 'Oh well, thought you'd like to know.'

He rang off and returned to his fleurie and his floosies, for Mac is a man of simple needs.

I was in Ross Gavney's flat, pouring fat tumblers of

twenty-year-old Scotch down my throat at an unpre-
cedented rate of knots. Ross and I go all the way back to
Holly Hill comprehensive but we keep up the old ties
despite everything. He thinks there is something richly
hilarious in my being a crime hack, nay, the chief crime
correspondent for a national red top. Ross does compli-
cated things with bonds and futures, thereby earning
himself more money than is humanly decent.

I am happy for Ross, especially when he calls me up
and invites me to empty his decanters. Generally we sit
around and rubbish each other's football loyalties. He,
God help him, is an Arsenal man.

In the old days Ross was a yuppy, one of Thatcher's
favoured children. He still has all the trappings, city
slicker suits, fluffed out hair, docklands flat.

We were in the aforesaid apartment, arguing the
toss over England's chances against Poland when Mac
bleeped. While I did my ace reporter bit, Ross poured
me another half gallon of single malt.

'What next?' he asked, after I had finished with Mac.

'Next?' I was puzzled. 'Nothing. I wait till the police
haul him out, dry him down and then pronounce him
dead. They're sticklers for that sort of thing.'

'How do you know it's a man?'

I flopped a languid wrist. 'It's either one or the other.'

Ross sipped thoughtfully. He persisted: 'When do
you know if it's a story? I mean, this could be another
Calvi case. All you crime reporters got that one wrong.'

This was unkind but true, which in my experience is
usually the same thing. Roberto Calvi, aka God's Banker,
aka head of the Banco Ambrosiano, where the Pope
lodges his pay cheque, was found swinging under Black-

friars Bridge in the eighties. Suicide, we all cried, conveniently ignoring every fact which screamed murder.

I sighed. It was a sigh custom-built to say, 'Listen, dear friend of my youth, I have in my left hand a glass of Glenfarclas, and in my right, a cigar worthy of my deepest appreciation. Why bother me with trifles?'

Ross is not a man who listens to sighs. He said, 'So, you boys wait until the police tell you what they've found and you just put it into English?'

This was a vile slur on my profession. I have never knowingly put anything into English. Tabloid-speak, yes, journalese if I'm pissed. But if ever a phrase in English pops up in my copy, we have trained sub-editors to throw it out.

I lowered my glass and looked Ross dead in the eye. I said, 'This is the picture. A body, male or female, is found floating in the dock. Today all over London, bodies have been found in bed – sometimes their own – under a bus, in hospital corridors, in Cardboard City, wherever. A few – only a tiny few – are tastefully decorated with bullets, needles or knives. The rest have been topped by the Great Serial Killer in the Sky. In short, no story.'

'What's the betting?'

'Eh?'

Ross said, 'I'll bet there's a story in it.'

'Balls.'

After this it developed into a sordid argument about the size of the bet (my fiver against a bottle of his whisky) and then I did the biz. Just to impress Ross, I even rang Scotland Yard's press bureau to see if they had anything on the story. I wasn't expecting anything from them. Usually they don't know what day it is.

'Good evening. It's Thursday,' I said helpfully.

'Oh, it's you. What do you want?' asked a young lady. Ruthie or Zeintab.

'You know perfectly well what I want but we've no time for that malarkey now. Just tell me if you have anything on a wet corpse in St Katharine's Dock.'

'Nope.'

'You have been ever so helpful. Thank you.'

As I switched off the mobile, I was alarmed to see Ross breeze into the room, a belted Burberry over the navy pinstripes. 'Ready?' he asked brightly.

I kissed my glass goodbye and donned my hack mac. Outside the May monsoon scythed in off the Thames, running through the gutters and putting halos around the street lamps.

'Let me make a few more phone calls,' I begged. But Ross strode off and I splashed away in his wake.

As I said, Magpie Court is hardly a kick in the pants off the dock, but by the time we got there I was drenched through. Under his golf umbrella Ross was dry and debonair.

We rounded a corner by a snotty wine bar and ran smack into the police tapes. Beyond them was a clutch of sodden coppers gazing into the dock for enlightenment. A police river launch was parked in the middle with its spotlight aimed at the pointy end of a white yacht. You couldn't make out its name. You couldn't see anything, what with all that rain between us and the action.

A beefy figure swam out of the waterfall. It was

Pennycuik, my friend H, a detective inspector of the old school. He'd tell me all about it. 'Hello, Harry,' I said warmly.

'Piss off,' he responded.

'Good evening, officer,' said Ross from about a foot above my head.

Pennycuik wiped his eyes and looked up at him. Clearly this stranger was not one of your scumbag reporters. Too distinguished for that. I could hear Harry's brain cell charging around in perplexity.

I said smoothly, 'Inspector Pennycuik, I don't believe you have met the Right Honourable Lewis Trefoyle, the junior Home Office minister.'

Ross didn't blink. He put out a nice dry pink hand and gave H a nice dry pink smile.

Harry said, 'Oh,' and stuck out a hand like a drowned fish.

'And what have we here?' asked Ross. His voice was just the right blend of fruity pomposity and blind ignorance we have come to expect from our political masters.

Our heroic DI favoured him with a yellow smile. 'It's a body, sir,' he said, displaying the lightning intelligence of London's finest.

'Suspicious?' I asked him.

Harry pretended I was dead. He addressed Ross. 'We got a call, about eight thirty, from a punter, ah, one of the customers.' He pointed towards the snooty wine bar.

'I cannot see the body,' said Ross peevishly. 'How could he?'

Harry said, 'It was before the rain. This just came

on. The call was passed on to the river police and they located the body.'

'Man or woman?' This was me again.

He spoke to Ross again. 'We believe it to be a male, but it is lying face down in the water so we cannot ascertain exactly.'

Ascertain! I love the way coppers talk when they are in the presence of their superiors, which is mostly all the time.

'They're taking their time hauling it ashore,' I observed.

Ross looked at his Longines. 'Yes, it's gone nine.'

Harry shook the rain from his brow. 'It snagged itself in the cable of that boat. It shouldn't be long now.'

At which point there came a distant sound, as of a waterlogged stiff being hauled into a rubber dinghy.

'There it is,' said H happily.

Ross looked down his nostrils at him. 'Is this, inspector, what one would term a suspicious death?'

Harry shifted his feet in a puddle. 'The caller said he heard sounds of an altercation shortly prior to the incident and then there was a splash.'

'That would probably be the guy hitting the water,' I said sagely.

H glared at me but let it pass. On the dockside a quartet of young coppers were falling over each other to unload the late lamented, now gift-wrapped in rubber sheeting.

The corpse, a skinny specimen, was manhandled past us, still face down. He was wearing a Casablanca trenchcoat, its white newness marred by ugly black oil weals from the yacht's hawswer. Behind us there was a waiting ambulance. As the bearers reached it, they turned their dripping burden over. And everyone did a double take. The stiff was not a he, or anything like one. These were the mortal remains of a beautiful and, guessing by the bumps in the rubber sheet, shapely young woman. Her dead white face was fringed with jet black hair and her huge dark eyes gazed back at us in dumb surprise. Her carmine lips were slightly open and her eyelashes were matted with rain.

And slap bang in the middle of her forehead was the neatest little bullet hole you ever did see.

'My God!' gasped Ross. 'It's Claudine!'

And so it was.